Cold Feet

Original stories by

Elise Juska

Tara McCarthy

Pamela Ribon

Heather Swain

Lisa Tucker

doWn tOwn press

New York   London   Toronto   Sydney

An *Original* Publication of POCKET BOOKS

DOWNTOWN PRESS, published by Pocket Books
1230 Avenue of the Americas
New York, NY 10020

Library of Congress Cataloging-in-Publication Data is available.
ISBN: 1-4165-0754-X

First Downtown Press trade paperback edition May 2005

10 9 8 7 6 5 4 3 2 1

DOWNTOWN PRESS and colophon are trademarks of Simon & Schuster, Inc.

Manufactured in the United States of America

Designed by Jaime Putorti

For information regarding special discounts for bulk purchases, please contact Simon & Schuster Special Sales at 1-800-456-6798 or business@simonandschuster.com.

Contents

Cold Feet

Perfect Weather for Driving

Elise Juska

I am shamelessly addicted to Dr. Phil, and it kills me to think how disappointed he would be in me right now. This is what I'm thinking as I ride shotgun in the Volvo, this and the fact that Joel still drives the Volvo, and the fact that I cheated on Joel, and that the long-sleeved black dress hanging in the back-seat is probably inappropriate for a July wedding and the sun-light bouncing off the windshield is strangely bright.

"Geez," Joel says, and nudges the visor down.

It is six-thirty on a Friday night, and Joel and I, like most of the eastern Seaboard, are inching toward New England. The sky is the perfect, cloudless blue tailor-made for family reunions and beach parties and summer weddings. Ours is the wedding of one of Joel's college friends, one of those three-day, three-hundred-dollar affairs. We left Philadelphia at noon, the inside of our car a minefield of tiny pink hearts. The dry cleaner's plastic hanging in the backseat: *We ❤ Our Customers!* The directions stuck to the dashboard: *Can't wait to see you! ❤ Nathaniel & Nicole!* The night before, Joel had counted out the exact toll change we would need, and the coins sit now, smug as sausages, in their designated compartments. The trunk is jammed with my red suitcase, his brown suitcase, martini glasses wrapped in paper the color of dimes. We've done the wedding thing so many times it felt like packing for a business trip.

I squint into the sun. The median is thick with trees, letting the glare sneak into shadow then pop out again, swallowing the cars, whitewashing the road. The windshield is exposed as filthy, every particle of dirt and dust magnified. A week ago, leaving for class, I'd discovered the Volvo had been soaped: YOU SUCK, ASSHOLE! I thought the fact they'd bother to insert a comma was hilarious; Joel did not. By the time I got home, he had scrubbed it off as best he could, but the sun finds those letters now, faint, translucent, like the silhouette of jellyfish lurking just under the surface of the sea.

"Dammit." Joel's mouth is a blond scribble, the rest of his face hidden under Ray-Bans circa 1989. He is wearing a short-sleeved shirt, sky blue. Sand brown shorts, sand brown sandals. Everything about Joel is sky blue or sand brown: hair, socks, belts, eyelashes. His eyes are the color of water. It was one of the first things I loved about him, this gentleness, beachiness.

Then he pokes the Ray-Bans up his nose with one finger,

like a pair of reading glasses, and there is no reason this should annoy me and yet it does, annoyance so intense that I gouge the door handle with my fingernails. Followed by a pause, a flip in the gut, and a groundswell of guilt.

"We'll never make it at this rate," Joel says.

He's swiveling the radio dial, looking for a traffic report. I focus on the square of driving directions stuck to the dashboard. It's affixed with a swatch of the Scotch tape Joel inexplicably stores in his glove compartment along with ruler, scissors, and penknife. They are poor substitutes for air-conditioning, cup holders, and power windows, but this is not something we joke about. When Joel and I moved to Philadelphia last year, my old Mazda was abandoned in favor of his older Volvo, a family relic from the 1980s. Joel is a firm believer in the theory of oil changes ensuring eternal life; at this point, the Volvo's very survival has become a point of pride.

"Here we go," Joel says. A female newscaster comes through faintly, crackling like a popping ear.

" . . . moving along nicely on Route Seven, with just a *little* minor congestion around Middlebury . . ."

The Volvo's engine starts chugging louder. Joel gives the dashboard a firm pat, like the shoulder of an old fraternity brother or a prize horse.

"But on I-89 northbound," the newscaster warns, "look out!" Her voice, though fuzzy, is irritatingly cheerful. "We're jammed from Exit One all the way to Exit *Ten*!"

"Great," Joel says. "We can forget the first course."

"How far do we have?"

"Forty-five minutes, at least. Maybe sixty minutes."

Only Joel would refer to an hour as "sixty minutes," though unfortunately, he's probably right. The sun is still blinding, the car barely moving. Our windows are rolled down; my right arm is burning. I scan the driving directions, skimming the ♥s and *loves* for the most important detail: Green Mountain Resort. Though I've acquired an exhausted indifference when it comes to most weddings, I always feel a stir of excitement about the hotels. They are the best part of any trip, in my opinion, and the most relevant. You might be visiting a different state, a different couple, a different country, but the hotel room is the place where you truly escape. You are stripped of your life, freed from yourself. Everything is unused, untouched, a sparkling clean slate.

The newscaster has moved on now to local listings. I see a flash of the ASSHOLE lurking in our windshield. "On Tuesday," she reports fuzzily, "a workshop on using e-mail will be held free of charge at the Rutland Free Library . . ."

I turn to Joel. "Isn't this static driving you crazy?"

"Not really." He pushes his glasses up his nose again. "Put on whatever you want."

As I reach for the dial, the sun finally slips below the tree line. All around us cars begin to reassemble themselves, sunbleached, flimsy, and move tentatively forward.

"What is this person doing?" Joel says.

I look up. He's talking about the truck directly in front of us, which is inching forward, then stopping, inching, stopping, inching, stopping. It has a Vermont license plate and a speedboat attached to the back.

"He's just being careful," I say, feeling defensive of the boatman. The side of the boat is painted, in purple letters, LOVE BOAT #9. "Would you rather be too careful or not careful enough?"

Joel pauses, considering. We always play these games with each other: Would you rather be too short or too tall? Stuck in an ocean or an elevator? Deaf or blind? Hot or cold? Joel is working on his Ph.D. in statistics.

"Too careful," he says. The truck's brake lights keep flashing, sluggishly, a watery red warning. "Not being careful breeds recklessness, and recklessness breeds selfishness. Before you know it, people would be ignoring the rules completely."

I glance at Joel, but his face betrays nothing. Lately comments like these have been hitting me hard, metaphorical, stinging. Did he know? Could he be insinuating something? But Joel doesn't insinuate, doesn't use metaphors. He never suspects anything. Sometimes I almost wish that he would.

Now he is mumbling again, swatting down the visor. Sun spots are collecting around the hull of the boat like bubbles in champagne. I feel tears rise behind my eyes and quickly scour the horizon, looking for an excuse to well up. There it is, of course: the sun, in all its brightness and difficulty, gorgeous bands of red and purple and orange suffusing the sky.

"It's kind of beautiful, though, isn't it?"

"What?" Joel says.

"The sun. Isn't it beautiful?" Ribbons of pink and lavender graze the treetops, the colors of artificial candy. "It's kind of—breathtaking."

I want Joel to look, to see what I'm seeing, but he keeps his eyes on the road. YOU SUCK, ASSHOLE! wavers in the windshield, like a ghost trapped inside the glass.

"I wonder how many car accidents are caused by sunsets," I say then.

Joel doesn't reply. The music seems to get louder, "This Kiss" by Faith Hill; the Volvo doesn't have a tape deck, much less a CD player.

"Tons, I bet."

"Tons of what?" Joel says.

"Accidents. Accidents that happen because people are distracted by beautiful sunsets."

Joel pauses, thinking. "Because they're distracted? Or because they're blinded?"

"Either," I say. "Both." It is the kind of ambiguity that irritates him, in exchange for the kind of logic that irritates me. The toll change trembles slightly, like children sensing tension. "I bet there's a statistic on it."

"I doubt that," Joel says, but not in the way you'd think. He's not being argumentative, just stating a fact.

"Why not?"

"It's not quantifiable. Too many variables." A bug lands on his arm; he blows it off. "You could be a bad driver, or talking on a cell phone, or overtired. You can't just blame the sun."

There's a pebble of tension lodged in my jaw, hard, sour, like a lemon seed. "Well, there should be," I say. "In fact, I'm sure there is. There has to be." I'm trying to sound confident, but I can't keep my voice from trembling. "People look at the sunset, and they can't look away, and then—wham!"

I slam both palms against the dashboard. The radio hops. The driving directions waft to the floor like a dry leaf.

"Wham?" Joel's eyes may flicker toward me for an instant; behind a pair of Ray-Bans, one can never tell.

"Yes." I lean toward the windshield, daring myself not to blink, and the brightness makes my eyes fill. "Wham!" It's so ridiculous a word, so cartoonish, that I burst out in a laugh.

This time Joel does glance over, catching me somewhere between laughing and crying. "What's gotten into you?" he says, a touch nervously, and in the eyeblink he looks away from the road we feel the solid thump of our car colliding with the boat.

The affair started nine weeks ago, though *affair* seems too strong a word. There was no sneaking around, no suspicion, no covert phone calls. There were no prolonged, sweaty bouts of sex in the daytime. There wasn't any sweat at all really, unless you count the smattering of drops that appeared on Max's upper lip during Week Eight: Curries.

Spice Appreciation was a nine-week course at the community college, the third cooking class I'd taken in the interest of keeping myself occupied. In the almost year since Joel and I had moved from Boston to Philadelphia, he'd been mired in his work at Penn and I had made exactly three friends: Ralph, my sixty-one-year-old boss at the mystery bookstore; Deb, a homeless woman at Broad and Arch who said I looked like her long-lost daughter, Shirley Temple; and Serena, the cross-dressing cashier at the Food Rite, with whom I shared a mutual love of Frosted Mini-Wheats that we discussed every time I came through her lane as if for the first time. These were good people, but not the kind you met for beers on a Tuesday. Still, rather than slump in front of the TV and admit defeat, I opted for self-improvement. I'd always been a bad cook, and our cabinets (with the exception of the Mini-Wheats) were close to bare. Cooking classes seemed like a sensible idea. Dr. Phil might call it a nurturing instinct, a nesting vibe; either way, he'd admire my initiative.

The first two classes I signed up for were Beyond Egg Rolls: A Tour of Asia and Introduction to Cheese. They temporarily transformed Joel's and my tiny galley kitchen into an explosion of the senses. Joel didn't mind. Or, care. There is subtle difference, but there is a difference. He ate whatever I brought home from class with equal enthusiasm—ginger chicken, fried shrimp balls, hunks of Camembert and Havarti and Asiago—pushing it into his mouth like feeding quarters to a video game.

"You're not even tasting it," I would point out.

"Sure I am," Joel would say and make a point of chewing harder. "It's really *good*."

But I watched him when he didn't know I was watching. He ate spicy garlic cucumbers without flinching. He slathered Brie on crackers in great insensitive swoops, like brushfuls of Spackle. One night I found him in front of his laptop, chopstick tucked behind his ear, drip of black bean sauce on the exact center of his nose. It frustrated me, this lack of passion, lack of awareness and sensitivity. I imagined myself grabbing up the leftover cheeses like our neglected children, wrapping them in plaid flannel shawls, and spiriting them away to a better life.

I imagined what it would be like if Joel and I had *actual* children, how I would console them before bed each night.

"Don't take it personally," I would say, smoothing their curls off their foreheads. When Joel and I fell in love we decided, as people falling in love do, that our children would be the perfect amalgams of ourselves. They would be funny (me) and brilliant (him). Good at Boggle, double-jointed, whizzes with a swizzle stick. In my best moments, they were carefree geniuses. In my worst, indecisive agoraphobics who would never do cartwheels and whose taste buds were shot.

"Daddy lives in his own world," I would tell them in my bedtime voice.

"What world?" The kids would be terrified. "Where?"

"Downstairs. He's working on his Ph.D."

"P H D," they would repeat, nodding solemnly, as if this were as vital a part of their vocabulary as *cookie* or *bye-bye*.

But inevitably, just as I was staring at the sidewalk, wondering how long it would take for Joel to notice if I up and left, he would do something endearing. This was the ebb and flow of our four years together: annoyance then endearment, and on and on, so on and so forth, one emotion catching up with the other in the nick of time. I would hear him wander into the kitchen, wash the dishes, uncork a bottle of wine. Then he would appear at the couch with two glasses. As he lifted my feet into his lap, I would feel my anger melting. I would look at his wrist, at the pale scar where he'd fallen out of a weeping willow when he was five trying to touch a full moon. At the Jazz Fest T-shirt we bought together in New Orleans. At the stubble

sprinkled across his face, glinting like flecks of gold. I would remember how kind he is, how awkward with words, with love.

He will never hurt me, I would think.

Spice Appreciation met on Tuesdays and had twelve stu-
dents: eight older women, one gay male couple, Max, and me.
Our teacher, Mrs. Battalgracia, was the stereotypical stern, bitter, flat-chested elementary school teacher who had turned sixty
and imploded: apron patterned with chile peppers, huge maniacal smile, bosom the size of a bread box, which shook when
she laughed. She made us call her Mrs. B.

"There are a few people I never trust!" Mrs. B announced on
day one. She tabbed them off on her fingers, which were the
size and shade of pork loins. "People who are too skinny. People
who eat frozen dinners. And people who don't like garlic." She
raised her chin and sang: "They can't be living life to the
fullest!"

"Hear hear!" shouted Max.

The group laughed. I glanced at him. He was what certain
generations might call "scrappy." Wry, lean, with a slightly
hooked nose, dark shaggy hair in need of a cut.

"Before we start," Mrs. B said, "let's form a circle, and everybody tell us how they came to find themselves in the land of
spice!"

She spoke as if we'd all stumbled into a foreign country
through some series of missteps and rabbit holes. Nonetheless,
like a cross between a preschool class and a self-help group, the
twelve of us shuffled dutifully into a circle to offer up our reasons for being there. Most of the women were in long marriages

and looking to vary their dinner menus. Todd and Bram wanted to reignite their relationship ("spice it up," they said and grinned). Gertrude's husband had died two months earlier; she'd since gotten her learner's permit, started ballroom dancing, and was eating "foreign foods."

"I'm Meg," I said, twisting the hem of my T-shirt like a dishrag. "I work in a bookstore."

I hoped this would speak for itself, but the group seemed to want more.

"Temporarily," I added, but still they waited, fixing me with their milky, sorry stares.

Then Max cleared his throat. "Hey, guys?"

This made me smile.

"I have a confession to make." His long face looked convincingly guilty. "I hate cooking," he said. "I just like eating. My wife's book club meets at our place on Tuesdays, and I needed an excuse to get out of the house."

The group peeked at Mrs. B, as if wondering whether this was grounds for expulsion. For a moment her face remained immobile, a chubby pink plate, then she let out a whoop. "You're all right!" she said and made the sign of a cross with her pepper grinder. When I smiled at Max, he was smiling back at me, his face bright across the room.

The car accident makes for a good story at Nathaniel and Nicole's not-rehearsal dinner. The rehearsal dinner was last night, the reception dinner tomorrow night. Tonight is the dinner for people not important enough to be in the wedding and yet not peripheral enough to just attend. We are the B-list guests, being served tonight in the Green Mountain Resort's Dining Room A. Our role is to sit through toasts, and more toasts, the only perk of which is the relative amount of champagne. Joel and I missed only the first few, arriving halfway through the salad course, as Nicole was flitting from table to table explaining in a shocked southern accent how there were just *so* many people to celebrate with they *had* to stretch the wedding over four days instead of two or three or even, hell, just one, like in olden times.

"There are about a hundred more people coming tomorrow," she told us as we sat down, her eyes like quarters, ringed with soft gray. "Isn't that truly hard to believe?"

It truly was, considering the size of the crowd already.

"It's all these darn southerners." She winked, and as if on cue, a posse of her girlfriends launched into an old cheerleading routine, something they probably all once performed together at Deep South High.

Table 14 is made up of northerners only: Joel and me, five of his MIT friends, and their five wives. These are couples we never see except at weddings. Over the four years I've been with Joel, they have all begun to morph in exactly the same ways: the men getting softer and balder, women getting softer and blonder. As the husbands' hair starts thinning, their wives' eyebrows follow suit, until they are sympathy slivers, the width of recipe cards.

Joel looks younger than the husbands by a good five years. I'd like to think it's staying unmarried that's preserved his youthful good looks, but the truth is he's always been this way. His mother, Anne (whom I love and wish was mine), has described him to me as a "milky" child. I know what she means. One of those pale boys who burns easily, whose skin picks up the imprint of whatever he's sitting on or leaning against, who sneezes not once but multiple times in quick succession. Anne told me that when Joel was fourteen he looked twelve, and he still has this boyishness about him. Tonight he is, as usual, almost groomed but not quite—his hair cowlicky, a few spots of stubble longer than the rest. To the untrained eye he appears disheveled, but this is merely a guise for his brilliance. The inside of Joel's brain is pristine, immaculate, orderly rows of numbers parading the membrane walls, a percentage sign drooping from the exact center of his cranium like a chandelier.

"The glare was in*tense*," Joel says.

The table looks politely rapt. Usually Joel and I are the oddballs at weddings: unmarried, unsettled, without home or leaf blower to call our own. But tonight, the accident has made us the centerpiece of Table 14, second only to the Vermont maple roasted nut sampler. Being in the spotlight is not a role I enjoy, but it's a welcome change from the usual breakdown: Joel and the husbands talking about jobs and sports, and I left alone with the wives—who usually have one child or are "trying"—as they nurse club sodas and talk in a disconcertingly candid way about the indignities of pregnancy: the swollen feet, hemorrhoids, afterbirth. One once used the phrase "placenta gushing out all over" while we were cleansing our palates with pear sorbet.

Tonight, all five of them are wearing what looks to be the exact same peach-orange shade of lipstick. I feel an irrational spasm of jealousy. Did they meet up together before dinner? Coordinate makeup without me? It wasn't always this way. When Joel first started bringing me to weddings, the wives were still the fiancées, and they would fuss over me, eager to indoctrinate me into their club. They lowered their voices to ask when Joel and I were "tying the knot" (some actually used this phrase) and looked concerned when I answered, "We don't really discuss it."

"Why not?"

I had the statistics on the tip of my tongue: the number of marriages that end in divorce, the increased likelihood of divorce if you're under forty-four, if your parents are divorced, if you live on the East Coast, if you live in a major city on the East Coast.

"It's just not a concern, I guess."

"But what about kids? Don't you want kids?"

"I don't know. Not right now. Not necessarily."

And this was the truth, as far as I knew it. The truth was, I wasn't sure if I wanted kids. The truth was, Joel was married to his work, at least temporarily. The truth was, I'd spent most of my childhood wading through my parents' sloppy, bitter mess of a marriage and at this point had little faith in the concept of semipermanent hair color much less being with the same person for the rest of your life. All I knew for sure was this: while the thought of losing Joel made me terrified, the thought of staying with him forever made me nervous, so I waded in this formless, nameless, ringless, statistically neutral middle ground.

But I couldn't explain this to fiancées, who would probably tsk it away with an easy explanation like "jitters" or "cold feet." I couldn't explain that there was something about their lives I didn't want mine to be, something that struck me as soft, generic, as playing it safe.

Instead I would smile and say, "Thank you for your concern," sounding for all the world like a bereaved wife.

"Anytime." The wives would smile back—sympathetically, it seemed—then one would say, "Joel is a really nice guy."

At the moment, the really nice guy is reveling in our accident story. It isn't that great a story, but he is taking pains to embellish it: adding new and dramatic details, editing out true and boring ones. It isn't like Joel to embellish anything, but tonight, in the presence of several gin-and-tonics and old friends who now own real estate, he is doing a surprisingly good job. He leaves out the hideous screeching sound that started as we crossed the Vermont border, the fact that we have a date with a mechanic tomorrow morning, the fact that our insurance premium will go up and we don't have money for extra expenses. And he keeps referring to it as a "boating accident," as if we were sailing on a yacht that gently nosed a coral reef, instead of the truer and more ridiculous version: a Volvo that slammed into the *Love Boat*.

"So we're going two miles an hour, maybe three," Joel is saying. His face is flushed, necktie loose. When he drinks, two perfect spots of red appear on his cheeks, like plums. He even gets drunk symmetrically. "Then from out of nowhere, this giant boat appeared."

This is accurate, if by "nowhere" he means three feet in front of us and "giant" he means the size of a couch.

"It's all stop-start, stop-start," he says, making jerking motions with his hands. The wives nod encouragingly. "Then Meg started yelling about the sun."

I wasn't anywhere near yelling, and am about to say so when I realize the entire table has fixed me with an affectionate smile. It occurs to me that we are being one of those couples who describe their private lives in public, making the arguments sound much lighter and flirtier and more enviable than they actually were. I'd always assumed those couples must be miserable, which is what compels them to pretend otherwise. I would imagine them later, without an audience, her silently removing her eye makeup, him silently pulling off his shoes.

But if Joel and I are faking tonight, no one seems to notice. The husbands are smirking, waiting for the punch line. Wives are holding on to husbands' hands. A team of waiters swoops in to pluck up our salad plates, mutilated, wet radicchio and shredded Cabot cheddar in puddles of country raspberry vinaigrette.

"So Meg's going on about how the sun was beautiful," Joel is saying, "and I'm saying the sun was a fucking nuisance—"

I look at Joel closely. He rarely looks so animated, rarely says "fucking." Suddenly he grabs hold of my hand, hard, as if yanking me with him into the finale. "And then, next thing you know—*wham!*"

I stare. He fucking stole my word. He even punctuates it with a slap of his hand on the table. It gets a big, round laugh, the Table 14 sign teetering from the impact. The wives are still smiling at me—at my feminine irascibility, I suppose—and I try to smile back but am still feeling the pressure of Joel's grip, and hearing the echo of his slap, and wondering what's going on inside his normally crisp, clear head.

"Are you a beef or a chicken?" says the waiter at my elbow.

We're both chickens, I think automatically, while Joel waves his place card with the word BEEF stapled to the back. My bitterness shifts then from wondering about Joel and my shortcomings to wondering why people rich enough to throw two rehearsal dinners and a wedding reception couldn't find a more sophisticated solution to the beef/chicken question than stapling the names of meats to place cards.

Joel releases my hand. The band strikes up "Walking in Memphis." My head feels fuzzy, fizzy, righteous with champagne. I wave my pink CHICKEN, as do all five of the wives, leading me to wonder if the BEEFs are deliberately blue for boys and the CHICKENs pink for girls, and if so, whether this offends me, and if not, why then I'm so angry, and either way, whether it's living with a statistician for so long that's made me question goddamn everything.

Joel pushes back his chair. He and the husbands are heading toward the parking lot to assess the damage to the Volvo. I watch the back of Joel's suit jacket as he walks, the endless sand brown of it, the watery, drunken swagger.

Then I feel a different kind of hand squeeze my arm, soft

and manicure-tipped. "I know just what you mean," a wife named Claudia whispers. "On our trip to Barbados last summer, the sunsets were like nothing I'd ever seen."

After class, Max was waiting. "I have a proposition for you."

Had I been at a party, or a bar, or one of Joel's academic receptions, I could have been witty. I can be witty under duress. But that night, standing in the dusty orange basement of an off-season high school, dressed in my usual cooking class uniform (sweatpants and a ratty Boston University T-shirt, worn for fear of being sauced or spattered) I was caught off guard.

"I need to convince you to kill time with me for the next hour," Max said.

He didn't seem dangerous, but you never knew, of course. He was shorter than me, funny-looking in a striking sort of way, lots of dramatic teeth and eyebrow.

"How come?" I said, hitching my backpack closer to my side.

"My wife's book club is still at our place. I was going to grab a cup of coffee alone, but if I drink coffee alone, then I have to be one of those angry-looking guys pretending to write in his journal." He made an exaggerated grimace. "I hate those guys."

I laughed.

"Is that a yes?"

"I don't know. No. I can't, really. I need to get—" Then I pictured Joel at home, hunched over his impossibly organized desk: the precise yellow stacks of Post-its, pencil jar a perfectly sharpened lead forest, framed diploma from MIT hanging on an otherwise blank wall.

"It's just a coffee," Max is saying. "Or a water. Any kind of water. Spring. Seltzer. Vitamin. My tongue's burning, isn't yours?"

It was.

"Wait—I got it." He actually snapped, mariachi-style. "*Spiced* coffee. Chai! Think of it as homework. Spicy extra credit."

I laughed again, and his face turned serious. "Meg," he said, and I felt an unexpected flutter at the sound of his voice saying my name. "They're discussing that *Ya-Ya Sisterhood* book." He clasped both hands together. "I am begging you."

Fifteen minutes later, staring into a chai latte with an extravagant head of spiced foam, I told myself I was ridiculous for worrying. The man had a wife, first of all. A *wife*. He was just looking for someone to kill time with. It was normal to have coffee with classmates; Joel had coffee with classmates all the time. Still, as I picked up my mug, I couldn't ignore the fact that I was too nervous to drink it. I took a huge swig to prove otherwise, then inhaled the cinnamon too fast and began to choke.

"You okay?" Max asked, instantly on his feet.

I was. It was the kind of choking where you are in fact fine but sound as if you're dying. I tried to make dismissive hand gestures, as all around the café people picked their heads up to evaluate my condition and ask themselves whether they felt confident enough to perform the Heimlich even though their certification ran out years ago.

Max bounded up to the counter and returned with a bottled water. "Here," he said, thrusting it at me. "Told you you'd need one of these."

I took a swig, still coughing.

"Will you make it?"

"I think so," I managed. "You start talking."

So, as I nursed my Naya, he did. I learned that Max Sutton had moved to Philly five years earlier from Tucson. That he had mixed feelings about the city: hated humidity, loved cheesesteaks. That while it was true he had a book club to escape, he was also a freelance food writer, so being in the class wasn't as coincidental as he'd made it sound.

"And you work in retail," he said, tapping one finger on the table. "Temporarily. That must make you an aspiring something else. Writer? Model? Actress?"

"God, no," I said and wasn't being modest. This was, quite honestly, absurd. I raked my bitten nails through a tangle of dirty blond curls to underline the point. "I just—" I didn't feel ready to come clean about the real reasons I was taking Spice Appreciation, about my loneliness, my friendlessness, the empty hours that needed filling. "Let's just say I needed a reason to get out of the house too."

Max nodded. "Fair enough."

I lifted my cup, took a tentative sip.

"Do you live alone?"

"No," I said. "Boyfriend."

"What does he do for a living?"

"He's a statistician."

"Really." Max raised both eyebrows.

"Well, he's not one yet, but he's working on his Ph.D.—in statistics."

Max seemed to consider this. "My wife's a chemist," he said.

"A chemist? Really?"

Both were the kinds of professions no one actually had. They sat between us on the little café table, near us but not like us, as foreign-seeming and awkward-sounding as fenugreek.

"My wife," Max said slowly, "Jill, is a raw foodist."

My wife, Jill. See? I sipped again.

"Nothing cooked at all," he added.

"That must be tough, considering the cheesesteaks."

Max laughed.

"My boyfriend," I offered—adding "Joel"—"is the opposite. Everything cooked. The more processed, the better."

It wasn't nice, and I regretted it instantly. I stared into my latte, its cheerful crown distorted now, like a cupcake dropped facedown.

"It's kind of exhausting, to be honest." Max sighed. "Raw foodism. All that infernal crunching and munching. It's so god-damn loud. And bland. A shrink would probably say I'm taking this class because I needed some—"

"Spice in my life," we said, at the exact same moment. The cliché was so obvious, it had to be gotten out of the way early.

Max grinned, but the grin softened, into not a smile but a kind of wry pretzel, an accident of the lips upon the face. "My marriage is very . . ." He leaned his head back, searching the tin-plated ceiling for the right words. "Practical. It's kind of the parsley of relationships." Then he winced. "God, that was bad."

"Terrible," I agreed.

We laughed, sort of, then said nothing. I glanced at my watch.

"Meg." Max leaned forward. "Let me ask you something."

Suddenly I felt afraid. "Okay."

"And I need a honest answer."

His voice was solemn, so I nodded.

"If you were a spice," Max asked, gravely, "what spice would you be?"

It took a moment to adjust, then laughter bubbled inside me. I thought: *This is fun,* at the same time I thought: *Joel would hate this game.* "Are you serious?"

He nodded. I chewed the inside of my cheek. "What would *you* be?"

"Jerk seasoning."

I laughed again, then stared into the bottom of my mug, the drowned spices strewn there like a fortune-teller's leaves. Then I lifted my head, smiling. "Sage," I announced, impressed by my own cleverness, when this could not have been further from the truth.

After the nonrehearsal dinner, Joel and the husbands go off for a nightcap. Joel uses words like *nightcap* and *evening* and *geez,* with what I always imagine is a *g* and not a *j,* although I've never actually seen his version in writing. I used to find his words old-fashioned, endearing. Is this inevitable? I wonder as I dip the key card into the door to Room 143. That what's familiar becomes annoying? And what's new is exciting? Given five years, would Max's sweaty lip and shaggy hair and bad food puns become draining, selfish, unbearable?

The lock blinks green, and I push the door open, catching it before it slams. The bedside clock beams 11:15. I turn on one lamp, then another, tapping the bases with my index finger, then gaze around at our hotel room, soaking in the details. Walls: sky blue. Bedspread: deep green. Carpet: pale green, extra-thick. Paintings: a mountain, a cow, a bowl of cherries. This inventory is an old reflex from childhood, when some of my happiest moments were spent in hotel rooms, on what my parents called "getaways." They were never longer than a weekend, never too expensive or exotic. My mother was uncomfortable around nature, so we usually chose a midsize city like Portland, Maine, or Hartford, Connecticut. Usually, these trips were prompted by my parents having a particularly bad fight, after which my mother would wander into the kitchen and say to my father: "You know what we need." Her voice was flat; it was less a suggestion than a prescription. My father would nod soberly as I scrambled from my chair, already mentally packing. It was like a deprived kid's version of "I'm going to Disneyland!"—the feeling less of joy than of relief.

Still, I lived for the getaways. Away from our house, my mother and father tried hard to act normal, unfolding and refolding maps, buying film, taking pictures of me eating chowder or sticking my head through a fake prison galley. This was when I was six and seven, before they formally gave up trying, and on some level I appreciated their effort, although all I really wanted was to get back to the hotel. All I really wanted was to be in a home that wasn't our home, far from the cramped duplex outside Boston with the orange rugs, the leaking beanbag chairs, the muffled sounds of late-night fighting, and the bathroom drawer with my mother's Xanax tucked carefully behind her panty liners and jumbo-size pink cotton balls.

Back at the hotel, I would fervently record the details. Wallpaper, paintings, carpets, bedspreads—I listed them on hotel stationery, committing them to memory, like a friend I knew was fleeting. I inhaled the smell of clean rubber in the bathroom and savored the feel of wall-to-wall carpet under my bare toes. I took comfort in the white noise of the fan in the bathroom and the endless supply of snacks in a machine at the end of the hallway, ensuring that the cabinets would never be empty.

In retrospect, these were cheap hotels, but I didn't know the difference, and had I known I wouldn't have cared. My parents were on their best behavior, and for that I would have lived there forever. At night, my father and I would go down to the hotel pool, where he would do five minutes of splashy laps, then hop out and shake off like a wet dog. Then he would sprawl in a lounger while I practiced what I'd learned in my swimming lessons: the simulated apple picking of the sidestroke, gentle bob of the dead man's float, tight scissor kick of the front crawl. Swimming lessons were one area in which my parents hadn't skimped; since I'd been out of diapers, my mother had been hauling me to the community pool down the street. While the other mothers chatted, she sat on a bench by herself, flipping through a magazine or staring at the sky. This only made me try harder. At the hotel pool, if my strokes failed to get a reaction from my father, I would hold my breath underwater as long as I could—once, worrying him enough to jump back in.

Back in our room, my mother would be waiting with an extravagant pile of chocolate and sugar from the vending machine. I would wriggle into my pj's, and the three of us would squash together in one big bed, drinking Cokes, watching TV, my hair drying in bleached clumps and skin taut from the chlorine. I knew even then that I had never felt more safe. What I didn't know, couldn't know yet, was that everything that seemed so special about those hotel rooms was really so generic it came wrapped in plastic, and that my sense of security was as false as the bad knockoffs of Renoir and Monet.

Now, looking around Room 143 of the Green Mountain Resort, I can at least say I've upgraded. The furniture is country-style light wood, the curtains checkered like tablecloths at a picnic. I kick my heels off and graze the desktop, touching all the courtesy pens and menus, each one branded with the same tiny, thumbnail-shaped green mountain. Next to the lamp I spot a tiny mesh bag of what look like M&M's but upon closer inspection I see are, unbelievably, N&N's. I peer at the silver gift tag: "Sweet dreams! ❤ Nathaniel & Nicole!" Ripping it open, I gobble a few without tasting them, then leave the rest lumped beside the notepad where Joel scribbled information about the mechanic. No, "scribbled" sounds too careless. Joel's handwriting is cramped, minuscule, fanatically neat. From a distance it looks like fleas.

With a jolt of regret, I realize that I never found out what Max's handwriting looks like. That I don't know his birthday or shoe size or what salad dressing he orders in restaurants. That even though his life revolves around restaurants, we'd never gone to one and never would. I remember how once—it was Week Seven: Peppercorns—he mentioned having been to a new Hawaiian-Asian fusion place, and I almost snapped, "Who'd you take? Your *wife*?" It was on the tip of my tongue, the snip of the jealous, the injured, but I caught myself in time.

Now, I stare out the soundproof window at the tranquil darkness. I can make out the faint tableau of distant mountains, a backdrop so perfect it might have been commissioned by hotel management to prove we are indeed removed from the world. When Joel and I and the Volvo collapsed in the parking lot five hours ago, the hotel seemed like an oasis rising from the endless, empty tracts of green. Now, it's making me claustrophobic. I look down at the parking lot, the rows and rows of unscathed cars gleaming serenely under the security lights. There it is, the Volvo, in the spot closest to the entrance; from this angle, you can't even tell it's been hit.

A champagne headache has taken root in my temples. I am assaulted by a queasy feeling, equal amounts giddiness and pain. I close my eyes and, like watching a movie of someone else, let myself remember the last time I was in a hotel room. There I am, in the parking lot, waiting in the shadowy pools of the security lights. The back of Max's head in the office window. The

VACANCY sign with its flickering orange V. As the office door swings open, I open my eyes, yanking the curtains closed and pressing them to my face. I breathe them in, only to realize that the fabric in this ludicrously country-style hotel smells, of course, of spices.

Unsteadily, I head toward the bathroom, shedding pants and blouse in graceless puddles, like the wreckage of some would-be affair. In the bathroom, I tear open a square of soap that looks like a giant mint, then stop and stare into the three-paneled mirror, my image reflecting over and over on either side of me like a house of cards. Over the course of the night my curls have become ugly corkscrews; my brown eyeliner is smudged. A slice of my right arm is burned bright pink, just one more of the sun's repercussions. I think back to Joel's "wham" performance at the dinner table, the way he clutched so tightly at my hand. There was something stirring in him tonight, distilled by the gin, like water shot through with a beam of light. Maybe there was more to his bravado than being around old friends. Maybe he sensed somehow that he needed to prove himself, that he was being upstaged.

Guilt rises thick in my throat, and I kill the light, the fan. Gently, I retrieve my clothes from the carpet and hang them in the closet beside Joel's brown suit. I dig in my suitcase for T-shirt and pajama bottoms, then pause to look at the suitcase next to mine. It's the same one Joel has had as long as I've known him, generic brown with gold zippers, his address printed carefully in the plastic window. It's our new address, the Philadelphia address, and I wonder when he sat down and changed it. I picture him hunched at his desk under the framed diploma, head lowered over the ID card, tongue poking from the corner of his mouth, and this time, the sight of his handwriting floods me with tenderness. I love his handwriting, I remind myself, fiercely. I love the way he holds his tongue when he's writing. The way he moves his left hand absently through his hair when he's deep in thought. I tear back the zipper, and the contents are as reassuring as I expected: Brown socks rolled into tidy doughnuts. Undershirts stacked and folded. Pair of flip-flops for the shower. Saline solution, cell phone charger, two Claritins in a Ziploc bag. *Life of Pi*, which his grandmother sent him because she thought it was about math, and secured tightly under a luggage strap, a manila folder and two pens.

I pick one up. They are expensive pens, heavy, marbled-looking. Joel got about a thousand of them when he graduated from MIT—"the smart man's alternative to cigars," his dad said. Each one is embossed JOEL WYLE in alert gold capitals. I love these pens. And I love his name: *Joel. Joel. Joel.* I love how it nestles roundly in the pit of my tongue, the *o* like a candy's chewy center. How it rhymes with the names of comforting things. *Oreo, Jelly roll.* I've developed a habit of repeating his name in my head, my secret mantra, any time I feel unsafe: walking home alone late at night, sitting on a plane about to take off. The first Sunday of every month, when I make my scheduled phone call to my mother. The Christmas Eve, two years ago, when I went to Chicago to meet my father's new stepfamily, and then almost constantly until I left.

Joel, I chant now. *Joel, Joel, Joel.* Sounds like *bell toll,* like *din-*

ner roll. If you weigh their names alone, Joel's is the clear winner. *Max* rhymes with the names of things that are harsh, blunt, disappointing. *Battle-ax. Imax. Anticlimax.*

On the other hand: *Alto sax.*

And on the other: *Droll. Troll.*

Would you rather date an ax or a troll? Would you rather have a climax or a dinner roll? I bite the inside of my cheek until I taste blood, then peel back the covers and wedge myself between layers of starch and polyester. There's nothing to debate, I remind myself, nothing to decide. The thing with Max is over; it was always going to be over. I tap the lamp off with one finger and lay the pen beside me on the pillow, JOEL WYLE just inches from my eyes, and in the muted light of the parking lot I stare at his name until it blurs.

At 1:30 I hear Joel come in, fumbling in the darkness. He turns on the bathroom light and lets it spill into the room, just enough to see by. The bathroom fan hums unevenly, punctuated by an occasional, almost spiteful chortle. I sense Joel moving around the room, emptying his pockets, stepping out of his shoes. His pants slide off, buckle hits the floor. I catch the faint, sweet smell of gin. The mattress dips as he sits on the foot of the bed, and seconds later, images of late-night TV are flashing past my slitted lids. Baseball, stand-up, music videos, steak knives. When I hear a faint clicking, it takes me a minute to identify: N&N's. Joel is chewing extra-quietly, but the tentativeness only makes his chewing more pronounced. I picture the inside of his mouth: tongue flicking, candy gently clacking, the silver caps on his molars like a tiny, terribly delicate constellation of stars.

He will never hurt me, I remind myself.

But the flip side is: *He will never make me fall apart. Or feel like I can't breathe. Like I'm falling off a cliff.* Is this normal, to want someone to make you feel this way? Or someone who at least could?

"The best verbs in the world," Max said, "are food verbs."

It was Week Three: Dessert Spices, and we were covered in a warm dusting of cardamom, allspice, and cloves. The week before, I'd explained to Joel that I'd met some people in my cooking class and we'd started going for coffee after, both of which were true. He didn't probe for specifics; he was probably happy to have the extra hours to work alone. If he noticed I'd stopped wearing sweats to class, he didn't say.

"Marinate," Max said, enunciating each letter. "Mince. Braise. Zest." He raised his eyebrows, my cue to join in.

"Boil?"

He frowned.

I thought for a second. "Flambé."

"There you go," he said, rolling the word on his tongue. "Flammmmbéééé. There's something intoxicating about it, isn't there? Food writing. It's terribly romantic."

"Is it?"

"Think about it. Cooking is all about passion and drama." Max puckered his lips to demonstrate. This was one of the things I liked about him; he didn't hesitate to look ridiculous. "Whip. Crush. Smother." He waggled his eyebrows. "Grind."

I laughed, in spite of myself. This was the soundtrack of our relationship: the groan that underscores the punch line, the rimshot that drives home the bad joke. To be fair, it was the tune of Spice Appreciation in general. The theme of our class was "spicing things up," for God's sake, and getting incrementally hotter each week.

"Don't turn this into some degraded S and M thing," I warned.

"Oh, it can be romantic. Don't forget simmer. Don't forget tenderize."

"Or melt," I threw in.

"Exactly. *Melt.* The language is practically sexual. Maybe that's why I became a food writer—you can act out your fantasies and it's socially condoned."

I laughed again. In a way, this described us too. In a way, because both of us were committed to other people, flirting felt more safe. We weren't physical, weren't technically unethical. We didn't talk between classes. We sent each other e-mails, but they had playful subject lines like "Thyme to Go to Work" and "Curry Up and Write Back." When I botched an attempt at "cumin" as "come in," he wrote back: "You're a nut—Meg."

It was harmless, I told myself, like dipping into a different language, just briefly in and then out again. Max and I were nothing more than conversation, cilantro, and coriander. But in retrospect, what we had may have been more dangerous than sex—it was the suggestion of romance, the possibility of something else.

*   *   *

The complimentary continental buffet at the Green Mountain Resort is your typically awkward group of wedding guests maneuvering politely and smiling vaguely across steaming vats of eggs, thinking they may have met the night before but not entirely sure now in the unflattering light of Dining Room B. Everyone looks paler, older, more sober. Joel is scraping a knife against a piece of burnt toast.

"Mark thought the noise might be coming from the alternator," he says.

We'd requested a wake-up call at 7:30 in order to get the car to the mechanic by 8:30; the buffet at this hour is largely older people and children under five. Dining Room B is too loud, too country-style, too strenuously charming. It seems deliberately designed to reprimand the hungover: the floors bare and creaky, the tablecloths a screaming blue-and-white-checked print. On each table sits a cow-shaped napkin holder and an assortment of local condiments: maple syrup, maple sugar, jams, jellies, medleys of cheese.

"In which case," Joel is saying, still studiously raking his knife across the toast, "I'd prefer to have it looked at when we get back." He is wearing glasses instead of contacts, and the lenses are smudged, the rims of his eyes hangover pink. "I could take it to that guy who fixed our rear brakes in October. What was his name? Fitzsimmons?"

"I think."

"I have it written down at home." He takes a bite of the toast, flakes of blackened crust falling to the table. "He seemed reliable. And we don't know anything about the mechanic here."

"True."

At the table next to us, a baby begins banging a spoon against her high chair.

"Except that they're flexible enough to take it on short notice," Joel goes on, raising his voice slightly over the racket. "But does that mean that they're unusually flexible, or that they do unusually slow business?"

He looks at me. I look into my oatmeal. It is thick, bleak; ever since Spice Appreciation, most foods seem bland by comparison.

A piercing scream goes up from the high chair, and a slice of country ham lands on my toe. The mother rushes over, picks it up, and silently mouths "I'm so sorry," as if she doesn't want to hurt the one-year-old's feelings by letting him hear.

"That's okay," Joel answers, smiling back. Then he notices my untouched plate. "How come you're not eating?"

I shrug. "I guess I'm not hungry."

Week Four: Fennel.

Max was eating away at me. At first he was just a goofy, after-class coffee partner; then thoughts of him began popping up all the time. A joke he'd made, an e-mail he'd sent, could buoy me through entire shifts at the bookstore. Riding the bus, I'd find myself smiling about something he'd said the week before. The city began to seem more tolerable, the aloneness more palatable, the bookstore more charming than decrepit. When I saw the comma in YOU SUCK, ASSHOLE! I laughed in part because I thought it was funny, in part because I knew Max would think it was as funny as I did.

"So let me ask you something," Max said, resting both elbows on the café table. "If you're so lonely with Joel, why do you stay?"

It was Week Four—early enough that this wasn't overtly suggestive. Still, the question made me uncomfortable. For a long moment, I was spared an answer by the shrieking of the foam machine. I stared into my latte, silently listing the reasons. *Because we've been together for four years, because we have a life together, because he's kind, and good, and makes me feel safe.*

I looked up, a touch defiant. "He makes me feel safe."

"Safety," Max said, "is an illusion." He smiled and took a deep swig of his latte, surfacing with a mustache of foam.

After breakfast, Joel and I return to the parking lot. Joel takes the wheel of the sand brown Volvo. I follow closely in a red Jetta that isn't mine. It belongs to Mike and Jaime, who loaned it to us for the drop-off. Mike and Jaime's Jetta has Norah Jones in the CD player and a cherry air freshener dangling from the rearview mirror. This seems easy, I think, steering gingerly. Not particularly original but easy. A red Jetta, Norah Jones, a cherry air freshener. Why couldn't life be like this?

I lower the front windows, relishing the small pleasure that is pressing a button instead of cranking a handle. The sky this morning is a cool gray, the air tastes sweet, and the world is a giant, rolling carpet of mist-softened, cow-speckled green. It would feel surreal except for the persistent screeching of the Volvo, a sound both strangely modern and primitive, somewhere between an offensive race car and an animal in pain.

I wonder if Joel even hears it; his ability to block out distraction verges on the robotic. I watch the boxy back end of the Volvo, its prehistoric taillights and Pennsylvania license plate, the Philadelphia parking decal stuck precisely in the bottom right-hand corner of the windshield, and the MIT (Joel, Joel's father) and Williams College (Joel's mother) alumni stickers in the middle. Through the glass, I can see the back of Joel's bent head, probably peering at the local map spread across his knees, on which he's traced the route to the mechanic's. Breathing in the cool, cherry-tinged air of Mike and Jaime's Jetta, I appraise our own capsule of a life: crushed fender, unidentified squealing, old graffiti clinging tenaciously to the windshield. Joel's head, as always, lowered in extreme concentration over something.

The squealing is getting louder. Even the cows look irritated, lifting their heads as we drive by, tails flicking like fans. I roll up the windows, turn up the Norah. It is early still, and the sky is soft with fog. In a fog, I think, you know to proceed with caution. It's the bright sunshine that deceives you; it is hazardous yet seems so perfectly safe.

Week Five: Saffron.

"If Joel were a spice," Max whispered, "what spice would he be?"

We were in class, half-paying attention while Mrs. B shouted about saffron. "The reds! The golds! It's *regal*!"

Max was like the nudge in the back of the classroom in junior high, slipping you notes, poking your spine, distracting and annoying but too charming to resist. We were cooking partners, which meant we shared a "kitchen," a blunt Formica island where we diced and seasoned and salted. It was an adult version of playing house. We chided each other for spilling, argued playfully about whose turn it was to clean. He'd taken to calling me Nutmeg. In between classes, our e-mail traffic had intensified to six, seven, eight messages a day. We weren't having an affair but had started to amass some light emotional baggage: jealousy, irritability, guilt. *Joel, Jill. Joel, Jill.* Their names rolled inside my mind like marbles in a pinball machine.

"So?" Max prodded in a whisper. "What spice?"

Ginger, I thought, but said nothing. I concentrated on adding raisins to our saffron-and-cashew risotto. I didn't feel comfortable talking about Joel anymore. "I don't think we should talk about Joel anymore," I said.

Max raised his eyebrows and shrugged. "Fair enough."

Week Six: Anise.

"How was class?" Joel asked.

It was nearly eleven; Max and I had stayed at the coffee shop until it closed. We hadn't talked about Joel or Jill, but I wasn't sure if this made things worse or better. Alone with Max, it was as if they didn't exist, but the moment I saw Joel, guilt engulfed me like a wave.

"Great," I chirped. "Really great." I was trying to sound artificial, to make him take notice, but he was faraway in a pool of lamplight, tapping a marbled pen against the back of his hand.

"There's this guy," I said then. It was part guilt forming the words, part desperation for attention, part the most basic desire to mention Max, out loud, to anyone. "In my class. He's a food writer."

Joel stopped tapping and turned. "Is he the person you have coffee with?"

"One of them," I lied. It was my first lie. I felt my stomach twist. "But don't worry," I said. "He's married. And—old." I walked over to his desk and set an anise apricot fritter on the edge. "Don't worry," I said again and summoned a reassuring smile.

"I wasn't worried," Joel said, but not in the way you'd think. It wasn't cocky, just true, and trusting.

He faced forward again, taking a bite of the fritter. "It's really *good*," he said, the exact same words in the exact same cadence I'd been hearing every week, like clockwork, since I'd accused him of not tasting.

"Thanks," I said but barely got the word out. I went upstairs, turned the shower on, sat on the toilet seat, and cried.

Week Seven: Peppercorns.

Max stared into his mug, looking miserable. His face was the elastic, dramatic sort that was incapable of concealing emotion. Happiness, sadness, boredom, frustration—he was as readable as a mime.

"Last night," he said flatly, "Jill made something called 'Could It Be Cake?'" His voice rose comedically on the question mark. "That's what the recipe was called: 'Could It Be Cake?'"

"Could it?"

"Not even close." He managed a pained smile. "That's the key to raw foodism. The recipes all have to sound self-consciously cute to make up for the fact that they taste like shit. 'Mock' this, 'faux' that. Or sometimes, these are my favorites, they just get lazy and call it what it's *supposed* to taste like but in quotation marks like"—he jabbed his index fingers in the air—"'Meat loaf.' Could anything sound less appetizing than 'Meat loaf'?"

I laughed, then bit my lip. "Sorry."

"Don't be. You should laugh. It's comical. It's also depressingly metaphorical. Pretend food—the perfect side dish for 'love' and 'happily ever after.'" The quotation jabs were getting more aggressive. "Here I am published in *Gourmet* magazine, and my wife's home with her book club eating something called Yummy Sunshine." He paused, and for a second his face registered genuine disbelief. "*Yummy Sunshine.* You'll notice it makes no mention of actual food, because it isn't."

"Maybe they should call it 'Could It Be Food?'"

But Max's face was serious. For a long minute he just watched me, not with tenderness, or judgment, or even a kind of vague consideration. His stare seemed made of eyes only, as objective as a flashlight's beam. It was impossible to look away.

Then he leaned across the table and covered my hand

lightly. "It's a good thing we drink coffee together, Nutmeg. I'd have a much harder time maintaining this façade of self-protective humor if alcohol were involved." He paused, and in the space between us I sensed a gaping hole I could fall into. Then he released my hand and tossed back the rest of his latte like a shot of bourbon. "God, I'm fed up," he said and smiled a humorless smile.

Week Eight: Curries.

Joel and I were eating our usual breakfast: cornflakes and an orange for him, Frosted Mini-Wheats for me. He did the crossword while I stirred my cereal. It looked grim, dry, the "frosted" like an actual crust of ice.

"Let me ask you something," I said suddenly.

Joel looked up, pencil poised over his crossword grid. I didn't usually announce myself this way. "Okay."

"If you were a spice," I asked, with what I thought was great flair, "what spice would you be?"

He paused only a beat. "Cinnamon."

"Why?" I pounced, praying for a good reason.

Joel thought for a second. "Because I like cinnamon," he said, then penciled something quickly in his crossword, as if an answer had been revealed.

When we return from the mechanic's, Joel joins the husbands in the Hunt Room, where the prewedding activities are getting under way. For the men, it's time for a little male bonding/freshwater trout fishing. For the women, it's those shapeless hours between the Friday night dinner and the Saturday night ceremony, where you reveal yourself as one of two kinds: those who steam-iron their hair and buff their toenails, or those who crawl back into their pajamas and revel in their aloneness.

First, I vend. Out drop a package of orange cheese-and-peanut-butter crackers and a can of Wild Cherry Pepsi, a meal I never order—much less encounter—except at hotel vending machines. Back in Room 143, I hang the DO NOT DISTURB sign, return to my pajamas, and climb into my freshly made bed. Cracking the Pepsi and flipping through the channels, I take just moments to find him: Dr. Phil. This is what I mean about Phil—he's always there when you need him. I love him for his reliability, for his no-nonsense brand of logic. He is a trusty moral compass, always there to cast the appropriate finger at the right or wrong.

I've often fantasized about being a guest on the show. Not just me, of course. Me and the varied cast of people who have wronged me: my mother, looking glazed and overmedicated; my father, scouring the studio audience for his stepkids; an assortment of ex-boyfriends, high school classmates, a gym teacher, a traffic cop in Northern Virginia. I would sit back and let Dr. Phil say all the words I always wanted to but never could.

You, he would reproach my father, *spending every holiday with your new family. You need to think about what kind of message you're sending to Megan. What are your actions telling her?*

In the audience, heads bob supportively.

And you, he would say, turning to my mother, *get therapy! Maybe then you won't need pills to escape from your life!*

The crowd erupts in a cheer.

But now, I would be chewed up if I went on. Phil doesn't like cowardice, and he doesn't like excuses. I imagine Joel and me sitting onstage, our faces pale as sand dollars above the vivid blue graphics. Megan: SAYS SHE'S NOT REALLY A CHEATER. Joel: MARRIED TO HIS WORK.

Now, Megan, Phil would say, as the camera panned out and the music—soothing and therapeutic but with an edge of un-rest—faded away. *You claim that Joel here is always busy and too focused on getting his doctorate in—what is it now, Joel?*

Statistics, Joel says. He's been brought on the show against his will but is ready to supply the facts.

That's right, Phil says. *A Ph.D. in statistics.* He pauses, mouth quirked. *Sounds like a pretty tall order to me, Megan.*

A few laughs from the crowd.

I mean, it's not like he's busy playing video games, now, is it? It's not like he's too focused on sleeping all day, or looking at porn on the Internet, am I right?

More laughs.

It's not just that he's busy, I interject, before I lose the crowd entirely. *He's oblivious—sometimes it's like he's completely inside his head. I moved here for him, Dr. Phil . . . and it's like I'm here alone.*

Well, let me ask you this. Did you ever tell Joel how you feel? Heads start moving enthusiastically. *How can you expect him to know what's bothering you if you don't speak up and say so?*

It isn't that easy, I protest, only to be met with Phil's trademark smirk. *I didn't want to hurt him.* I appeal to the audience. *I—I didn't want to lose him.*

But Phil isn't having it. His head cocks, smile widens, southern accent grows exponentially thicker. *So now, let me get this straight. He was busy, and you were lonely, so you figured—heck, what better way to solve this problem than go out and cheat?*

Teleprompters flash: BOO!

Joel is looking confused, bereft. The camera finds a doe-eyed woman in the audience whose expression says she thinks he's cute and would appreciate him far more than I do.

I wasn't planning to. It just happened! All of a sudden, he was consuming my thoughts. I—I just couldn't resist him.

Sorry. Phil chuckles. *Not quantifiable. Too many variables.*

Teleprompters: HISS! SPIT! SHOW DISGUST!

Phil keeps laughing and shaking his head, Joel working a confused hand through his hair, until their two faces merge into one: sharp brown eyes poised over a sprinkling of stubble, a gray mustache, and a pair of Ray-Bans wrapped around the package like a mirrored bow.

I turn the TV off, throw the bedspread back, let it slide to the floor. Grabbing the key card, I charge down the hall toward the elevator. I recall that I'm wearing pajamas only when I catch my reflection in the warped glass of the elevator doors beside a poster of the deluxe Vermont Cheddar Cheeseburger available in Dining Room A. The elevator arrives, and I step on it, joining an older couple with Tennessee accents. They stop their conversation to give me the pinched smile they've reserved for northerners who are "quirky." I smile back, undaunted, ride merrily down to the lobby, and march into the cubby beside the reception desk.

The cubby contains tiny, overpriced versions of things you may have forgotten to bring with you—mouthwash, toothpaste, plastic-wrapped toothbrushes; when had hotels stopped providing free emergency toothbrushes?—plus Vermont magnets, Vermont mini maple syrups, Vermont mini wedges of cheese. I am beginning to hate Vermont. And cheese. In the far corner are two boxy, cream-colored computers with faded clipart signs advertising "Surf the Web!" I plant myself in front of one and check my e-mail, not pausing to wonder why I'm checking my e-mail until I find my in-box empty and realize just how much I'd been hoping to hear from Max because seeing that I haven't makes me sad—no. More than sad. Used. Deserted.

I see Max's old spice puns wavering on the greenish screen. I should erase them, but I can't. I fantasize about firing one back:

This message brought to you with MACE.

Yours sincerely, Red Pepper—CRUSHED.

You are, as it turns out, jerk seasoning!!!

But it was ending anyway, it was always ending, and I have no right to be so angry. Yet I am. Angry that I'm here, that I'm alone, that our car is broken, and that Joel thinks the accident was all my fault when as far as I'm concerned it only proved my point: the sun is dangerous.

"You can't just blame the sun," I can hear Joel say.

Seconds later I'm on Google, typing in "accidents statistics sunsets," my fingers tiny mallets on the keys. I wait while the machine searches for results at a tedious fifty cents a minute and am just about to feel ridiculous when, lo and behold, a document appears. "Safety and the Sun," it is called, and as soon as I begin skimming I know I've found what I'm looking for. "At sunset, light reflecting off a dirty windshield can momentarily blind you." Yes. "It is thought to be a leading cause of accidents at dusk." Vindication! I send it to the printer, watch as the evidence comes chugging out. "Dangerous when there's too little sunshine," it says, "dangerous when there's too much. In the glare, it's impossible to see the shadows being cast on the road before you."

Week Nine: Chile Peppers.

"Last but not least!" announced Mrs. B.

It was our final class. Max and I were standing in our pretend kitchen. Our arms were folded, elbows barely, inconspicuously touching. We were ascending the ranks of the pepper, a fitting end to our tour of spices, our increasingly fearless palates and increasingly thick skins. Before us on the counter were a pile of seeds and a nest of mangled, brightly colored stems. We had started with jalapeño, then chipotle and cayenne, and were now staring down the barrel of a flame-red habanero that Mrs. B dangled in front of her nose like bait.

"This, my partners in spice," she said, "is a test of courage." She smiled mischievously. "Who's up for it?"

We glanced around the room. Generally, all of us tried everything; the trying was as important as the cooking. More important than the deft slicing of a chipotle was the courage to pop it in your mouth, to splash Tabasco into salad dressing, drop a few fennel seeds on the tip of your tongue. But in the face of the habanero, we were withering.

Then Bram's hand shot up. "I'll do it!" he shouted. Around Mrs. B, it wasn't unusual to find yourself shouting. "Wait!" His hand dropped back down. "Tell me the Scoville first."

Scoville units, we had learned, represented the amount of capsaicin—the chemical that determines hotness—in a given pepper. After the capsaicin lights your mouth on fire, the brain releases a rush of endorphins. "The higher the Scoville," Mrs. B liked to remind us, "the better the rush!"

Now, she lowered her voice with something like reverence. "Three hundred thousand."

The class rippled appropriately with awe and terror. Bram stuffed his hand in his pocket and shook his head.

Mrs. B began roving the classroom, swaying the fiery pepper in front of her gigantic bosom like a hypnotist. "Who will it be?" she mused, bypassing me and stopping in front of Max, her favorite. "Feeling daring, Sutton?"

Max paused only a second, then flipped an imaginary cape over his shoulders. "Always."

Everyone cheered as Max strode forward. Gertrude leaned over to me, clapping, and whispered, "Shame he's taken." Then we all waited, breath drawn, while Max accepted the pepper, displaying it first for his rapt audience like a magician with his dove before he makes it disappear.

* * *

That night, Max and I didn't speak. Sitting on the café table, our lattes looked ridiculous, foamy, frivolous, relics from a time when we were only hypothetical. When finally he said, still recovering from the habanero, "I would tell you I'm on fire, but it seems too obvious," I wanted to laugh, but I couldn't. We left the shop with our cups untouched. Max hailed a cab. From the backseat, he leaned forward to speak in the driver's ear, quietly, as if not to implicate me in where we were going. When he sat back, staring out the window, he held my hand so tightly it hurt. Still we didn't speak. After nine weeks of nothing but wit and verbs, puns and metaphors, our final evening together would be virtually wordless. When the light in the cab blinked on, Max paid and I stepped onto the sidewalk. He went inside the office. ACANCY, the sign said. The V was flickering crazily, the traffic swishing in the distance. I waited in the parking lot, safe in the shadows of the security lights, my brain a rushing gorge of endorphins, washing away all conscience, doubt, thought. For the first time, I would leave a hotel room without remembering the details: not the wallpaper, or the bedspread, or the number on the door. All I would remember was the sound of it shutting behind us and how, when Max's lips found mine, they felt exactly as I knew they would: hungry.

Joel returns from the fishing trip and throws the key card on the desktop. The sound is not as satisfying as actual keys; it's like a paper clip falling.

"The mechanic called."

I pause in front of the mirror, where I'm simultaneously applying liquid eyeliner, watching TV, and wondering again why I brought a long-sleeved dress to a July wedding. "And?"

"The damage is more extensive than they thought."

"Is it expensive?"

"Extensive," Joel repeats.

"No, I know—but is it expensive?"

"Of course." He yanks his shoes off and throws them on the carpet. Spending money, especially spending that could have been averted, is the thing that upsets Joel most. "It's outrageously expensive. It's probably more than the car's even worth."

I don't bother asking whether we would consider getting rid of it; this, I know, is not an option.

"Not only that, but cell reception is practically nonexistent, so I'm paying analog roaming rates. And we may be stuck here until Monday."

Now it is my turn to feel alarmed. "Monday?"

"Yes."

"That's the soonest they can fix it?"

"Since they're not open on Sundays—yes." He's undressing as he speaks, stuffing each piece of clothing in the plastic bag he brought to separate his dirty laundry. "They took us on short notice as it is. And offered to bring the car here when it's finished. I can't exactly ask them to hurry."

I look beyond his bent back, at the checkered tablecloth curtains, the cow in a frame, the blanket of green yawning outside the window. Suddenly the prospect of two more days here feels unbearable. "So, you mean, we'll have to book the room for another night?"

Joel straightens, blocking my view. His mouth twitches slightly. "Unless you want to sleep in the car," he says. "At least then it would be good for something."

He swipes one of my damp towels from the floor. I notice then that he is badly sunburned, pink down to his collar and halfway up his arms, like a flesh-colored shirt.

"Does that hurt?" I ask, but it's too late. He is heading for the shower. I hear the overhead fan rattle, water slap the tub floor. Maybe he's frustrated with me about the accident, maybe about many things, but now, I know, is not the time. We have to get to a wedding.

Every wedding is about many other weddings. The ones you've had, the ones you wished you had, the ones you had and wished you didn't. There is the couple in the center, glowing, feeding each other delicate slivers of cake. There is the couple on the top of the cake, eternally happy, made of molded plastic. There are the older couples—majestic, battle-scarred, jewel-encrusted—flanking them at the head table and presiding over all the other couples in the room, all of them the stars of their own love stories, stories about love and not quite love, an endless sequence of clasped hands and drained champagne glasses, secrets shared and secrets hidden.

"To have and to hold," the priest says.

Nathaniel and Nicole face each other in front of the altar. Her dress is embroidered with tiny flowers, hair drifts in soft wisps around her face. She looks radiant. Light spills through the high stained-glass windows, illuminating haphazard details of the congregation: a ringed hand, a glittering earlobe, a smooth swatch of face. I gaze around the room and think about how being surrounded by love's perfect beginnings puts every other relationship in high relief. It highlights what's there, magnifies what isn't. It reminds you of what love is meant to be and leaves you with either a renewed feeling of passion or a more certain sense of despair. You drink and dance and wake up the next day in your hotel room, feeling recommitted to the notion of spending the rest of your life with the person in bed beside you or feeling hollow, rising quickly, starting to pack, ignoring the gnawing feeling that you are missing something.

Nicole is crying as she says her vows. Nathaniel reaches out to brush a tear from her cheek. "I promise to be true to you," she says. "In good times and in bad."

I've been to a million weddings, heard these words spoken a million times, but this time I pay close attention.

"For richer or for poorer," she says, voice trembling. "In sickness and in health. I will honor and be true to you for all the days of my life."

As I listen to these words, really listen to the magnitude of them, the absolute and startling promise, I realize how incredible it is that people say them. That to do so may be the most genuinely dramatic act of courage, the most daring leap of faith. As I watch the exchange of rings, I feel myself welling up. I am getting emotional at the wedding of two people I barely know, and as the tears come, I realize the other thing about staring into the sun: after it dazzles and blinds you, it can make you cry.

Then I feel a hand on the small of my back. Joel's hand, and I am surprised by how strong it is, how steady. I look up at him, expecting embarrassment, or confusion, but what I see in his face is something else—a twinge of panic, shame, and something firm, like dignity—and I realize in that instant that he knows. That he's probably always known. And I think suddenly about what it would feel like to lose him and I can't breathe. I feel like I'm falling apart. Like I'm falling off a cliff. And I cry and cry as the husband kisses his wife because it's all so beautiful.

When we left the hotel, it was almost midnight. Max's hug was loose as a shawl.

"You know," he said, standing on the sidewalk, "if my situation were different . . ."

He let the line drift into ambiguity. It sounded crafted, right down to the ellipses, which were probably designed to evoke wistfulness. They came across sounding weak.

"But it isn't," I said, finishing for him.

"No," Max said. His voice sounded tender, but his face had lost all its light.

I wanted him to say something more, something meaningful, but then his arm moved and a cab eased to the curb, as agreeable as a stunt car waiting in the wings. Max touched my shoulder and leaned into the curl of my ear. "You," he whispered, "are everything nice."

It was his parting shot, his final punch line, and in retrospect it was only appropriate we ended as a joke.

*   *   *

Sunday afternoon. Joel and I are alone together in the aftermath of someone else's wedding. All pretense has been dismantled. The guests are gone, the N&N's eaten, the rugs newly striped with vacuum tracks. The hotel staff are busying themselves with towels and sheets, syrup and cheese, making way for the next event. The newlyweds have flown off on their honeymoon; Mike and Jaime drove away in their Jetta. Everyone has moved on while the Volvo sits useless in a garage in the middle of nowhere, and despite the fact that we're far away from home with all the trappings of a getaway—a thick carpet and idyllic mountain view and maids who make our beds each morning— real life feels more immediate than it's ever been.

Still, Joel and I are valiant in our attempts at escaping. We haven't talked about my crying yesterday, what he saw in my face and what I saw in his, and I don't know what he suspects is wrong, whether just that I'm unhappy or something more concrete. He's been abrupt all day, asking only the most practical of questions—"Can you pass the sugar?" "Do you want to shower first or should I?"—and I find myself longing for his obliviousness. Now he is the opposite of what's always frustrated me, and it's terrifying.

At the moment, Joel is effectively cloistered in Room 143, text-messaging people at Penn about his absence tomorrow. He spent an hour this morning outside on his cell phone, hunting for a pocket of good reception; when I looked out the window, he was roaming the parking lot, a near-empty grid of painted lines and numbers. I watched as he paced, in fits and starts, testing different spots as if in a giant game of tic-tac-toe. When he came back to the room, he made instant coffee in the bathroom sink and started typing in his cell phone.

"I'm going for a swim," I tell him now, wearing a fluffy hotel bathrobe and Joel's oversize flip-flops.

"Okay," he says, without looking up.

The Green Mountain Resort pool is completely empty, and comfortingly manufactured: the hum of an unseen motor, water the color of Windex, air thick and steamy with chlorine. Giant green plants in giant terra-cotta pots anchor each corner, and the walls, true to their name, are done in green mosaic: slick, damp shards of tile arranged in rudimentary mountain shapes.

I slough off the bathrobe and ease my way down the metal staircase, past the placard that says NO DIVING. When I'm sub-merged to the waist, I dive to the bottom and run my palms over the smooth pool floor. Everything else I leave on the sur-face: my boyfriend marooned in our hotel room, the Volvo ma-rooned at a vacant garage, my pressing desire to go home, leave, explode, when we're surrounded by nothing but all this aching beauty and stillness.

As I start swimming, I savor the fact of motion: the orderly gulp, splash, and kick of it, the feeling of my cupped palm slic-ing the water, the sense that I am getting somewhere, if only the wet concrete edge on either side. I try to empty my mind, to focus on nothing but the space I occupy. It is a physical space only—made of aches and endorphins, limbs and breath. But the memories are encoded. I know too well the resistance of water, the moment of connection when, palm like a blade, the water parts, sending rivulets streaming from the fingers like a speedboat's wake. As I layer lap upon lap upon lap, I realize I am chanting my secret mantra: *Joel, Joel, Joel.*

When my shoulders start aching, I tread water. Sunlight slants through the beveled ceiling, winking like mica on the surface of the pool. I look around at the bright, empty water, the mountainous mosaics, and for a minute I am inside an elementary school diorama: everything perfect and motionless and fake. Tilting my head back, I squint at the sunlit ceiling, then suck in a deep breath and dive under. I open my eyes to gaze at the soft, smudged pool bottom, the wavy bars of the drain, pale tendrils of my limbs. In the center, the Green Mountain insignia wavers like a mirage. Out of old habit, I find myself holding my breath, letting the pressure build in my chest, and it feels daring and dramatic until it occurs to me that there is no one here to jump in if I needed to be saved.

I break the surface, gulping air. My fingertips are puckered, my eyes starting to burn. I climb up the steps slowly, chest aching, hair streaming water, and dry off as best I can. When I arrive at the door to Room 143, it opens instantly. It's as if Joel has been waiting on the other side, listening for my approach.

"Meg," he says.

Something about the tone of his voice makes my heart leap into my throat.

"We need to talk."

It isn't a question this time, not an either-or situation. The statement is so true there is no room for debate.

I sit on the foot of the bed. This fluffy robe feels heavy. It isn't fresh anymore, isn't anonymous but overused, a robe wrapped around a million bodies, a bed slept in by a million couples. Joel is looking at me with a mixture of affection and apprehension, and no matter what happens, I love him for being the one brave enough to speak.

"Are you unhappy?" he says, quietly. "With me?"

"No." I pause. "I don't know."

"You seem unhappy."

I look at my hands, lying wrinkled in my lap. "Sometimes I am. But I don't know if that's being with you, or in a new city, or how busy you've been . . ." I pinch the thick carpet beneath my toes, squeezing it like sand. "I didn't even know you noticed."

"I noticed."

"Why didn't you say anything?"

"Why didn't you?"

We are silent for a long moment, and I am afraid to keep talking, but when you're alone together in a hotel room far away from home, there is nowhere else to go.

I look into his face. "Why don't you want to marry me?"

"Do you want to marry me?" Joel asks, but not in the way you'd think; it isn't a proposal, just a hypothetical.

I answer him honestly. "I don't know." It is a relief to admit it, though I don't know what it means, or where we go from here. As Joel moves toward me, what I do know is that I need to come clean and tell him everything. I am about to when he folds his hands around my face.

"You look"—he says, lifting my chin toward him, and to my surprise I see his eyes filling, his mind working as he searches for a new word—"dazzling."

Dusk, Monday. Joel and I survey the damage. They fixed the Volvo well enough to get us home, even power-washed the windshield. All traces of graffiti have vanished now, but the fender is still crumpled, and one headlight is smashed, not to mention all the damage on the inside. The car is no longer a showpiece, just a reality: expense and inconvenience. We stare at it for a minute, then walk silently to the back.

Joel opens the trunk and begins loading. The parking lot is nearly empty, unlike when we arrived on Friday. Then, we were relieved just to make it here before we broke down. We thought the hotel would save us; maybe, in a way, it has.

"What's this?" Joel says.

He's looking at my suitcase, at the article I found on the Internet peeking from the side pocket.

"Oh, it's just a—" I pause, unsure how to explain. "It's a story. About sunsets causing accidents."

He looks confused. "Where did you find it?"

"The Internet."

"You mean you looked for it?"

"Yeah."

His face softens, hand moves to his hair. "Here? At the hotel? You got on the computer in the lobby to look up that— that sun statistic stuff?" I can see him processing this information, trying to make sense of it. He takes his sunglasses off, looks again at the thick sheaf, then turns to me with his pale blue eyes. "What did it say?"

"It said it's true," I tell him, but there's no vindication in it. Suddenly I'm wishing that I'd never found it. "It said—there are accidents caused by sunsets. That people look into this bright light, and then—"

"Wham." He says it softly.

I say nothing. For a minute we just watch each other, and I can see the instant when the shadow crosses his face, the shudder of understanding in his eyes as the right memories in the right order collide into place. He shoves the article back in the suitcase, puts his sunglasses back on, and slams the trunk down. He gets into the car; I follow. We sit in the front seat, the air heavy with his breath.

"It comes up on you so suddenly," I whisper. "The sunset. That's the whole thing. And it's so beautiful. You don't know not to trust it."

Joel's head is hanging, hands opening and closing on the steering wheel.

"You don't know it's going to be like that. It's so sudden."

Joel lifts his head and looks straight ahead. "I don't see why it would be sudden," he says. "The sun sets every day."

Then he starts the car. The sky is overcast, perfect weather for driving. We roll cautiously through the parking lot, past the sign where someone has removed CONGRATULATIONS NATHANIEL & NICOLE and is replacing it with HAPPY ANNIVERS—one letter at a time, an endless game of taking apart and piecing back together. At the exit, Joel looks both ways, pulls onto the road, and we drive off into the sunset. Except it's not that kind of sunset. The sun is invisible, hidden behind a mass of gray clouds, and it's not clear what lies ahead but it's easier to see straight.

Losing California

Tara McCarthy

Alison Beyer, twenty-nine years old with hair in a low, wet ponytail, is perched on a surfboard, riding a roaring wave. In the Pacific, watching her from a distance bobs Bob Gunn—a stout fortysomething. He's straddling a surfboard.

Alison spins around on her board, which shoots up into the air as she dives into the surf. She pops up, shakes her hair out, climbs back on her board, and paddles toward Bob. She says, "What happened, Bob? Come on!" She wipes some water from her eyes with the top of her wrist. "Today's the day," she says. "I can feel it."

Bob smiles and says, "I know! I know!" But he's not sure today's the day, and to be honest, neither is Alison. Quite frankly, he's the worst student she's had this summer. Possibly ever. But then another wave comes, and with Alison's encouragement, at the exact right moment, Bob rises up, plants his feet on his board, and extends his arms. He's doing it. He's riding the wave.

Alison screams, "Yes! You got it! Go! Yes!" She sees another wave coming, paddles, catches it, rides it to the shore, where Bob has collapsed in the shallow surf.

He lies back in the water and throws his fists up, victorious. "I did it!" he squeals. "My God! I never thought the day would come."

Alison thinks, *Tell me about it,* as she jogs to his side, her surfboard tucked under her arm. She says, "That's what we do here at Leo's Land of Surf, babe. We make dreams come true." She says it all cheesy-like, but that doesn't mean she doesn't believe it. She's a romantic, our Alison. That's important to the story.

She holds out a hand, helps pull Bob up, then looks at her chunky watch. She checks to see that her ring's still on her finger and that her diamond's still in her ring. Colin hates that she wears it in the water. He says, "It wasn't cheap, you know." When she first got engaged, it was simply that she never wanted to take the ring off—almost immediately felt naked without it. Lately it feels like it's more to prove a point. She says, "It's insured, you know."

"Can we go again?" Bob asks.

"Mnn. That's our time. Sorry." On any other day she'd stay—particularly with such a promising set of waves rolling in—but she's having dinner at her parents'. They're finalizing some details for the wedding. Somehow, Alison still can't believe it's come to this—seating charts over surfing, the wedding over waves. She would've been happy getting married right there, on the beach, but Colin would have none of it.

After a quick trip to the showers at the Surf Shop, Alison drives an old blue Volkswagen Beetle, windows down. Hair half dry, now in shorts and a tank top, she pops a tape in, listens to a snippet of the song, hits Rewind, then Play. She cranks up the volume—loud—and bops her head along to a vigorous rock song. It's not a song many people would recognize, but that's not important. What's important is that Alison loves it. It's by the band the Deductibles, and it's a well-known fact among Alison's friends that she likes them a little bit more than would be considered normal. Especially when you consider they hail from *Canada*.

Outside the apartment complex where she lives, Alison pulls over, honks, and bangs out a beat on the steering wheel. Colin Kraig—that's Alison's fiancé of a year, live-in boyfriend of two before that, regular ole boyfriend of *another* two before that—emerges from the building and opens the passenger-side door. He slides in, reaches for the volume, turns it down, closes the door. He says, "We've got to get you to a record store."

"Why?" she wants to know. "What's wrong with this?"

"Oh, nothing." He looks out his window, fighting a smile.

Alison looks over at him, starts to drive. "I play other stuff. Sometimes."

"Yeah! Other Deductibles stuff." Colin, well aware of his fiancée's silly Deductibles obsession, has often joked that maybe Alison should run away and become the groupie she's meant to be. He's probably never imagined, though, that it might actually happen.

"I like what I like," she says. "What can I say? And you better be warned. The new album comes out next month."

"Oh, great." Colin shakes a tape in the air; he's made it special for her Beetle, lacking as it is in CD technology. "So anyway, I think I've finally got it," he says. "Our first dance. Can I pop it in?"

"Sure," she says, as she drives off in the direction of her parents' house. "Go for it."

Colin puts the tape in and hits Play. Alison has always hated the song that comes blaring through the speakers. Colin would have no way of knowing this; it's not like they've ever had occasion to discuss this particular song before. She knows that things like this aren't supposed to mean anything. People love songs and hate songs for inexplicable reasons. But somehow she's starting to wonder whether these kinds of things mean *more* than anything, whether Colin even gets her at all. She also knows that two weeks before her wedding is probably a bad time to think about this. It's not on her "Two Weeks Before" to-do list.

When she pulls into the driveway of her parents' house, another car has just arrived. Colin and Alison linger a moment in the car until the song playing ends.

"Well?" Colin wants to know.

"I don't know," Alison says with an upward lilt. She doesn't have the heart to outright reject yet another song, though it's true Colin's suggestions have been getting progressively worse. Firmly in avoidance mode, she cuts the ignition and gets out just as her father, Steve Beyer—fit in his fifties—gets out of the car in front. He says, "They have new Beetles now, you know. Hi, Colin." The men shake hands.

"Yeah, they had new Coke once, too." Alison kisses her father on the cheek; he walks down the driveway. He says, "I'm going to grab the mail."

Colin grabs Alison by the arm. "Hey. Can I get one of those?" Kisses, he means.

She smiles, kisses him on the cheek, then on the lips.

"Hey, Colin," Steve calls out. "You'll be part of the family soon enough. Make yourself useful, will you? Bring the recycling can out from the garage."

Alison says, "I'll see you inside."

Inside, she sets her keys and bag down on a counter in the kitchen. Music blares from another room: "Wooly Bully." "Mom!" she calls out.

No answer.

Alison goes to a Crock-Pot on an adjacent counter, lifts the lid. Steam rises up. She inhales deeply, lifts a spoon, stirs, puts the spoon down, covers the pot again. She peeks into the living room: nobody there. She crosses the room—turns down the volume on the stereo she passes—goes down a hallway, and pokes her head into the study with a "Boo!" but there's nobody there either. She returns to the living room, looks out the sliding doors, sees a glass of iced tea on the diving board. A net skimmer floats in the pool. She hears her father shout, "I'm home," as she heads for the sliding doors. She steps out onto a patio, sees a dark mass at the bottom of the deep end.

"Ohmigod!" She breaks into a run, heading straight for the pool—"Mom!"—but at the water's edge, she stops short, almost against her will, and waves her hand in circles to keep from falling in. She's like Wile E. Coyote, skidding toward a cartoon cliff, only *she* somehow stops before going over.

The world is spinning; her feet are cement blocks. She wills them to move, tells them to propel her body forward into the water, but they've shut down. They're not listening. And why would they? As long as she's standing *here,* she can pretend it's all in her head—a trick of the eye or some horrible dream.

Behind her, her father screams, "Oh, Christ! Evelyn!" He rushes past Alison and jumps into the pool, fully clothed. Steve takes heavy steps toward the side of the pool. Evelyn's body—dressed for dinner—is draped across his arms, half submerged. Colin appears by Alison's side.

"Colin," Steve says. "Call 911."

Alison stands paralyzed, thinking, *My God, not my mother, my God, not my mother.* It's not until the ambulance arrives—too late, they were all already too late—that she thinks, *My God. My wedding.*

Six months later—word of the postponement spread quickly, some deposits were lost, others returned, the honeymoon canceled, the funeral held, the coffin put in the ground, the wedding dress put in a closet—sirens sound inside a rock club. On top of the chatter of the crowd, voices, maybe ten of them—Alison's included—chant a singsong "De-DUCT-ibles, De-DUCT-ibles" punctuated by random whoops and yells. A thumping bass note marks out a beat. The band's lead singer (inasmuch as there is one; they all write and they all sing lead on the songs they write), Trevor Walsh, neo-hippie hip with glasses and shaggy hair, steps up to the mike. "Okay," he says. "This crowd is awesome."

More cheers; more bass thumping; more sirens (they're part of the song). The band is touring in support of that new album, which is all Alison has been listening to since it came out about a month after, well, you know. Seriously, *all*. It's the *only* album she has played in months.

"So I think Michael's going to start off this next one," Trevor says into the mike. "Michael?"

Isolated girls in the crowd shriek with glee. Guitarist Michael Madsen—nerdy cool with Buddy Holly glasses—leans into his mike. "Yeah?"

"Are you ready to rock?"

Michael just laughs, adds a guitar riff to the mix. Alison can't take her eyes off him. She has always loved his songs best, but the new album has solidified her devotion. The longing in his songs, it just does something to her. She doesn't mind the look of him either.

Trevor turns to the crowd. "How about you, L.A.? Are you ready to rock?" The crowd goes nuts. Drummer Adam Lindy—broad-shouldered, ruggedly handsome, sweaty—has drumsticks at the ready.

Michael looks at Trevor and leans into his mike. He says, "Are you?"

And they're off. It's that song from the car, the one that had Alison rocking out the day that, well, you know. Now she's ten feet from the stage. Eyes glued to Michael, she sings along. She knows every word. Beside her stands Kara Kraig—less hip, less enthused, but singing occasional phrases because you can't be friends with Alison and not know at least a couple of Deductibles songs.

Alison says, "I'm in love." She's said this about Michael on any number of occasions before. To Kara, even—and Kara's Colin's sister, which you might have deduced from her last name. This time Alison feels funny saying it, though. It's like she means it.

Kara doesn't seem to notice the change. She just rolls her eyes and says, "I'm going to the bathroom."

After the gig, Alison and Kara retire to the front bar. They're sitting on barstools with almost empty drinks when Kara yawns and says, "Can we go now?"

"Just a few more minutes," Alison says. "The rest of them are already out; he'll probably be out in a minute."

Kara looks over toward the end of the bar, where rhythm guitarist Dan Blaine—friendly, easygoing—is talking to a few fans, showing his toothy smile. "I like his songs best," she says. "I bet he's the only one of them who isn't an asshole."

Alison sips her drink, scans the room. Trevor is talking to two guys just ten feet away.

Kara says, "We're really too old for this, you know."

Alison turns back. "Too old for what?"

"To be groupies."

"I like to think of myself as a fan, not a groupie." Michael appears at the far end of the bar. "Ohmigod," Alison says. "There he is."

Kara turns to look, but Alison grabs her. "No, don't. What if he sees?" Kara turns back and says, "And the difference between a fan and a groupie is . . . ?"

Alison looks over toward Michael; his gaze falls on her briefly, moves on. He spots something or someone across the bar, starts to move that way. As he passes behind Alison and Kara, Alison absentmindedly strokes the back of her neck; she has a tattoo, an intricate Celtic design, on the back of her right shoulder. Michael gives the tattoo a double take as he walks by, but neither of the girls notices. How could they, busy as they are looking so uninterested? When she believes he's out of earshot (he is), Alison says, "Fans keep their distance."

Kara says, "Fans are chickenshit."

Alison finishes her drink, swirls the ice in her glass. "I could talk to him," she says. She knows she wouldn't do it, though, not with Kara there, with Kara being who she is. She thinks if she were with another friend, or alone, she might, though. She's more drawn to him after hearing this last record, and seeing this show, than ever. "Why don't you think I'd talk to him?"

Kara reaches for Alison's left hand and lifts it for inspection. "That's a pretty nice diamond my brother got you."

Alison pulls her hand back and says, "Come on. Let's go."

She takes one more look at Michael and thinks, *I wish I knew you. I wish my life* allowed *me to know you.*

Back at home, Alison tiptoes toward the bed, where Colin sleeps. She slips off her jeans and shirt, climbs on top of him, and kisses him awake.

"Mmmmn," he says. "I thought I told you to go because Alison would be home soon."

"Very funny."

"How was the show? You keep my sister out of trouble?"

But Alison has other things on her mind. She's coming on strong, groping under the sheets; she wants to be made love to now.

Afterward, Colin (no fool, for all his failings) says, "The Dedictibles should come to town more often."

"What are you talking about?" Alison says. Though of course she knows exactly what he's talking about.

"I haven't been able to get you that worked up since—"

Alison shoots him a stern look. She gets up, pulls on her jeans.

"Oh, come on, Al. I was *joking*!" He watches, mouth agape, as Alison heads for the door. "Where are you going?"

When daylight dawns, Alison's asleep in a lounge chair beside her parents' swimming pool, a blanket pulled over her. Her father emerges from the sliding glass doors, throws his towel on a chair, and jumps into the water. The splash wakes Alison; Steve notices her only when he resurfaces. He says, "Whatcha doing?"

Alison stretches. "Nothing much."

Steve swims over, rests his arms on the edge of the pool. "Come on in. The water's fine." He splashes her and she flinches. He has started to suspect the truth, which is that Alison hasn't been back in the water since the accident. She's been building a website for Leo's Land of Surf, but that's more of an excuse than anything.

Alison says, "Dad, just leave it alone, okay?"

Steve pushes off a wall and floats on his back across the pool. "Had a fight with Colin again?"

"Yeah."

Steve dunks his head under the water, reemerges. "Well, he's right that it's time to set another date. You two should've been married by now. *Would've* been by now. You can't wait forever."

"Well, maybe there's a reason it didn't happen, did you ever think of that?" It's the first time Alison has expressed out loud to anyone even the tiniest possibility that she's having second thoughts about marrying Colin. That maybe general compatibility and similar backgrounds and five years together aren't enough, that maybe she expected there to be something *more*. Like do-or-die. Like really can't live without you. Like *passion*. "God, Dad, how can you swim here?"

Steve grabs on to a ladder, pulls himself up out of the water, reaches for his towel. He says, "Come into the house. There's something I want to give you."

Inside, there's a decorative box on the kitchen table. *Oh, great,* Alison thinks. *Flowers and shit.* She imagines there's something wedding-related and frilly inside, something meant to inspire her to get back on the horse and walk it down the aisle. "What is it?" she asks.

"Some of Mom's stuff," her father says. "Looks like from before I met her. I thought maybe you'd want it."

Alison opens the fridge, grabs a bottle of water. "That's okay. You can keep it."

Steve wipes his brow; he's clearly at a loss. "You have to let her in again if you're going to let her out."

"What," she says. "So I can 'get over it' and get married and make everybody feel better?"

"That's not what I mean." Steve knows it's best not to try to talk to Alison when she's like this. "I'm going to get dressed," he says. "Take it or leave it, love."

Alone in the kitchen, Alison sits at the table. She opens the box and starts to sift through loose letters and postcards, then picks up a card addressed "To Evelyn on Sunday." (Her mom's name, you may recall, was Evelyn.) Alison sets it aside and digs deeper into the box; she pulls out a stack of letters tied up with a red ribbon, sets them aside. Then she pulls out a 45 record with a handwritten label: "To Evelyn on Thursday." She puts it back in the box, picks up the box, and leaves.

Back at her and Colin's apartment, Alison puts the box down, goes straight to the hall closet, and opens it. Her wedding dress, which Colin insisted cover her tattoo, stares back at her. She almost loses her breath. Then she reaches up for a Technics box bearing a picture of a turntable.

When Colin comes home after work that evening, Alison's

on the floor by the stereo; a breezy pop song blares: "Lie back and look up at the sky/Relax and let the hours go by . . ."

Colin enters and shouts "Al!" She's oblivious.

"Alison!"

She looks up, jumps up, turns down the music.

"What's this hippie shit?"

Excitement drains from her face. "You know? You can be a real asshole sometimes."

"What? Is this the *Deductibles*?"

Alison lifts the needle off her turntable, off "To Evelyn on Thursday." She's too disgusted to answer, though the reality is that the frequency with which she's been listening to that new Deductibles CD would drive any sane person off a cliff. Colin, until now, has been remarkably tolerant. He collapses on the couch and, with uncharacteristic force, says, "We need to make a decision about the wedding."

"Col—"

He steamrolls. "And you won't even talk about it. And you just can't seem to let me help you through all this. Or maybe you think I can't. Either way, it's like that thing you talk about in surfing. When you're stuck in one place because of the tides."

She looks at the record on the turntable and thinks of that horrible, horrible song that Colin wanted them to dance their first dance to. She says, "Someone wrote this song for my mother."

"Al, you're not listening." Colin drops his head into his hands, then looks up, strained. "Maybe you should go away or something, take some time, figure stuff out. Cause I can't go on like this. You need to commit to another date or we need to call it off for good. I'm going to stay with my sister for a few days, give you some space." He gets up and goes into the bedroom to pack a bag.

After Colin has left, Alison sits at a table in her living room, her fingers on her laptop. The Deductibles blare from the stereo unabashedly now. She thinks back to the show the night before, to Michael, whose songs *move* her, as corny as it sounds. They seem to open her heart up, the way she imagines true love should. Marriage shouldn't feel like closing off or a shutting down; it should feel like an opening up. Right? She has a memory, then, of her mother's first impression of Colin: "He's a little stiff, isn't he?"

But to have such a shameless, irrational schoolgirl crush at her age! When she has a fiancé! It's embarrassing. Humiliating! To think she has spent the better part of the day imagining a scenario in which Michael wrote a song about her. (And to think someone actually wrote a song for her mother! Her *mother*!)

Alison, of course, is not the only girl ever to lose her head over someone she's never met, and certainly not the first to do so over a member of a band she likes. Her problem is that she can't seem to quash it—Colin and her presumably soon-to-be-rescheduled nuptials notwithstanding. She tries to trick herself back into reality by signing on to her wedding registry—she wishes one of the early gifters had sprung for the comforter. And what was she thinking registering for fine china, anyway?

At this rate, she and Colin will one day be able to throw a swanky dinner party for three and a half people. She even looks at her calendar, tries to figure out when would be a good time to get married. The two-hundred-person bash they had planned just isn't going to happen; she's off the hook in that way; even Colin's parents agree it's inappropriate. But maybe they can elope somewhere tropical with their immediate families in tow? Alison only ever wanted something small to begin with.

The trickery's not working, though. Setting the calendar aside, Alison types in the URL for the Deductibles' website—she's responsible for countless hits in the last several months—and then she clicks on the link for E-MAIL MICHAEL.

She gets up, goes to the fridge for a beer, and returns to the computer, steeled. "I have no idea why I'm writing," she writes, a little bit startled that she's actually come to this point, "except to say that your music gets inside me in a way few things do. Last night I felt alive for the first time in months. It was all I could do to leave without introducing myself. I'm not sure why I think I'm any different than other fans, but sometimes, I just do. I can't shake the feeling that if we knew each other we'd like each other."

She types for a while more, and when she finally stops, she sits back, reads—"I don't even know if you're single but you don't wear a wedding ring"—shakes her head, hits Delete. Out loud, she says "I'm pathetic."

She sits for a moment and considers Colin's suggestion that she get away for a few days. She finds herself checking airfares to Canada, then closes out of her browser. "Worse than pathetic," she mutters, then decides to take a shower.

In the bathroom, she starts the shower, then stares at the water spiraling down the drain. She takes a few deep breaths, drops her robe, climbs in, washes frantically, gets out, sighs with relief. Six months, and that's as close as she's gotten to catching a wave.

The next morning, Leo Mancao of Leo's Land of Surf—compact, Hawaiian—pulls on a wet suit in his shop's back room. Nearby, Alison rubs down a surfboard with a bar of wax. She says, "He thinks I'm doing a reef dance." Colin hadn't been able to recall the exact term, just the idea of being in a rut.

"And what do you think?" Leo wants to know.

"I think he might be right. But I don't know. God, it's all so stupid."

"Your thing for the guy in the band?"

"Yeah," she says. "I mean, you're my *boss* and you know about it!" Alison puts the wax bar down, lifts the board, hands it to Leo, who tucks it under his arm and walks out of the shop and onto the boardwalk.

Leo says, "Well, what is it about this guy?"

"I don't know." Alison stands next to him on the boardwalk. "There's just something about his songs." She looks out at the water. The haze is burning off so fast you can practically see it disappearing. It's promising to be an amazingly gorgeous day, and Alison has a pang. She misses the water. "It's like being out there," she says.

Leo looks out at the water, nods.

"I almost bought a ticket to Nova Scotia last night; their tour just ended, and that's where they live. Halifax."

"Well, he said you should maybe get away for a few days . . ."

"I'm pretty sure that's not what he had in mind."

"Well, I hate to say it"—Leo picks up his board and puts it under his arm—"but you've built the website, and that's great, we needed it. But if you don't get back out there for real, and soon, I don't know how much longer I'll be able to keep you on the payroll." He walks off toward the water, stops and turns. He says, "Don't spend too much time asking all sorts of supposedly rational people like me whether you should go or not."

"Why not?"

"Because I'm giving you a couple of days off." Leo looks at his watch. "And airport traffic's a bitch."

In less than an hour, Alison has booked a plane ticket, made a hotel reservation, checked in for her flight, found what she believes to be Michael Madsen's address in Halifax, and alerted her father and Colin that she's leaving town for a few days. ("Be careful," said one; "Do me a favor and don't tell me where you're going," said the other.) In less than four hours, she has packed, gotten to the airport, and boarded her flight.

On the plane, her hair in pigtails, she listens to her mom's song over and over on her Walkman. She reaches down to grab the bag beneath her seat and pulls out her mother's letters. There's something about them—the red of the ribbon, the special care her mother took to bundle them just so—that intrigues her. Scares her. She has yet to read them. She fiddles with the ribbon, turns and catches the eye of the passenger next to her, half-smiles, then puts the letters back in her bag. She reaches for an in-flight magazine, comes to an article about Belize, where she was supposed to go on her honeymoon, puts the magazine down. She closes her eyes, nods off, and wakes up upon arrival.

Halifax International Airport ain't no LAX. It's a tiny building, hardly any gates, one baggage claim conveyor. Alison comes out of her gate, looks around, and heads off in the direction of a sign that reads TAXIS. As she steps in line behind a fortysomething businessman, she notices that the third driver—two taxis back—appears to be in her early twenties, quirky, also pigtailed; she's out of her car, wiping down her windshield. This is local (sort of) hipster Lisa Garey, though of course Alison doesn't know that yet.

The next taxi pulls up; behind it, Lisa gets into her cab. (Such as it is: It's not a yellow cab, just a run-of-the-mill gray car with a car service company placard on the dash.) Alison turns to the middle-aged couple behind her and says, "You can take this one."

Alison steps aside as the couple gets into the cab, then pulls her suitcase toward the trunk of the next cab—Lisa's—but Lisa shouts out the window: "The latch is broken. Can you take it in the backseat?"

As Alison does just that, Lisa pushes the cigarette lighter in, picks up a dispatch walkie-talkie. "Car two to base, come back."

Static. "Stupid fucking thing. Bobby! Airport. Picked. Up. Last. Fare. Calling. It. A. Night. Day. Whatever."

Lisa puts a cigarette between her lips, lights it. "Where to?"

Alison, just a wee bit scared, says, "The Sheraton, please."

"Mind if I smoke?" Lisa says as she exhales.

"Nope," Alison says. She's staring out the window, twirling one of her pigtails, thinking about how insane she is, how easy it would be just to hole up in the hotel for three days—it's got a casino and she likes to gamble. She could make up a story for Colin when she gets home. *Who? Me? Nova Scotia? Never!* I mean, really, what is she *thinking*?

In the front seat, Lisa glances in her rearview mirror and checks Alison out. Then she slowly, casually, pulls out her own pigtails, combines them into a single ponytail, and drives on. Alison, noting this, thinks, *Okay. Whatever. Freak.*

At the hotel, Alison gets out, and Lisa does, too. She says, "I'll bring your bag in." Alison says, "Thanks," and proceeds to the reception desk; the ringing clatter of slot machines fills the air.

Lisa wheels Alison's suitcase up. "Anything else I can do for you?" she wants to know.

Alison surveys her taxi driver for a moment—there's something about the streaky hair, the dramatic lipstick, the tilted chin and defiant stance, hand on hip, that makes Alison think, *Do or die.* "Actually, yeah." She pulls a piece of paper from her bag. Covering the word "Michael" with her thumb, she holds it out to Lisa and says, "How far away is this address from here? Do you know?"

Lisa looks at the address, pulls the paper out of Alison's hand, and then looks at the clerk behind the check-in counter. As he hands Alison a card key tucked into a small cardboard folder, Lisa says, "Does that room have a minibar?"

Two double beds; pastel paintings. Lisa's crouched down by a little refrigerator. "We plowed through the gin," she says. "You want vodka? Michael drinks vodka."

Alison, sitting on the terrace floor, calls back to the room, "Then vodka it is." Lisa joins Alison on the terrace, where there's a spectacular view of Halifax harbor. Cigarette butts fill an ashtray. They've been here awhile.

"So let me make sure I've got this straight so I understand exactly how much of a loser I am." That's Alison. Her speech is a little sloppy from drink. "You came here six months ago because you thought you were destined to be with Trevor Walsh."

Lisa says, "Yup." She lights another cigarette as Alison pulls one from the pack for herself. "And things didn't work out but you decided to stay anyway."

Lisa lights Alison's smoke.

"And since then at least three other women that you know of—"

Lisa nods, "That I *know* of."

"—including yours truly—have come here on similar Deductibles pilgrimages."

"You got it. But you trump them all, Ms. Beyer. Don't forget."

"Why's that?"

"Because you, my dear, have a fiancé!"

Alison runs her fingers through her hair—hard. "God, I'm such a jerk. We've been together forever. I mean"—and even as she says this she wonders if it's ever really been true—"he's my best friend."

Lisa snorts. "Well, *that's* reason enough not to marry him." She pats Alison on the leg and says, "You should get some sleep."

"Mmn. Good idea." Alison puts her cigarette out, gets up, sways a bit. "How is it that I'm bombed and you're the picture of sobriety?"

"How do you get to Carnegie Hall?" Lisa heads for the door as Alison crawls into bed fully clothed.

"Hey, Lisa?" At the door, Lisa turns. "I don't exactly have a plan. Will you help me?"

Lisa hesitates in the doorway a moment. She says, "I'll pick you up at eight."

After her nap, Alison's perched on the closed toilet in her underwear. She watches the bathtub fill with water, turns it off. She stands, steps closer, as if bracing herself, then lifts one foot and steps into the water. She steps in with the other foot and stands there, staring at her feet. She bends to sit but stops halfway. She thinks, *A person can drown in an inch of water.* Panicked, she steps out, releases the drain, resumes her position on the toilet.

After taking a few deep breaths, she gets up, goes to the sink, turns on the water, takes a glass, and starts to pour water over her head. She takes shampoo and begins to wash her hair. When she's done, she sits with wet hair at the room's desk, where she has connected her laptop to the Internet. Throwing off her towel, she goes to a popular search engine. She pulls out her Walkman, puts the earpieces in, and hits Play. Her mom's song plays, and Alison types lyrics into a search field: "Lie back and look up at the sky/Relax and let the hours go by."

She hits the Enter button; a window appears: NO MATCHES FOUND. She gets up and gets ready to meet Lisa, who is parked in front of the hotel smoking at the appointed hour. Alison approaches the cab, gets in.

"You're looking pretty hot tonight, Beyer. I wasn't sure you had it in you."

"Well, gosh, aren't you sweet." She's wearing jeans and a nearly backless black halter top, and she's wearing her engagement ring on her right hand.

"Yeah, well, don't get used to it." Lisa starts to drive. "So I've been thinking about your little saga, and there's something I don't get."

"What's that?"

"Why now? What brought on this existential crisis of yours?"

"My mother died."

"Wow." Lisa nods her head seriously. "How unbelievably clichéd."

Alison looks over at her, stunned. "Fuck you!"

"Oh, calm down." She reaches over and pats Alison on the

knee; Alison notes that Lisa's nails are painted deep purple. "How'd she die? No! No! Wait! Let me guess! Breast cancer!"

"If you must know," Alison says, snarkily, "she slipped by the pool, hit her head, and drowned."

Lisa hits the breaks, pulls to the side of the road, stops. She looks at Alison, eyes alight with excitement . . . or *something*. "Really?"

Alison nods.

"Do you realize how completely awesome that is?"

Alison feels like she's been slapped, and her face gets hot. For a second she thinks she's too stunned to speak, but she's not. She says, "Do you realize what a complete bitch you are?" then reaches for the handle, opens the car door, and hisses, "Go to hell."

But Lisa grabs her arm. "Beyer! Wait. I'm sorry. I know I must sound awful."

Alison pulls her arm away. "Yeah," she says. "You do."

"It's just that my life is so fucking boring and you—"

"What about me?" Alison snaps. "You don't even know me. It's not my problem if your life sucks."

"No." Lisa sits back in her seat, looking deflated. "It's not."

Alison's half out of the car but wondering what to do. They haven't gone very far, and Halifax looks like a safe enough town, sort of like a little London. She could probably walk back to the hotel without incident. What she wants, though, is for Lisa to give her a reason to stay.

"I'm like a dime a dozen, Alison." Lisa sighs. "But you . . . you've got drama. I mean, you're a runaway bride! So don't go. I mean, you've come all the way here and, well, destiny awaits. I'm sorry. I'll behave."

Alison slowly pulls her right foot into the car and closes the door. The two of them look at each other, and Alison says, "Okay then."

And so Lisa puts the car into drive, and soon, they're at a bar. It's an empty little dive. Alison feels compelled to note aloud, "There's no one here."

"That's the point, babe. Because in the end, it's all about the seats and who has them. And who's going to have them, Beyer?"

"We are."

"Atta girl. We are." Lisa leads Alison to a big wooden booth in a back corner.

"I can't believe I'm doing this."

"Yeah, well, guitars make women do strange things."

"Sometimes I think imagination is a curse."

"You think you're going to be disappointed with the real Michael?"

"Will I be?" Alison asks. She's relieved they've snapped back into friendly mode.

"Depends." Lisa shrugs. She's relieved, too. "I mean, if you expect him to have a twelve-inch penis and shit hundred-dollar bills, then yeah."

"Jesus!" Alison says. "Is that your idea of the ideal man?"

Lisa smiles, thinks. "I guess not, no. Ow."

Alison smiles and says, "So you never told me exactly what happened with you and Trevor Walsh."

"Nope, I never did." Lisa pulls out her wallet. "All right, Beyer, pick your poison."

Maybe an hour later, the bar is full, the ashtray, too. There are fresh drinks in front of the girls as a bar back clears empties away.

Lisa says, "So what's this wedding of yours supposed to be like anyway? You don't seem like the poofy dress and paraffin type."

"I don't even know what paraffin is," Alison says.

"Neither do I," Lisa says. "Sounds like a wedding thing, though."

"I wanted something simple, but the families kind of took over and it was going to be a two-hundred-person thing. Big sit-down dinner. Sushi stations. Raw bar. Swing band. The works. I'd have been happy to get married on the beach, but Colin hates getting sand in his shoes."

"Well, he sounds like one cool guy."

"Don't be like that. I feel bad enough already."

"Yeah, well, get ready to feel worse," Lisa says, coolly. "They're here."

Alison looks toward the bar, sees Trevor Walsh, and says, "I think I'm going to be sick."

"Well, don't go tossing your cookies yet. It's just Trevor and Dan. They're getting drinks, looking around for seats, bingo." She waves at them. "Oh, and by the way, probably best to pretend you've never heard of the band."

"But—?"

Trevor says, "Hey, Lisa. Mind if we join you?"

"Would it stop you if I did?"

As the boys sit, Trevor says to Dan, "Well, at least she's in a good mood."

"Trevor. Dan. This is Alison, a friend of mine from L.A."

"You have friends in L.A.?" Dan says.

"You have friends?" Trevor says.

Alison notes that his nose is bigger up close. He'd be cuter if he got his hair cut. It's shaggy, overlong. Like the guy from Scooby-Doo. Shifting her attention to Dan, Alison remembers Kara's assessment and wonders whether Dan might really be the only one of them who isn't an asshole. Now that she's here in Canada, it's occasionally occurring to her that Michael could turn out to be a real prick. With guys in rock bands, you just never know.

Lisa says to Alison, "Trevor and Dan have a little rock band they're in." She turns to Trevor. "What's it called again? The Co-payments?"

Dan sips his beer demurely as Trevor laughs an exaggerated laugh, holding his belly. To Alison, he says, "So, you work in the film industry or something?"

"No, actually, I teach surfing."

Lisa bangs a hand on the table, nearly spits out her drink. "No shit, Beyer!"

Dan says, "So you two are obviously real close."

Swiftly changing the subject, Lisa says, "So where's you two's better half tonight?"

"Adam's on his way," Dan says. "And Michael's on a blind date, if you can believe it. At the casino, no less! I give him two hours before he shows up here without her."

Lisa kicks Alison under the table as Adam, newly arrived, with a drink in hand, approaches the table. "Anybody up for pool?" he wants to know.

Lisa says, "Alison'll play. If I remember correctly, she's a shark."

Alison says, "As a matter of fact, I am."

As Alison squeezes past her, Lisa says, "I swear, Beyer, you get better by the minute."

In the back room, Alison swiftly kicks Adam's ass. The rematch is in full swing when Lisa pokes her head in. "Hey, surfer girl," she says. "Need a drink?"

"Sure."

"Adam?"

"Please."

And Lisa ducks away.

"Surfer girl?" Adam says.

"I'm a surfer. I give lessons back in California."

Adam surveys the pool table. "You could give pool lessons, too." He takes a shot and misses; Alison moves forward to the table, lines up a shot, nails it quickly. "Are you a guy in extremely convincing drag?"

Alison laughs. "No, why?" She gets another shot.

Adam leans his cue stick against the wall. "I don't know. I mean, not to be sexist, but pool? Surfing? Pretty traditionally masculine pursuits."

Alison's left with the eight ball, lines up a shot. "I'm a poker fiend, too." She gets the shot easily, rests her cue against the wall.

"I'm glad you don't play drums," Adam says.

"I'd never be as good as you are," Alison says.

"How do you know I'm any good?"

Ooops.

Lisa arrives with drinks just then.

Alison says, "Lisa told me." Then adds, "Hey, where's the ladies' room?"

Adam says, "There's just one for both. Over there."

He points, and Alison goes, thinking, *Whew, that was a close one.* Thinking, too, of Michael and whether he'll turn up tonight at all and whether she's officially losing her mind. She does her business and starts singing one of Michael's songs—it's called "Losing California," and it's one of Alison's favorites. It reminds her of when she was little and learning about her home state, and how she'd go to bed at night and wonder whether California would ever really break away from the rest of the continent. Would her house float? she wondered. Her whole block?

Unfortunately, Alison's still singing when she opens the door and runs right into Adam, who says, "Catchy tune."

So much for never having heard of the band.

In the car on the way home, Alison tells Lisa what happened. Lisa pounds on the steering wheel as she drives. "Goddammit."

Alison says, "I'm screwed."

"I don't know," Lisa says. "Shit. At least he didn't say anything. Maybe it's not a big deal. I mean, they act like they don't like it when groupies infiltrate their inner circle, but I mean, come on! They wouldn't look twice at a girl who didn't know who they were. Their egos couldn't *stand* it."

"Well, we tried." *And Michael never showed up anyway,* Alison thinks. Is that a sign she should just go home? She twirls her engagement ring around on her right finger and thinks, *I am a terrible, terrible person.* Because she doesn't want to go home. Even though she knows that Colin's hurting, that she's already betrayed him by coming here at all.

They pull up in front of the hotel, and Lisa says, "Don't give me that defeatist crap. We'll regroup and strategize tomorrow."

When Alison enters the Sheraton, the lure of the casino is too much. Imagining, with a combination of disappointment and relief, that Michael and his date have long since moved on, she turns into the vast room and wanders through the aisles, wondering whether she's retracing any of Michael's footsteps. She thinks of Vegas, the only place she's ever gambled, and she remembers how she once told Colin she'd marry him that night if he drove her straight to Sin City. He'd said, "Don't be stupid. Our families would kill us." It doesn't make him a bad person, she told herself at the time (and it should be noted that Colin has many fine qualities, most of which Alison just can't recall anymore, having fallen, clearly, out of love, whether she's ready to admit it or not). It might have been the first time, though, that she wondered whether he was the right person *for her.*

She comes across the blackjack tables and approaches, taking a seat beside a couple in their fifties. She pulls out her wallet, pulls out a hundred Canadian dollars, puts it on the table.

The dealer takes it, says, "Changing one hundred." He stacks chips, pushes them toward her; she places a bet.

The cards are dealt. Alison has a three and an eight. The dealer's showing a two and a four.

The dealer attends to other players as Alison readies chips. She says, "Double down," when it's her turn, and the dealer hits her with a ten. Hits himself twice, for a total of twenty-two.

Someone behind her says, "Lucky break." It's Michael, but she doesn't know that yet. She says, "First one all day," then turns to see who she's talking to.

Holy shit.

Michael's on his way to sitting down two stools away. And he's alone. At least, there's no date in sight.

They look at each other a moment too long. Michael reaches for his wallet, finally breaks their gaze. He says, "You from around here?"

Alison manages to say, "No."

He puts his money on the table. "You look familiar."

Alison quickly realizes this has all become too real and quickly collects her chips, her hands shaking the whole time. She asks the dealer, "Is the bar still open?" He nods, she nods at the fiftysomething couple, and she's gone.

At the bar she thinks over and over again that Kara was right. Fans are chickenshit. Or at least Alison is. She can't believe this is all actually happening—Michael. Right there in the casino. Saying she looks familiar. Which means he's noticed her. Maybe even thinks she's attractive? And yet what does she do? She runs away! Then again, she could've gone straight up to her room and she didn't. So maybe she's plotting something else, maybe she's building courage.

Her drink is down to ice, her racing mind beginning to calm, by the time Michael joins her at the bar. Approaching her from behind, he says, "I hope I didn't scare you off."

Alison turns. "No. I just didn't want to push my luck." Which is kind of funny when you think about it. She's flown across North America in the hopes of falling in love with a complete stranger—and of him reciprocating—in spite of having a fiancé, but she *doesn't want to push her luck?*

Michael flags down the bartender, who acknowledges him while taking another order further down the bar. "Can I buy you a drink?"

"I think I've had enough for one night," she says. "But thanks anyway." She's freaked out seeing him up close: his black glasses and salt 'n' pepper hair and pointy nose and blue eyes. She'd never have guessed blue.

"Okay, here's the situation." Michael claims the barstool next to Alison's. "It would go some ways toward restoring my otherwise shattered male ego if I could buy you a drink, even order you a glass of water."

Alison smiles. "Well, then how can I refuse?"

Michael says, "Water? Straight up?"

The bartender approaches.

"Definitely not water," Alison says. "Make it a Wild Turkey on the rocks."

"That's more like it." Michael turns to the bartender. "Vodka on the rocks for me and a Wild Turkey on the rocks for the lady."

Michael reaches for his wallet, and the simple manliness of the gesture nearly makes Alison swoon. She can't remember the last time she had such a visceral attraction to a man, or the last time she noticed the lines of Colin's arms as he reached for his back pocket. "Did that feel good?" Alison asks.

"You have no idea."

"Glad to be of assistance." The bartender places a Wild Turkey in front of her. She asks Michael, "Do I have to drink it for this to work?"

Michael smiles. The bartender sets a glass in front of him, and he slides a few bills across the bar. "So let me ask you something, since you're a completely random, impartial, woman"—*Gulp!*—"and I mean no offense by that.

"Do women take pleasure in shooting men down?"

She can't help but be playful. "That's the stupidest question I've ever heard."

He smiles. "Er. That's a joke, right?"

Alison nods and fidgets with her drink. "So what happened?"

"Oh, you know. Insert bad date story here. Why is it that people can't just cut past the bullshit? Life would be a lot easier if people said what was really on their minds, don't you think?"

Alison's demure sip turns into a large swig, and she's think-

ing, Yes, maybe it's as simple as that, maybe it's as simple as saying what's really on her mind. "Okay, here's the deal." She slams
her drink down, again with the *do-or-die.* "My fiancé and I were
supposed to get married months ago. But then my mother died
in a freak accident and we postponed the whole thing and ever
since then, I've been walking through life like a zombie and listening to nothing but your new album and driving people absolutely nuts with it. I guess with everything suddenly seeming
so meaningless, certain things started to seem more and more
meaningful in their place, and somehow, because of your music
and how it affects me, you—"

She points at him.

"You specifically—have come to personify all of my unful-
filled dreams in life, like you represent whatever it is I'm looking for. So when my fiancé said that I should maybe go away
and get my head together, I decided to come here, to meet
you and get it, whatever *it* is, out of my system. So I spent the
last couple of hours pretending I was old friends with this in-
sane cabdriver Lisa and lying to the rest of the band, pretending I'd never even heard of the Deductibles and was just here
on vacation and waiting for you to turn up, which you
didn't."

Michael takes her drink away. "Well, you were right about
having had enough." Alison strokes the back of her neck
and starts to get up. It's a gesture that triggers a memory for
Michael in three . . . two . . . she says, "I'm going to go crawl
under—" . . . one . . .

"That's where I recognize you from."

She stops midsentence.

"L.A. Two nights ago. And other gigs, too. You have this amazing tattoo right here." He touches the back of her right shoulder. "I've wanted a tattoo for as long as I can remember, but I can never decide what to get. It's pathetic." He sips his drink; she watches and waits. He looks at his watch. "I should probably get going."

"Yeah, it's late."

They both get up and start to walk.

"By the way, I'm Michael."

"I know."

"I know you know. But it seems rude or maybe just weird to not introduce myself."

"I'm Alison."

They're in the lobby, can walk no further without parting ways.

"So, Alison"—the name seems to catch on his tongue, and he looks at her more deliberately than he has yet, taking in this girl who thinks he's her destiny—"are you going to see the sights while you're here in lovely Nova Scotia?"

She likes the way he talks, the sound of his spoken voice, the light dusting of wit over everything he says. "Well, to be honest, that wasn't exactly part of the plan."

"No?" He smiles. "What was the plan?"

"Um." He's making fun of her, and she likes it. "I didn't really have one."

"Well, you have one now." He backs away, jiggling his car keys. "I'll pick you up at ten."

When he leaves the lobby through revolving doors, she looks around, as if seeking a witness to the fact that what just happened really happened. There's nobody there.

Alison steps out into the day, and Michael waves from the far side of a tiny orange car. It's the smallest car imaginable; Alison studies it and laughs as she approaches.

He says, "Hey, don't mess with the Pumpkin."

"But what the hell *is* it?"

They get in and buckle up.

"It's the first model Toyota they ever made." He starts it up; it putters. "Hear that?"

Alison nods.

"Motorcycle engine."

"You're kidding."

"I kid you not. And apparently a dopey looking car that runs on a motorcycle engine suits me perfectly."

"Why's that?"

"Because it makes up in eccentricity what it lacks in balls."

Michael drives on. He starts to drum on the steering wheel.

Alison feels her stomach flip at the sight of his lanky arms on the wheel and says, "You're very calm about this whole thing."

Michael looks over, shrugs.

Alison says, "I know I'm not the first."

"Ah, but you're *my* first," Michael says. "Deductibles pilgrims tend toward Trevor or Adam."

"Adam scares the shit out of me." She looks out the window,

sees what looks like a botanic garden. "He's just too manly or something. I'm intimidated by men that good-looking."

"Oh, thanks!"

"I'm sorry. But his songs are so esoteric, too. I don't think I get any of them."

"You should see his paintings."

"He's a painter?"

Michael shifts gears as he shakes his head in mock disgust. "And you call yourself a groupie."

Their destination turns out to be a church. As she walks down the aisle with Michael—*Here comes the runaway bride*—she knows she should feel guilty. She should feel awful, really. But she doesn't. In fact, she's surprisingly calm today. Like this is just something she's supposed to do, someplace she's supposed to be, someone she's supposed to be with. It's as if that puzzle she's been working on for years, the one where she's trying to fit the circle into the square, has been replaced with one where a circle fits into a circle. She wonders if this is what people mean when they talk about the knowing, the clicking, the coming home.

Michael leads her to a metal object jutting out of a wall; it's covered in glass. He looks at it and seems mesmerized. Alison doesn't quite. "What is it?" she asks.

He rolls his eyes. "It's part of the *Mont Blanc,* which was one of the two ships that collided causing the Great Halifax Explosion of 1917, is what it is."

"Well, excuuuuuuse me."

"Didn't learn about that when you did Canadian history, eh?"

"I must have blinked when we covered Canada."

"Well, it was only the worst ever human-caused explosion before Hiroshima. Actually, when our second record came out and there were a bunch of other pretty good bands playing around, a local reviewer said that we were likely to cause the second Great Halifax Explosion."

"That's pretty cool."

"I thought it was the stupidest thing I'd ever heard."

"It could have happened."

"It didn't."

"It still might."

"If I thought you really believed that I'd kiss you."

Alison's eyes meet his; her gaze drops to his mouth, returns to his eyes.

"You don't have to look so scared," Michael says. "I know you have a fiancé." He nods toward the aisle. "Come on."

Meanwhile, Lisa pounds on Alison's hotel room door. "Up and at 'em, Beyer. Rise and shine. Come on! The day's a-wastin." Getting no response, Lisa harrumphs, walks away.

Back in her car, she picks up her walkie-talkie, presses a talk button. "Car two reporting for duty." She releases the button. "Because I have nothing better to do." A crackling voice comes through the walkie-talkie in response; it's nearly indecipherable, but Lisa understands. "I know. But if you need me to take a fare or two, let me know."

She gets out of the car, goes to the trunk, opens it. Inside, there are a few bags of clothes, makeup, shampoo, stray shoes, pillows, blankets, a guitar. Lisa takes out the guitar, closes the trunk, sits atop it, and starts to play; it's immediately obvious she's not very good. It's obvious, too, that she lives in her car.

Alison and Michael face an arc of granite tombstones in a cemetery. A nearby sign reads TITANIC.

"There's a story in my family that my great-great-grandmother had a ticket but got sick and never got on." Michael bends and plays with a blade of grass. "There are a hundred and twenty-one here, nineteen more in another cemetery, and ten in a Jewish cemetery, too." He stands. "Did you see the movie?" Alison nods and he says, "C'mere."

He leads her over to a specific gravestone: J. Dawson.

Alison says, "I promise I'll never let go, Jack."

"This poor guy's actually *James* Dawson, a coal trimmer from Ireland. He's probably cursing James Cameron now that tourists are taking his gravestone's picture all the time."

"How come you know all these little random facts?" Alison wants to know.

They turn to walk.

"I read a lot, especially when we're on tour. And I guess I picked up a lot of Halifax trivia just because I've spent most of my life here. For example, did you know that Halifax has the highest concentration of Ph.D.'s in Canada?"

"I did not know that."

"But it gets better. It also has the most bars per capita of any Canadian city."

"Well that's a great combination."

They exit the cemetery, approach the Pumpkin.

"Isn't it? A city full of drunken intellectuals."

"It beats where I'm from. A city full of overcaffeinated anti-intellectuals."

"Oh, L.A.'s not that bad." He unlocks her door, walks around to his side.

"Oh, this from a guy who wrote a song about how California should drift off into the ocean."

Michael talks to her over the car. "For your information, missy, that song is about the fact that California *will* fall into the ocean, not the fact that it should. What *will* happen and what *should* happen are entirely different things." Which might be an interesting concept for Alison—heck, for all of us—to pause to ponder, but she's having too much fun.

"So what is this," Alison says, "the death-and-dying tour of Nova Scotia?" They're at their next stop—a lighthouse behind them, the water of Peggy's Cove in front of them. Michael carries a kite, which he hands to Alison as he unravels some string.

"I'm sorry." He backs away with the kite's twine in hand. "I guess it is all pretty morbid. I just like this place."

"It's okay. It's just if I didn't know better, I'd think someone from home put you up to it."

"What do you mean? Okay, you can let go."

Alison launches the kite into the air. "The Great Halifax Explosion, the *Titanic*"—she gestures out toward the water—"Swiss Air Flight whatever it was. Lots of freak accidents involving water."

"You mentioned the accident," he says. "Not the water bit." They sit and gaze up at the kite, now soaring above their heads in the wind. "Do you mind talking about it?"

"I don't know, really. Not much to say. Best we can tell, she was skimming the pool and she slipped, hit her head, and fell in and no one was around. It's been all I can do to even take a shower since then."

"Well, you know. Who needs water anyway?"

Alison half-laughs. "Unfortunately I do. To make a living anyway."

"Fisherman?"

She shakes her head as a wave crashes on the rocks below and sprays mist at them.

"Evian sales rep?"

She shakes her head again.

"Hydroponics farmer?"

She feigns shock. "I can't believe you actually guessed it."

"Are you serious?"

"No." She looks out at the water again. "Surfing teacher."

He raises his eyebrows, taken aback, looks back up at the kite. "See, now I actually would have believed hydroponics farmer. You don't seem like a surfer."

"You don't seem like a rock star."

"That's because I'm not."

"You kind of are."

"That's like being a little bit married."

"Touché."

He hands the kite off to Alison and sits down on the rocks, looking up at the sky. "Rock star." He shakes his head. "Now *that's* funny."

She says, "You seem pretty down on the band."

"Yeah, I don't know." He lays back and perches on his elbows. "Right now we do okay, money-wise, but I want to be able to support a family someday—soon, actually. Unlike *some* people I know, I *want* to get married soon."

"Don't make fun."

"Anyway, the point here is to figure out your life, not mine, isn't it?"

"Don't remind me."

"What was this wedding supposed to be like, anyway?"

"Big. Expensive. Everything I didn't want it to be."

"Ice sculptures?"

"Check."

"Cheesy band?"

"*Swing* band."

"Ugh. Horse-drawn carriage?"

"Check."

"You must be joking."

She smiles. "Yeah. But if somebody had thought of it, no doubt it could have been arranged."

"Yowsa."

"Yeah."

Michael looks at his watch. "Shit. I have to get going. Band meeting." He takes the kite from Alison, starts to reel it in. She watches his hands and thinks, *He's doing that to me, too.* She wonders whether he knows it.

"What's the meeting about?" she asks.

"Oh, you know." The kite dives into the rocks beneath their feet. "The usual."

Alison notices Lisa's cab in the parking lot when Michael drops her off. She waves good-bye, waits for him to leave, then approaches the car. Lisa's asleep on her back in the backseat, her legs bent up at the knees. Her T-shirt says, "You call me a bitch like that's a bad thing."

Alison wakes her with a knock, and Lisa rolls down the window. "Why are you sleeping in your car?" Alison wants to know.

"We can't all afford swanky hotels."

Lisa climbs out of the backseat, opens the trunk. Alison follows her to the rear of the car, sees all of Lisa's stuff. "You live in your *car?*"

"It'll be a good topic for interviews when I'm famous. I'll be like Jewel and that chick that played the guy in *Boys Don't Cry.* Come on, I'm feeling lucky. Like I just might win enough to get me a bed to sleep in."

They walk toward the hotel and go into the casino. Lisa has a handful of coins, strolls down a row of slot machines. "So where the hell have you been, Beyer? I can't play matchmaker if you're going off and doing, well, what were—"

Alison can't contain herself. "I met him. Last night. Totally by fate. I mean by accident. Isn't that amazing?"

Lisa puts a coin in a machine, pulls the arm.

"I was playing blackjack and he just turned up. And we started talking and I told him everything, and—"

"You told him everything?"

Alison nods.

Lisa moves to the next machine. "Man, you've got balls."

"We spent all day together, and he wants to see me again tomorrow."

Lisa puts a coin in and pulls: a few coins sputter out. "Are you going to do it?"

"Why wouldn't I?"

A woman approaches the machine Lisa played before this one, puts a coin in, and wins big. Lisa watches with disgust as the woman collects her booty. "Uh, because of a certain someone you left at home, maybe? I mean, wasn't the point to get it out of your system?" Lisa collects her coins, pulls out a few bills, takes them to a cashier.

Alison follows. "Yeah. And it's not out yet."

"What's it going to take?" She turns to the cashier. "Ten dollar chips, please."

"I don't know."

The cashier slides two chips through the gate.

"What if he wants to sleep with you?"

"He doesn't."

"What if he does?"

"He doesn't."

The two walk through the casino; Lisa spies the roulette wheel. "I don't get you, Beyer. Didn't you come here wanting him to want you?"

"I guess so. But I counted on the fact that he wouldn't or that he'd be with someone else. Then it's out of my system. Then I can go home."

"But he's not with someone else. And anyway, it's not about that."

"Well what is it about, since you seem to know everything?"

They're at the roulette table now, watching it spin and spin as the white ball pops around.

"Don't get pissy with me. Because you know as well as I do that it's not about Michael Madsen. It's about your not being able to grow up, and face your own mortality, and commit to your fiancé, or to anyone."

"You changed your tune pretty fast."

"What's that supposed to mean?"

"It means that yesterday you were all gung-ho to introduce me to him. 'You're a runaway bride!' And 'destiny awaits' and all that crap—"

"Take your pick. Black or red?"

"I don't know."

"Well that figures." Lisa bets on red, and the wheel begins to spin.

"—and now that it looks like it might actually happen, you're acting, I don't know, jealous."

"All I'm saying is that telling him everything isn't the route I would have chosen. Groupies aren't attractive."

"Well, you said they can't stand it when people don't know who they are, either. So which is it?"

Lisa's eyes are glued to the wheel. "Oh, I don't know, Beyer.

But you're better off not listening to me. Half of what I say is crap anyway."

The ball lands on black as the wheel slows; Lisa huffs. "Any chance I could crash in your room for a few hours?"

Alison just looks at her.

"Oh, come on." Lisa shakes her hair out, faux sexy. "You know you want me."

Alison and Lisa are sleeping. There's a knock at the door, and Alison stirs. She gets up, pads over, opens it. It's Michael. She says, "Is it tomorrow already?"

"No, but I don't know, I felt like going out. I thought you might want to go for a drink."

"I'll meet you downstairs." She closes the door, looks at Lisa, decides not to wake her. She quickly dresses, brushes her hair. She spies her mother's letters—nope, still hasn't read them—stows them in a dresser drawer, puts on some lipstick, quietly leaves the room. She and Michael walk in silence to a nearby bar, where there are four nerdy guys in their twenties—all in jeans and ratty T-shirts—on a small stage. Michael and Alison enter as a full house sings along with the band. They cross the room and slide into chairs across from each other at the end of a long table. Alison looks around: hordes of hip twentysomethings are singing "Wildfire."

"Okay. This is freaking me out. I haven't heard this song in years. Decades even. How does everybody know all the words?"

"Give it time." Michael taps the side of his head with his

index finger. "Your brain probably just needs a few minutes to reset itself to the seventies."

A waitress approaches, and they each order a Guinness.

"This is all they do," Michael says. "Covers of seventies soft rock hits."

"That's hilarious."

The band starts a new song—about a girl named Aubrey—and the crowd whoops and claps recognition. Alison turns to Michael. "Ohmigod." She reaches across the table and grabs his forearm. "For years I begged my parents to let me change my name." Her eyes fixate on her hand on his arm.

Alison looks Michael in the eye. "My mother said someday I'd understand why they wouldn't let me. I don't think I did until this very moment." She smiles and releases her grip on his arm as the drinks arrive. Alison takes a gulp of her Guinness. When she puts her pint down, there's foam on her lip.

"You have a little . . ." He points to his own lip. She wipes her mouth with a cocktail napkin. "Better?"

He looks at her mouth. "Much."

When she turns back to the band, she starts to sing along with the crowd. Michael just watches her, then looks down and strokes the condensation on his pint glass, then looks at her again. She's still singing. And he's still watching. To the casual observer, even, this much would be obvious: he's falling for her.

Alison turns to drink more of her beer, asks Michael to lean forward across the table with a wag of her finger. She looks around to make sure no one's listening. "They're terrible."

He smiles. "I was wondering whether you were going to notice that."

"Oh, I did. Immediately. But it doesn't matter somehow." She turns and sings along some more, and Michael joins in now too. He figures what the heck.

When Alison and Michael emerge from the bar, the sound of music still fills the air. They start to walk. He says, "You knew the words to every song."

"I know." She's wide-eyed, invigorated. "Isn't that wild?"

"Is that the kind of stuff your parents listened to when you were a kid?"

"I guess so. There was always music in the house. But you'd be horrified if you knew who I looooved when I was a kid."

"All right. Horrify me."

"Actually, the worst part isn't that I liked him as a kid, it's the fact that, well, I'm still genuinely moved when I hear . . . are you sure you want to know?"

"Yes, yes."

She winces. "Barry Manilow."

"No!"

"It's bad, right?" Their pace slows. "But what was so weird about knowing all those songs tonight is I always thought I had a bad memory for stuff like that. I always thought I wouldn't even know any lullabies to sing if I had a baby."

"I could write one for you."

Alison stops in her tracks. "Please don't joke about that kind of thing."

"Who says I'm joking?"

They continue to walk and arrive in front of the hotel. Alison's looking sullen.

"Did I upset you?" Michael says. "Because I had a really great time tonight, and I'd hate for it to end on a sour note."

"I found this old 45 in my mother's stuff. I think someone may have written a song for her, but I don't have any way to find out who."

"You could play it for me. Maybe I'd know."

Alison shakes her head, stares at her feet, pulls out her room card key. "I love it too much. I'm afraid you wouldn't like it." She thinks of Colin then, and wonders what song Michael would want to dance *his* first dance to.

"I just took you to see a band called Yeast, whose set consists almost entirely of Bread covers. I think you're safe."

Alison drops the card key; they both bend down to get it and bang heads. "They're called Yeast?"

"Yeah."

They stand up. Alison takes a deep breath and smiles. "Hey, how'd the band meeting go?"

"Good. Real good." He nods, lips flat and tight. It's obvious he's not going to say any more on the subject. "We still on for tomorrow?" he says.

"Sure."

He looks at her, but she's looking away; then she turns and looks at him, but he looks down. "So, I should go," he says.

"Yeah." Now she looks down. Because she can't do it. No

matter how much she wants to. It would make her a terrible person. There will be no kiss tonight.

Michael doesn't appear so convinced of this point. He lingers a moment, even leans in, but senses her tense. Getting the idea but not wanting too, he turns to walk away, hesitates, looks at her again, then goes.

At the door to her room, Alison struggles with her card key; she's had a few pints. The door whips open from the inside, and Lisa pulls her into the room, where Trevor, Adam, and Dan are sitting around looking none too pleased.

Alison says, "What's going on?"

Adam says, "What have you been saying to Michael?"

"Nothing. I don't know."

He says, "Well, you must've said something."

Lisa explains: "Michael quit the band tonight. Something about how Adam does his paintings and Dan deejays and runs a label and Trevor's so popular and involved in so many charity events and stuff that he could run for mayor if he wanted to, or how he's little Mr. Canada—"

"Which, for the record, I just have to reiterate, is *insane,*" Trevor interjects.

"—and how he, Michael, doesn't have his own thing and how he wants to be able to move to California if he wants to and have a life of his own."

Alison sits down on the corner of a bed, not quite absorbing anything beyond the idea of Michael's—even for one second—considering moving to California. "That's impossible," she says.

"Afraid not," says Trevor.

"But I didn't say anything. I mean, we haven't talked about . . ."

Adam says, "Well, you must have. So this little existential runaway bride crisis of yours"—Alison looks sharply at Lisa—"has gone and fucked up all our lives. And we want to know what you're going to do about it."

"I don't believe this." Alison runs her fingers through her hair, wanting them all to just *go*.

"Are you seeing him again tomorrow?" Trevor wants to know.

"Yeah."

Adam says, "Well, fix it."

They get up to go, and Lisa follows. The three guys exit and Lisa turns back. She says, "Sorry!" But she's not really sorry. She sees a new opportunity to capture Trevor's attention the way Alison has captured Michael's. So she goes straight to her car, plugs her cell phone into the cigarette lighter, and sets about finding a phone number for one Colin Kraig. It may be a shitty thing to do—it's absolutely a shitty thing to do—but Lisa would rather not admit that right now. Right now, she's dialing information, thinking she's not about to let Trevor's band go down without a fight.

Alone in her room, Alison spots the hotel services directory on the dresser and picks it up, flipping intently; she stops at the page that pictures the indoor pool. She changes her clothes and, a few minutes later, sneaks into the deserted room, where the water shimmers under dim lights. She strips down to her swim-suit and steps up onto the diving board. She gets down on all fours and crawls to the end, where she lies on her stomach. Then she closes her eyes, grabs the sides of the board with both hands, and in one swift motion, rises up and plants her feet like she's surfing. She surfs goofy-foot—that's left foot forward—and wonders why she can't, at least sometimes, just do what everyone else does, like get married when they've said they would, and be happy.

At the far end of the room, a door creaks open. Flashlight beams scan the water's surface and find Alison's bare feet and legs. "Sorry, ma'am. Pool's closed." Alison turns to see a security guard. "Anyone ever drown in this pool?" she wants to know.

"No, ma'am," he says. "And I'd like to keep it that way."

Alison steps off the board, gathers her belongings. "Oh, I wasn't going to go in."

He says, "Looks to me like you were."

The next morning, Michael sits in the Pumpkin's driver's seat, engine idling, in front of the hotel. Upstairs, Alison is about to exit the room. She pauses, retraces her steps, picks up her Walk-man, puts it in her jacket pocket.

Outside Michael's still waiting. The passenger-side door opens, and Lisa slides in. She slams the door. "I wish you could realize how lucky you are. To have what you have. The four of you. It makes me sick."

Michael just stares straight ahead.

"Just for a day, I wish you could be a Deductibles fan instead of who you are. I wish you could drive this stupid-ass car some-where with the Deductibles blasting and discover it. You'd never walk away from it if you could do that."

They sit in silence.

"Just don't throw it away over some random girl."

Michael finally looks her in the eye. "Oh, why should I lis-ten to you, anyway? It's always been a hunch, but I've got a feel-ing that you're a random girl the same way she is. What exactly are you doing in Halifax anyway, Lisa?"

And this, of course, is what Lisa hasn't told Alison. That she never even *told* Trevor Walsh she came to Halifax to meet him. Lisa is still more living proof that fans are not always the bravest of the brave.

Alison emerges from the hotel, sees Lisa get out of the Pumpkin and slam the door. As Alison approaches, she says hey and nods toward the car. "What was that about?"

"Just saying hi," Lisa says. But her tone is snippy.

"I don't know what you're mad at *me* for," Alison says.

"I'm not mad," Lisa says in a tone that makes it clear she is. "Have fun today."

Alison gets in the car and says, "What was that about?"

"Nothing worth mentioning."

"So, where are we going?"

"Whale watching," Michael says.

Alison looks terrified.

"Trust me," he says. He then drives on to the Nova Scotia Museum of Natural History, where the two are soon staring up at a huge whale skeleton. "See? Not one drop of water in sight."

Alison just looks up.

He says, "You're very quiet this morning."

"Why didn't you tell me you quit the band?"

He looks up at the whale now. "Okay. I preferred the quiet." They walk around the skeleton, stop at a placard describing it. "Kind of ruins the fantasy if I'm not in the band anymore, doesn't it?"

"Technically, the fantasy was ruined the second I met you."

He smiles wryly. "You do have a way with words."

She nudges him. "Oh, that's not how I meant it."

They walk on, stop at a display of sea turtles suspended in air with a seascape painted behind them.

"No offense," Michael says, "but you really don't know me well enough to give me a hard time."

They walk on.

"Well, three-quarters of the band were in my hotel room last night blaming me."

They step up to a collection of starfish pinned to a wall.

"It's not your fault, Alison," Michael counters. "There've been a lot of problems with the band for a while now. But it's true that the fact that you took off on a whim and came here made me think about following some of my own whims without having to take a band vote. I need to figure out who I am without the Deductibles."

"But see, that's it! It was a whim. I'm this totally fucked-up, fickle person. I'm a mess."

"You're not a mess, Alison."

"Normal people don't abandon their fiancés and fly across

the country believing that someone they've never met is their destiny."

"Maybe they should. Especially if they're right."

Alison's stomach clenches tight, and she can feel her heart thumping. She says, "You think I'm right?"

Michael's eyes look bluer than blue when he says, "You tell me, Alison. Are you?"

She wants desperately to say yes, but something is holding her back. Everything's happening, *changing* so fast.

He says, "Come on"—he doesn't want to push—and leads her back out onto the pier. This is Purdy's Wharf, which is straddled by two office towers that shoot right up out of the water.

Alison says, "I wouldn't work in either of those buildings for a million dollars."

"You have to admit they're kind of cool, though. The water generates the air-conditioning; it's an architectural first."

"Do I sense a pro-water theme developing?"

"I felt bad about the death-and-dying tour."

They walk on.

"Am I how you thought I'd be?" Michael wants to know.

"Well, you're not very rock 'n' roll. I mean you don't smoke. You're not an asshole. You don't have tons of women hanging on you."

"Yeah, I'm still pretty pissed off about that last bit."

Alison smiles, then says, "You seem like who I hoped you'd be."

He says, "So what does that mean for your fiancé?" So maybe he *does* want to push.

The two stop and stare out off the end of the pier, the shops in the distance behind them. Alison says, "You can't quit the band because of something I said or did."

"You're deflecting. Anyway, it's too late."

"But that's not how it's supposed to work," she protests. "It's like if this were an episode of *Quantum Leap* and I was Scott Bakula and realized I'd done something that would affect the course of history, I'd set out to fix it."

"I quit the band, Alison. There's nothing you can do about it."

Alison turns to face the pier, notices a sign for a tattoo parlor. "You sound pretty decisive today." She points at the sign, and Michael turns.

"Yeah, I am," he says. "I'll do it. But you have to promise me one thing."

"What?"

"You'll never mention Scott Bakula ever again." He walks off toward the parlor, where they begin to gaze at walls of tattoo designs. She says, "What's it gonna be?"

"I was thinking 'I heart Alison.'"

"You were supposed to be a complete asshole, you know. Or at least have a girlfriend."

"I did. Up until a couple months ago."

"What happened?"

"What ever really happens? You decide you don't want to marry each other; sometimes it takes a few seconds, sometimes a few years." He stares at one wall of tattoos, and Alison stops beside him. She says, "He doesn't even like my tattoo."

"Doesn't make him a bad person," Michael says. He looks at her and says, "You going to help me pick one?"

Alison raises her eyebrows.

Michael turns back to the designs. "Okay, okay. I get it."

Nova Scotian hills dot the background. Lisa cruises alongside Trevor in her taxi; he's walking, stapling posters to telephone polls: "THE DEDUCTIBLES at the Electropolis—THIS FRIDAY NIGHT."

"You think he's really serious?" Lisa wants to know.

"I guess we'll find out. He agreed to this gig. After that, who knows?"

"You all write. You all sing. The Deductibles could go on without him."

"You know that's not true." Trevor whacks the stapler, attaches another poster to a poll.

"It's funny because we think of Michael as our hit writer. He is. He writes our hits. Only none of our hits have ever been hits."

"You wrote 'Bust Out.' That was a hit."

" 'Bust Out' was a bust." Trevor pulls a poster from a roll Lisa's holding out her window.

"So you think you have to be super-successful at what you do in order to do it?"

"No. I mean think of how many crappy bands there are out there that never go anywhere. But the problem is we're not crappy." He whacks it, walks on; Lisa inches the car ahead.

"All those other bands probably don't think they're crappy either."

"I think people know when they suck."

"Don't I know it," Lisa mutters.

"What?"

"Nothing." She hands him another poster.

"It wouldn't bother me so much if he were leaving because of creative differences or whatever. He's leaving because he's got himself a pilgrim. Because he thinks it's what he's supposed to do now. Settle down, have a family, grow up."

"Maybe he's right."

"Maybe he is. Fuck it, Lisa. Let's get hitched and make babies!" He shakes his head like it's the most ridiculous idea ever, whacks another poster.

Michael drives with Alison in the passenger seat. He's got a bandage over a patch on his right arm. She says, "For a second there I thought you were going to break my hand."

"Sorry about that."

"You did it. That's the important thing."

"Yup. And now it's your turn." They pull into a hotel parking lot. "Don't worry. I haven't reserved the honeymoon suite or anything."

Inside, Michael approaches the guy working behind the front desk; Terry Madsen, a younger version of Michael, nods hello.

Michael says, "This is Alison. Alison, my brother Terry. You have what I need?"

"Yeah, but be quick about it. A few guests have already asked why it's closed; I said it'd be open in a half hour or so."

"Excellent. Thanks."

"What are we doing?"

Michael leads Alison down a long hallway, jiggling a key his brother gave him.

"You'll see." And with that, Michael opens a door: In front of them looms a 180-foot waterslide with a huge pool at the end of the chute. The area is deserted. "I figured this way the emphasis is taken off the water and put on the fact that you're falling a hundred and eighty feet. You're not afraid of heights, just water."

Michael takes a seat in a lounge chair. Alison just stares up in awe. "Why don't you go?" she says. "I'll watch."

Michael points to his bandage. "Can't get it wet."

Alison looks at him, distraught. "It's really sweet of you to think of this, but I can't do it."

"Come 'ere," he says.

She goes and sits on the edge of his chair, starts to cry. "I was the first one to find her. And I didn't jump in. I just couldn't."

Michael pulls her close.

"If I do it now, it feels like a betrayal." Wiping her eyes, she reaches inside her jacket pocket and produces her Walkman. She hands Michael the earpieces, and he takes them, puts them in his ears. She hits Play. The faint sound of music comes from the headphones. Alison watches him as he listens. After a moment, she curls up closer to him and takes one of the earpieces and puts her face beside his, holding the earpiece to her ear. It's the introduction to her mom's song. "I'm leaving tomorrow," she says.

"I know." Tomorrow's Thursday. He doesn't mention Friday's gig.

They settle in more comfortably as the song kicks in.

> *Lie back and look up at the sky*
> *Relax and let the hours go by*

Michael puts an arm tighter around her; starts tapping a foot. Alison looks up at him, but his eyes are closed. Then they open and the song builds and she says, "This is the best part." To the sound of a swirl of lush harmonies, Michael kisses her. And they kiss and kiss . . . When he pulls away, she says, "I wish you could've met her."

"I feel like I just did." Michael takes the headphones off, hands them back. "Come on. There's someone we should go see."

"Michael, Michael, Michael." Michael's uncle Max—about sixty years old, with an unruly gray coif and beard—shakes his head, crosses his den, and starts to finger a row of records. Evelyn's song blares from his stereo. "You should know this." He pulls out an LP and holds it up. The jacket says *The Turn of the Century: Spinning.* Max stops the tape, gingerly pulls out the vinyl twelve-inch, and puts it on an open turntable. He lifts the needle, places it down. Alison's mom's song fills the room again.

Alison and Michael look at each other and smile. Alison asks, "What's it called?"

"Only the obvious, dear. 'To Evelyn on Thursday.'"

"I don't believe it."

Max hands Alison the LP jacket.

"The Turn of the Century. West Coast surf music avatars of sorts. But they only sold about fifty thousand records before they fell into obscurity. Too mellow for FM, too psychedelic for AM. They were a bit like your getup." He nods at Michael. "All seven of them were songwriters." He opens a drawer in a huge chest of cabinets and pulls out a CD copy of "Spinning." "In fact, young Alison here may have led us to exactly what you need right now." Max hands the CD to Michael. "Give this a whirl before you unplug and throw yourself a pity party."

When Alison gets back to her room, there's a poster for Friday night's Deductibles show taped to the door. She takes down the poster carefully, opens the door. She sits on the bed, stares at the poster, picks up the phone, dials her home number in L.A. She hears her own voice on the machine, then takes a deep breath. "Hi, it's me. I'm sorry I haven't called. I'm fine, but there's been a slight change of plans and I'm going to be away another couple of days. Please don't be mad."

Hooking up to the Web, she quickly changes her flight and then finds a home page for the Turn of the Century. "Unbelievable," she says. Scanning a list of band members, she pulls her mother's stack of letters out and slides out a postcard signed "Andrew." Sure enough, an Andrew wrote the song.

*   *   *

At the crack of dawn Lisa's sitting by the airport gates with a "Colin Kraig" placard perched on her lap. The flight from L.A. is delayed, and she nearly falls asleep on the job. Resting her head on one arm, she's just shy of dozing off when a figure approaches. It says, "I'm Colin Kraig."

Lisa rubs her eyes, sits up straight. She says, "Well, it's about fucking time."

That same morning, the morning she was originally supposed to leave, Alison goes down to the pool as soon as it opens and sits by the edge, her mother's packet of letters on the floor beside her. She's listening to her Walkman, singing occasional phrases. Michael appears at the far end of the room, stops, listens. Alison sings a few more stray lines. When the door closes, it catches her eye. Michael comes forward as she pulls the headphones off. "You're singing my part."

"How'd you find me?"

"Just a hunch." He sits down beside her, notices the letters. "What are these?"

"Old letters of my mom's. From before she met my dad."

"What's in them?"

"I don't know. I can't seem to bring myself to read them. To be honest, I wish my father never gave them to me."

Michael picks up the letters and goes to throw them in the pool.

"No! Don't!" She grabs at them, but he's already handing them back to her. She clutches them close now. "I think they're from Andrew Hennesey, the guy who wrote the song."

"Really? They're all I've been listening to. It's so depressing that a band that brilliant never made it."

"The way I see it, they did."

"How do you figure?"

"We're talking about them thirty years later."

Michael cocks his head, surprised by the thought. He nods at the letters again. "What are you afraid you're going to find?"

"I don't know. I guess that she married the wrong guy."

"Ouch."

"What?"

"That was on behalf of your father."

Alison nudges him with an elbow.

"We're playing tomorrow night."

"I know. I changed my ticket."

They look at each other and their arms fly around each other and they kiss and then he says, "Alison."

She pulls away. He runs his hand through her hair. "I have to go in a few minutes. We're rehearsing."

Alison wipes her mouth, resumes her sitting position.

"Can I ask you something?" he says.

Alison nods.

"The first night I met you, you said this all had to do with my songs, how they affect you. What did you mean?"

She thinks for a moment. "You've never surfed, have you?"

"Uh. No."

"Doesn't matter. You can imagine. I mean I always loved the band, but that night in L.A. it was, I don't know, it was as if I could feel this wave forming inside me, but also somehow beyond me, like I could see it taking shape out there but knew I was driving it or was part of it, and the anticipation of its getting to me was this scary and wonderful thing. It's that feeling of being infinitesimally small and infinitely large at the same time—and a feeling, too, like I was going to be okay, in spite of everything. Your songs, they're like instant ocean for me—they make me scared shitless and I like it. I hadn't felt that feeling in a long time. Not since my mom died. Maybe not even the whole time I've been with Colin. Isn't that awful?"

Michael shrugs. "You're not the first person who's ever broken off an engagement."

They sit in silence for a moment; Alison looks at the letters. She says, "She thought I was going to marry him."

He says, "She thought you wanted to," then he squeezes her hand and gets up to go.

Alison takes a deep breath and unties the stack of letters. She roots through them, all addressed "To Evelyn." She rifles some more, finds a letter in different penmanship, her mother's, addressed "To Andrew." She unfolds the pages, begins to read:

You were amazing last night. I've never experienced anything like it. Seeing you doing what you love to do. There's nothing like it. I'm amazed by it every time. I couldn't sleep for hours. I must have replayed every moment of the show in my head ten times, wondering where this great gift of yours comes from, marveling over it.

Here comes the hard part. We can't see each other any-

more. I'm not cut out for it. The double life. The drama. Maybe I'm a coward, but I'm choosing a different kind of life for myself. One that doesn't reach for the stars so much. I don't know if I'll ever even mail this letter, but either way you'll find out that I can't see you again and that I'm going to marry him. He's a good man. Not that you aren't. I just don't know if I have it in me to follow you wherever your life takes you. Be well always . . .

Back in her room, Alison pulls her swimsuit out and lays it out on the extra bed.

She goes to the phone, picks it up, dials, waits; her father's machine picks up. "Hey, Dad . . . Everything's fine. I just wanted to say hello and I'll be home soon. I love you." There's a knock on her door. She hangs up, goes to answer it.

"Colin," she says.

He looks up and down the hall. "Can I come in?"

She steps back, looking at him as if she's seeing a ghost. *This is Colin,* she reminds herself. *My fiancé.* She figures he's here to win her back, and he figures that, too. Though Colin hasn't missed Alison near as much as he thought he would. That, however, is another story for another day.

"What are you doing here, Al?" he says. "Why don't you come home?"

"I don't know, Col. Right now, being here . . . I don't know why, but it's helping."

"But I want to help, too."

"I don't think you can."

"Have you slept with him?"

"No!"

"Do you want to?"

Alison doesn't say no fast enough. She doesn't say it at all.

"This was a bad idea," Colin says. When he goes to leave, she doesn't stop him.

Alison wakes to a knock at the door; she gets up and opens it; it's Lisa. "Nothing happened between me and Trevor, okay? I never told him. He has no idea I came here to meet him, that I'm like this girlie girl pining away for him."

Alison waves her in, closes the door behind her; Lisa notices the swimsuit, flops down on the bed. "When I first got here, I found out about this party they were playing at, and I went. And this girl Fiona got up and sang with the band for a couple of songs. And when they did "Superpowers" she harmonized the whole song with Trevor, and it was like effortless, and I knew I couldn't compete. The way he looked at her, like even he was in awe . . ."

"Is he with her now?"

"No, he's never been with her. That's not the point. The point is that people with talent gravitate toward other people with talent. Or passion, or whatever it is. And I've tried and tried, but I suck. My guitar playing sucks, my voice is just okay, and I have nothing to say."

Alison laughs.

"What's so funny?"

"It's just the idea of you having nothing to say. It's funny."

"But it's true! Why do you think I try so hard to be wacky and out there or whatever? I'm hundreds of miles from home, living in a car, and I'm in love with a guy who I think will reject me because I can't play a G-minor seven."

"I've got you beat. Sorry." Now Alison flops back on the bed. "I'm a surfer who can't swim."

"What do you mean?"

"Haven't been in the water, haven't even taken a bath or a proper shower since."

"That's fucked up, surfer girl. But I still might have you. Get a load of this." She hands a letter to Alison, who reads it and hands it back to Lisa, who wants to know, "What do you think?"

"I think you should give it to him. It's perfect."

Lisa groans, pulls a pillow over her head. "Then why do I feel like such a loser?"

"Because the world is fucked up. I mean, everybody wants everybody else to like them. But if you like someone and they don't like you, you're made to feel like you're doing something wrong, which is so screwed up."

"But what if we're just these little groupies and we don't even know it?"

"Well, then, you know what? So what? I mean, what's so bad about being a groupie? I'd rather be a groupie than somebody who doesn't give a shit about anything. If he doesn't take it as a supreme compliment—no matter how he feels about you—then fuck him."

Lisa gets up. "Yeah!"

"Yeah!" They high-five.

Lisa says, "Fuck him!"

Alison says, "Yeah!"

"I'm going to deliver it before I lose my nerve."

"I'm going to do something before I lose my nerve, too." Alison picks up the phone as Lisa goes to leave; Lisa stops, turns.

She says, "There's something else I need to tell you."

Alison just waits.

"I called him. Colin. He's here."

Alison can't wrap her head around this right away. She just assumed he'd decided to come on his own. "Why would you do that? What did you say to him?"

"I don't know." Lisa shrugs. "Because I'm evil. I told him you and Michael seemed to be hitting it off, and that he should come here and show you what he's made of."

"Ohmigod, Lisa."

"I know. I'm ridiculous. I was jealous. I thought if I somehow saved the band or whatever that Trevor would think twice about me."

"Well, it was a really awful thing to do."

"I know that now. Really. I do."

"Okay, okay." Alison sighs. "For whatever reason, I just can't seem to be mad at you right now." She smiles and says, "But I want to reserve the right to do so at a later date."

Lisa smiles, too. "You turned out to be all right, Beyer."

"Yeah, well, you're not so bad yourself. Now get the hell out of here. Destiny awaits and all that."

"Yeah yeah yeah."

No more than ten minutes later, Lisa's stuffing her letter into one of many post boxes in a nearby apartment building. Trevor comes in through the front door, and Lisa, startled, tries to hide the letter.

Trevor says, "Whatcha got there?"

"Nothing."

Trevor approaches, reaches from behind her to grab the letter. "What is it?"

Lisa clings to it, but Trevor has managed to get a strong grip on the letter. "It's nothing," she says.

"Well, why are you trying to shove it in my mailbox if it's nothing?" Trevor tugs once more, and the letter comes free in his hand.

"Fine. Take it." Lisa storms out in a huff. Trevor opens the envelope, unfolds the letter, and starts to read. He turns toward Lisa as the lobby door swings closed. His eyes are alive with surprise.

Michael approaches the Dartmouth Surf Shop. Inside, the guy working the desk looks up and says, "Can I help you? Hey, wait. Aren't you . . . ?"

"Yeah."

"You want to learn how to surf or something?"

Michael runs his hand across a surfboard. "This is going to sound really strange. But I just want to rent all the gear and get out there, see what it feels like."

"Uh. Okay."

"Would that be all right?"

"Yeah, man. Whatever you want. That's cool." He climbs off his stool. "Follow me."

Alison and Colin stand staring up at the waterslide. There's loads of activity: kids sliding down the chute, splashing in the pool; parents lounging in chairs, eyeing the slide nervously. Alison starts to peel clothes off; she's wearing a swimsuit. "Will you do it with me?"

"Of course." Colin peels off his shirt, and the two start to climb. Alison reaches a perch at the top of the slide first; Colin steps up next to her.

She can't explain why she wanted him here, needed him to bear witness to this. Maybe because he was *there,* when it happened, when everything changed. Maybe because you don't throw five years away just like that. "I feel like it'll change things," she says, looking down at the pool.

"If there's one thing we agree on, Al, it's that things really have to change."

"What we had doesn't change, though," she says, squeezing his hand. She thinks for a second, then nods. "We were great . . ." She trails off.

He nods, too. "We were," he says, with a sad smile, "for a while."

She tries to imagine anew what "their song" might've been. It'd be bittersweet, maybe even with a few dramatic orchestra swells, about a girl and boy who thought they had it all, only to discover they wanted more.

Alison kisses him hard on the lips. In an instant she's

gone, plummeting 180 feet, water swishing around her. As she's dumped into the pool, she closes her eyes and is submerged in a world of wet. It feels scary and wonderful—like love.

Voices are chanting "De-DUCT-ibles." Alison's at the bar of the Electropolis, which is packed with hip, young types. She pays for two drinks and carries them through the crowd, where Colin's waiting, a few feet from the stage. She hands him a drink as the Deductibles chants are replaced by applause and howls when shadowy figures appear on stage.

Alison says to Colin, "You really don't need to be here."

"I can't explain it," he says. "But I do." He's not quite ready to let go yet, you see. *Almost* ready. Just not quite. That's the thing about closure (if such a thing even exists). It comes differently for everyone.

As the band launches into a high-powered rock song, Lisa appears, grabs Alison by the arm. "We need to talk." She says to Colin, "She'll be right back," and leads Alison out of the room into the front bar. It's quieter there, but the band can still be heard rocking out. "I gave it to him," Lisa says.

"That's awesome."

"You think he read it?"

The bartender approaches, and Lisa orders two shots of tequila.

Alison says, "I hate tequila."

"They're both for me."

"He probably read it, yes. I mean, wasn't that the point?"

"He's going to think I'm such an idiot." Lisa pays for her shots.

"Well, if he does, then he's the idiot."

Lisa downs a tequila. "You look different."

"I went swimming."

"Way to go, surfer girl."

"And I realized something, too. This thing with Michael? I don't want it out of my system."

"Well, I could have told you that. But have you told him that?" Lisa downs the other shot, cringes, shakes it off.

"He knows."

"With your fiancé hanging around?"

"Shit. We left him alone." She turns to go, and Lisa follows.

They rejoin Colin by the stage. Alison looks up to Michael just as Colin bends to say something into her ear. Alison sees Michael look at Colin, then look away. She hasn't made eye contact with him yet tonight. A drumbeat starts; guitar riffs are added.

"Okay," Trevor says, "anybody know the words to this one?"

Loads of people in the crowd raise their hands and scream. Trevor scans the crowd, spots Lisa, holds out his hand, gestures for her to come closer. Lisa moves forward, looks back at Alison as if to say, What's going on? Trevor grabs her hand, pulls her up onto the stage.

Trevor starts singing as Lisa stands there onstage, perplexed. He encourages her to join him at the mike with a wave of the arm, but she shakes her head. Adam tosses her a tambourine, which she catches and starts to shake. Trevor tilts his head away from the mike, still singing, and reaches out, pulls Lisa closer; she goes for it this time. They sound fantastic together. Then Trevor drops out, and Lisa's suddenly singing alone and doing a damn fine job of it.

Alison looks at Colin, lifts her eyebrows to say, Who knew?

"I'm going to the bathroom." Colin works his way through the crowd, exits the room, but he doesn't go to the bathroom. He goes to the bar and orders a shot. Alison's world isn't his anymore. Maybe it never was. To tell the truth, he's never thought the band was especially good, and he'll be happy never to have to hear a song of theirs again. Ever. To tell the truth, he's been thinking for a while now that some other couples he knows seem happier than he and Alison did. That maybe *he* could be happier with someone else—someone a bit more grounded and driven, someone a bit less . . . *Alison.* Closure, it seems, is closing in.

Trevor and Lisa finish out the song. Trevor gives Lisa a hug, and she climbs back down into the crowd and joins Alison. Lisa says, "I'm shaking."

Alison says, "You were amazing."

The two smile and grab hands.

In a while Alison says, "I'll be right back." She approaches Colin at the bar; he sees her and gets up, starts to put his jacket on. "What's up?"

"It's time for me to go, Al."

In the other room, the band starts a new song. It's instantly recognizable to Alison as the Beach Boys' "Surfer Girl." She instinctively looks toward the back room. When she turns back, Colin's gone. She feels guilty, sad, but also relieved.

Alison rejoins the crowd and works her way up to Lisa as Michael—turns out he's playing solo—rips through a fast, pissed-off version of the song. He bangs out a loud power chord at the end and drops his guitar, which overloads the system with feedback. People cover their ears as Michael walks offstage.

Lisa turns to Alison and says, "Told you so."

Outside, moments later, Alison's leaning on the Pumpkin. The back door to the club opens, and Dan emerges, walks toward her. He's carrying a guitar case. They look at each other as he goes to open the trunk of a car beside the Pumpkin.

Alison says, "Hey."

"Hey." He puts the guitar in the trunk, slams it closed, starts to walk away.

"Hey, Dan?"

He stops and turns.

"I never meant to cause any trouble."

"I know. My girlfriend was a fan, too. Before she was my girlfriend."

"Will you tell him I'm out here?"

"That won't work." He looks at the Pumpkin, reaches in through an open window, and switches the headlights on. "I'll tell him he left his headlights on." He disappears inside, and she waits. In a moment, Michael emerges, sees her, stops, walks toward the Pumpkin determinedly.

"What the hell was that all about?" Alison wants to know.

There are other people hanging out in the parking lot now, wrapping up their evenings. "Don't make a scene," he says softly, looking over his shoulder as a couple approaches the car next to his.

"Oh," Alison says. "You're one to talk."

He opens his car door. "Get in."

"Fine." Alison strides around to the other side, goes to open the door, but it's locked. Michael leans over, opens it. She gets in, slams the door. He's fiddling with the cassette player; there's a snippet of a Turn of the Century song before he hits rewind.

"What the hell was that 'Surfer Girl' stunt about?" she says.

He hits Play again, then Rewind again. "Stunt?" he says. He shakes his head.

"Yeah, I mean, what are you so mad—"

He hits Play again, and the music drowns her out. The Turn of the Century blasts from the stereo; not Evelyn's song but another one. Alison sits quietly for a moment, contemplating her next move. Then she roots through her bag and pulls out a cassette. She ejects the Turn of the Century tape.

"What are you doing?" Michael says.

She puts *her* tape in and hits Play. She says, "Listen to this the same way you've been listening to that."

It's one of Michael's own Deductibles songs.

"Oh, for Christ's sake, Alison." Michael ejects the tape. "I know what my own band sounds like."

"I don't think you do." She just stares at him.

He looks at her and starts to sing Barry Manilow, badly. It's the one about how he writes the songs.

Alison says, "Don't be a jerk."

But he keeps on singing.

She talks over him, loudly. "So this is who you are without the Deductibles?"

He stops singing. "Yeah, that's it. I quit the band and I turn into an asshole. You can go back to California now."

"Is that what you want me to do?"

"I think you're going to do whatever you want to do no matter who gets hurt along the way. Isn't that what you do?"

"That's a low blow," she says. She looks out her window and shakes her head. "This isn't how this is supposed to work."

"God!" He grabs on to the steering wheel and fake bangs his head against it, repeatedly. "You keep *saying* that! What the hell does that even *mean?* I'm not some rock star fantasy anymore, and now you don't want me?"

"No!"

"I'm falling in love with you. Isn't that exactly how this is supposed to work?"

"Yes."

"Then what's the problem?"

"I'm trying to figure out why you're so mad."

"Your mother thought you were going to marry him, and I can't compete with that."

"It's not like that."

"Well, then spell it out for me, Alison. Because I honestly have no idea what's going on and what he's doing here."

"Yes, she thought I was going to marry him. But she also thought she was just skimming the pool and was going to have dinner with us that night . . . and loads of other nights. Everything's changed. And I'm here now, and there's you."

"You're not going to marry him?"

"No."

Michael takes an audibly deep breath, turns to her. "How do you know you haven't picked the wrong guy?"

"If I have to explain," she says, "then maybe I have."

And that's all it takes. He reaches for her, slides a hand to the back of her neck, and pulls her into a kiss. She feels free and happy and alive and *relieved*—and he does, too. The kiss dissolves into as tight an embrace as is possible in the front seat of the Pumpkin.

"Your hair." He breathes deeply. "It smells like chlorine."

She nods and says, "I went back to the waterslide."

"I would've gone with you," he says.

"Colin came with me. And he stormed out of here and I want to talk to him before he leaves but I don't want you to be mad about it. I didn't ask him to come. Lisa did."

He looks confused.

"Long story," Alison says. "Can you drive me to the hotel?"

He kisses her again and puts the car in gear.

Back at the hotel, Michael pulls the Pumpkin up to the entrance. "You want me to wait?"

"No," she says. "I'll be okay."

"Well, if you need me, I'll be back at the Electropolis. I kind of skipped out before making sure everything was packed up."

Alison just nods; then she leans over and kisses him, pulls back and opens her car door.

"Hey, Alison," he says.

She turns.

"The Manilow bit. I'm sorry. You've got really great taste in music."

"I know." She gets out, sticks her head back in, and says, "Unfortunately, my favorite band recently broke up." And before he can respond, she closes the door.

Back out on the road, Michael turns the radio on and starts scanning stations. Suddenly Barry Manilow's voice fills the car. Michael says, "Oh, you've got to be kidding me." Barry's singing, "Looks Like We Made It."

At a stoplight, Michael stares at the radio. Alison's tape is perched on the cassette player. He shoves it in. It's his own song again. He drives on, rolls the window down, turns up the volume, and tries to imagine he's hearing it for the first time. He has to admit, it sounds pretty great.

Alison knocks on Colin's door. There's no answer. She knocks again. Still nothing. Knocks once more, waits, starts to walk away. She hears the door open and turns to see a groggy Colin. She says, "Can I come in?"

Colin steps back to make way, then leads Alison out to his terrace. They both lean on the railing, hinged at the waist and looking out at the harbor. Colin says, "You know Jean Fisher from work?"

"Yeah."

"We had a lunch this week. A few of us. She said you and I were the most stable couple she knew."

"Col . . ."

"I'm not saying it to make you feel bad. It's just, well, I don't want to be stable. I may not be the most passionate guy on the planet—"

"Aw, Col."

"—but I want more than 'stable.'"

They stand in silence.

"You don't have to explain," he says. "I felt it. I knew it at the top of that stupid waterslide. Maybe the second I got here and saw you. You seem different somehow. More relaxed. More calm."

"You don't think I'm crazy?"

"Maybe just a little." He turns and pulls her into a hug.

She feels tears welling up, and then he pulls away.

He says, "I guess this means we have to return the presents."

"Yeah," she says, wiping her eyes. "I'll take care of that."

He says, "Damn right you will," a little bit more harshly than he'd planned but decides not to take it back. He figures he's owed at least that much.

The Electropolis is practically empty. Trevor and Lisa sit at the bar, Trevor with a beer, Lisa with a glass of water. Dan and Adam are talking nearby. Trevor leans in to Lisa flirtatiously and says, "You were a hit."

"Yeah, well, it was one of the top five moments of my life so far. So don't ruin it by mentioning that stupid letter I wrote you."

"It wasn't stupid. It was sweet."

"Ugh." Lisa hides her face with her hands.

"What? It was. I'm sorry. I just don't think of you that way."

"I don't think I even think of you that way anymore. But I had to at least put it out there . . . before I left."

"You're leaving?"

"I have to get a life. Or at least an apartment."

"I'll miss you."

"I'll miss you, too, Trev."

"In a weird way."

Lisa shakes her head. "You couldn't just leave it alone."

Michael comes in, and Trevor turns and says, "Well, lookee here."

"So, er, guys?" Michael takes a seat at the bar. "That stuff about quitting?"

Trevor says to Dan, "I don't remember anyone quitting. Do you?"

Dan shakes his head, pretending to be bewildered.

Trevor says, "But there's one problem."

"What's that?" Michael wants to know.

Trevor says, "We have a band rule against lame tattoos, especially tattoos of—"

"Trev," Michael says. "Can you just leave it alone?"

"How long have we known each other, Michael?"

"A long time, Trev."

"Do I ever leave anything alone?"

"Not to my knowledge, no."

"Speaking of which, I'm thinking of running for mayor, and I want to run a clean campaign if you know—"

"Oh, God," Michael says. "Here he goes."

*   *   *

A soaking wet Alison is in a wet suit, straddling a surfboard, looking out at the horizon, where the sea swells. Well, kind of. She's still in Nova Scotia and the waves are—how do you say?—lame. She looks over her shoulder as Michael struggles to climb onto the board behind her. He's wearing a wet suit, too. He says, "Knock me off again and I'll kill you."

"I'll be good," she says. "Promise."

He settles in behind her, and the two just sit, the board bobbing as swells of waves pass. She's thinking of how maybe it wouldn't be so bad if California broke away one day and gained another coastline; Nova Scotia floats, California would, too. Would the waves suck this bad, though?

"We're going to have to be bicoastal if this is a good surfing day here."

"Okay." He shakes his hands around in the water. "But can we never again use the word *bicoastal*?"

She smiles and says, "I'm thinking something small. Maybe on the beach."

"Whatever you want," he says. "The sooner the better."

She says, "Okay, here comes one."

He perks up a bit. "Where?"

Alison points. "There. You see it?"

"Yeah. I think I do."

They share a moment of quiet anticipation as the wave undulates toward them. Alison's thinking about her mother and California and the kinds of earthquakes that happen inside of us every day. Michael's just watching the wave; he wants to be careful not to lose it.

Finally it's upon them, and he slides his arms around Alison's waist. He says, "Are you ready to rock?"

The wave lifts them high as Alison folds her arms over his and leans back to steal a kiss. She's ready for anything. She says, "Are you?"

Sara King Goes Bad

Pamela Ribon

I am the kind of woman who still writes people letters. Some might say that makes me antiquated, but I think opening an envelope, unfolding a piece of paper, and reading a handwritten statement carries much more importance than an e-mail, a message on voice mail, or even a stammering conversation across a fancy meal that has turned cold from neglect. I'm about to write possibly the most important letter of my life.

As I smooth the sheet of light blue stationery across my lap desk, I get my first shot of nerves. I'm about to do something people wouldn't expect from me. It's what keeps me moving forward, when absolutely every molecule inside of me is terrified at what I'm about to do to my life.

I catch a glimpse of myself in the mirror across the room. I'm on my bed, looking up as if trying to remember something. My mouth is open, my tongue pushing forward against my bottom teeth, folding out like a dead fish. My blue eyes peek from bangs that need a trim. The rest of my dishwater blond hair is flopped over its own ponytail. I resemble an exhausted, confused waitress at a truck stop diner. I wonder if this is the face I show people when I go to the store, when I order something off a fast-food menu, or when I try to give directions.

I see myself slowly shaking my head, but I don't feel my neck twist. I've outsourced my existence to a girl living in my skin. She knows to tell everyone her name is Sara, but she doesn't seem to know how to feel about anything. I want to yell at her, "Wake up!"

I put pen to paper.

DEAR MITCHELL. I'VE MOVED OUT. I'LL
SEND FOR MY THINGS.

My love of the written word does not come across in my handwriting. I might use fine papers and a Cross pen, but my scribbles look like those of an angry child writing an impassioned missive to his parents, declaring his intentions to move out and take all of his stuffed animals.

As I shift my position on the bed, I can see I've rumpled the covers. The blue comforter is bunched under my left knee. I scoot forward, hoping to even out the edges with my butt. A messy bed drives Mitchell crazy. Some mornings he'll go back into our room after we're done getting ready just to smooth the corners. If I had written this letter sitting on a sloppy bed it'd look . . . well, just so *deliberate*.

I crumple the paper. I start over.

SWEET MITCHELL.

I never call him that. Start over.

MITCHELL, IT'S SARA.

Unbelievably stupid.

I'M LEAVING YOU. ARE YOU MAD AT ME?
CIRCLE YES OR NO.

It's better to leave now, when there's still two weeks before the wedding, when there's still time to call everyone. Knowing Mitchell, he'll deliver the bad news like a weather report—succinctly, with a hint of apology. "You might want to bring a jacket if you're going out tonight. I'm afraid it's getting rather chilly out. Oh, and it appears I won't be getting married after all."

"Three kids," Mitchell had said to me in this very bed, not too long ago.

"No," I returned, louder than I had intended. "Not from *this*." I protectively held my hands over my crotch.

"You don't want kids." He said it as a statement of defeat, as if he should have known all along I was going to thwart his plans, decide his future. He ran a hand through his black hair, then lifted his head to rest it on his palm.

"I do want kids," I said. "I just don't need three."

"You don't know that yet."

"Neither do you," I said, trying to be gentle. "Can't we try one first?"

"That's how they usually arrive."

Mitchell's chest hair forms a perfect rectangle across his torso. I love the symmetry of it. Tracing my finger around the edges of the dark, curly tangle, I paused to push each mole on his tanned skin. "One. Two. Three," I mouthed to myself as I connected the dots.

Mitchell's hand rubbed the curve of my shoulder. Then he shook me gently, like he was trying to wake me up.

"I think we'd make beautiful children," he said, whispering as if he wanted only my subconscious to hear.

We had been engaged for six weeks.

I knew I had to leave Mitchell when we received our first wedding present. It was a blue dish, square and small, darker in the middle than around the edges. A card in the box held a one-word message scribbled in red pen: "Congrats." No return address or receipt.

"Who sent this?" I asked Mitchell like a game-show hostess, holding the card in one hand and the plate in the other. For a moment I was sure our registry had been switched, like babies at a hospital, and now we were going to get another couple's linen and silverware. A hopeless fear crept inside of me; I was positive they had registered for sixteen bath towels in lime sherbet.

Mitchell took the card from my hand, read the one-word scrawl, and laughed. "Gotta be Toots."

Now that I'm thinking about this, it actually was right then, right when I found out Mitchell had a friend named Toots, that I knew I had to leave him.

"Toots?"

"My roommate in the frat house, freshman year at State. Toots." He had the tone people use when they think you know everything about them. Like I'd just read *Mitchell's Life* for my book club.

"Is he married?" Suddenly I had to know all about the wife of Toots. What kind of woman is attracted to a man famous for his flatulence? Perhaps she has a charming nickname of her own. People like Toots tend to seek their own kind. "Toots and Spitlips are coming over. Better flip the couch cushions to the stained side."

"Toots will never get married," Mitchell said, interrupting my vision of us one day vacationing in Maui with the Tooter family. "He promised us."

Mitchell can make three innocuous words become the newest thing I'm fascinated with.

"Promised?"

"Back in college," he said, interrupting himself to chuckle and shake his head.

Oh, Toots. You're such a card.

"Toots was the loser of our frat. Legendary. Failing out of classes, messed up every relationship he attempted, owed money to half the guys on our floor—I think there was even a death pool going for him because he'd get so wasted we'd sometimes find him passed out by the mailboxes in the morning. Then one night he lost at our weekly poker game, and of course he didn't have the money to pay us back. So we made him swear off women for a month. Started as a joke, I think, because he'd recently asked out someone's sister. Have I been talking for a long time?"

Mitchell's paranoid that people think he's a babbler. He interrupts his own stories, right when they get really good, to make sure people still care about what he's saying. Sometimes he'll even decide to stop talking, if he's bored himself enough. It makes people get reinvested with what he's saying right before he gets to the good stuff. I now think Mitchell does it to make sure he has as much attention as possible before he finishes his story. He's smart like that.

That's why I have to leave him.

"Go on." I stared into the dish in my hand, as if the story might begin playing on the tiny blue square.

"By the end of the month he'd gotten his grades up, found a job he loved, and had almost enough money for a down payment on a car. Toots turned his life around. He decided women only led to problems, so he was never going to get married. He went up to each of us, returning whatever it was he owed—CDs, cash . . . I think he washed some guy's car because he'd let

Toots borrow it one night. He was like some kind of mission-ary, spreading the word of how women were the reason every-thing had gone wrong for him, but now, girl-free, he was truly living life."

"And now he's gay?" I asked, making the logical conclusion. But the question threw Mitchell. Frat guys have this reaction when someone questions the sexuality of a man they shared close quarters with.

"No, he's not *gay*. He swore off women. That doesn't make him *gay*."

"Sorry."

"You want everybody to be gay."

"Yes, Mitchell. I want everybody to be gay. That's my *thing*."

Mitchell was quiet, reflecting on those good times, those days when he had no idea he was going to meet me.

"What is this I'm holding?" I finally asked.

"It's a sushi dish. For dipping."

"I didn't register for this."

"I did," Mitchell said, giving a sheepish grin.

Our wedding registry had resulted in a weeklong argument over which thirty-five items we absolutely needed. Fifty guests; thirty-five items. Mitchell had come to that numeric conclu-sion, and I had agreed. There was no need to make a wish list that rivaled a five-year-old's letter to Santa. This meant every candle, every pillowcase, every tumbler had to be discussed and debated. We both had to sign off on the style, the color, and the quantity. I will never get back those hours of my life when we finalized the items that would start our new life together.

One month after the registry was declared finished, Mitchell discovered sushi. People who love sushi have to talk about it all the time, like a religion. Raw fish and Jesus—two topics about which you have either everything or nothing to say. Mitchell's new love affair with rice, seaweed, and eel has resulted in us being the proud new owners of a flat bowl. What good is a flat bowl?

"Why are you opening our presents?"

The guilt shot down my chest. "It was our first present."

"It's bad luck to open presents before the wedding."

"It is?"

He dropped to his knees quickly, fast enough that there was a hollow clunking sound on our floorboards.

"Kiss me," he said, his hands resting on my forearms as he leaned in close to my face. "Quickly. Erase the bad luck."

His lips were dry and salty. He had just come back inside from a walk, and I could smell the outdoors in his hair, his clothes. We kissed until I felt my shoulders relax, the tension slipping away.

"There," he said, giving me one last, small kiss on the bridge of my nose. "Bad luck erased."

I've kissed sixteen men in my life. Ten of them have seen me with my shirt off. I've held three different penises in my hand. Two have been in my mouth. But only one, only Mitchell's, has been inside of me. I thought I should mention that because it's inevitably going to be the reason he gives everybody for why I've left.

In high school, I foolishly assumed I'd be able to find someone who would treat my virginity and me with the respect we deserved. But every boy was rushed, hurried and sweaty. The places available for my deflowering included an abandoned playground, a cleaning closet in the back of a movie theater, or half of a bunk bed with the bonus feature of a nearby sleeping younger brother. There was never the perfect match of location and boy that made me feel ready to enter a new realm of womanhood.

Eventually enough time passed that I went from being a novelty—the supposed Mount Everest of Lakeside High—to what could only be assumed was damaged goods. Not giving it up by seventeen meant I must have the kinds of issues that would have me weeping by second base. Admitting I was a virgin was verbal saltpeter. The pressure to be my first lay was too much for these young men, and inevitably they'd give me the We're-such-great-friends-and-I-don't-want-to-spoil-it line, and it'd be back to me and my pristine hymen.

Then I went through a six-month period when I was flinging myself on every boy-whore in our school. But rumor travels faster than truth, and by the time I'd get my shirt off, the boy would be positive I was the girl who had gonorrhea of the mouth, or was raped by her stepdad, or had a secret kid and was looking for his new stepdaddy.

I met Mitchell in line at the bank two summers after I graduated. He was opening a checking account. I was making a deposit into savings. The line was enormous, and the computers kept going off-line. We talked for more than half an hour before we made plans to go to dinner that night. Last month, on our three-year anniversary, we stood in that very line again and opened a joint checking account.

Mitchell met me right when he was turning his life around. Dating a virgin, the opposite of everything he knew about girls, was just what he needed. After what Mitchell went through in college, he no longer wanted to party. He needed a woman who wouldn't want to drink until three in the morning and then run down the street naked. Mitchell said he liked how slowly we could take it, how every experience we had together was momentous for me.

I have this niggling feeling that I'm not very good at sex. I think I might be all limbs or have an awkward rhythm. Maybe my skin is rubbery to the touch, or when I'm aroused it gives off a weird smell. I might feel wrong inside. I'll never know if it's true because Mitchell says I'm beautiful, which is the right thing to say. I can't take his word for it. He loves me; he'll say anything. I have to leave him before he becomes my husband and I'll never know the truth about myself.

Mitchell's mother is going to have a field day when she finds out I've left. Judy will probably call the local paper, hand-deliver a photo of me, and convince them to run the story with a notorious-sounding nickname—like Runaway Bride, if that didn't already exist. Actually, she'll call me exactly that, thinking she's so clever.

When Mitchell and I first started going out, Judy told her son she knew I was no good for him by the way I answered the phone. She believes she can determine a woman's entire personality by the words and manner used when she takes a call.

A simple "Hello?" with a bit of a lilt at the end, halfway a question, halfway a song, means that the woman is eager to please, happy to make friends, and always there when you need her.

If she answers, "This is" and then her name, it means she puts herself first and always thinks she's right no matter what the situation. She's quick-tempered and fiercely loyal to her friends, even though she secretly thinks she's better than they are.

"Yes?" means she's a snobby bitch who always has some wildly stupid opinion she's decided is fact and uses it to make sure her son never gets married. Call Judy sometime. See if I'm wrong.

I answer "Hello," but apparently I say it like a statement, not a question. This means I'm unstable, unpredictable, and carry a U-Haul of emotional baggage I unload on anyone who gets close to me. This is the gospel according to Judy.

Dealing with Judy has often made me wish my parents were still alive so I could call them up and commiserate, tell them how lucky I am to have two completely sane parents who would never judge me by the way I say a single word. Every time I see Judy these days I have to discuss up to fifteen topics about the wedding—from guest books to napkin colors. She wants nothing more than for me to turn to her, eyes full of tears, pleading, "Judy! I can't do this without you! Help!"

I wonder if Dad would have offered to help us. When I was

very little, young enough to sit for hours at a time on his knee, I'd make him plan our wedding. I even drew it once in my sketchbook, Dad and me walking down the aisle to where Mom was standing. The three of us were getting married and would live together forever in a tree house next to Disneyland. I had it all worked out.

In a perfect example of how every plan you make changes beyond your control, I lost my parents the day before my college classes started. Mom and Dad were surprising me with a new car, a gift that was equally selfish on all of our parts; it was meant for me to drive home as often as I wanted, and I wanted to drive home every weekend. They had left their house very early in the morning so we could spend the day together. The police think Dad fell asleep behind the wheel. The car was hit three times before it came to a stop on the other side of the highway.

I started classes the next day. My parents had worked hard to get me into a good college. I wasn't about to let them down. I swore to be the best version of myself. I studied relentlessly, obsessively, adding hours to my course load until I was able to double-major in English and physics—one major for Mom, the other for Dad. I graduated with a 4.0. I still don't own a car. I don't even have a license.

New piece of paper.

MITCHELL—

One word down. The easy one.

I LOVE YOU. YOU ARE A WONDERFUL
PERSON. YOU DESERVE EVERYTHING.

My heart is racing, and my hands are trembling too much to
write. I put down my pen and pick at a hangnail on my thumb.
Get it out.

WE CAN'T GET MARRIED ANYMORE
BECAUSE I THINK I'M NOT THE RIGHT
PERSON FOR ME.

"What does that even mean?" I ask out loud, too loudly. My
voice is sharp, and I can hear it echo in the corners of our badly
decorated bedroom. We never could agree on what we should
hang in here, and so now there's nothing but blank blue walls.
Robin's egg blue. Mitchell made fun of that color as we painted,
saying it sounded like we were smearing the walls with smashed
baby birds.

The phone rings. I run into the kitchen and find the cordless.

"Hello." *You've reached the office of Unstable, Unpredictable,
and Baggage. How can I help you?*

"Sara?" It's Patrice, my maid of honor. "What are you
doing?" she asks, rushing through the words because she's got
something to tell me that's going to take a while. I walk back
into the bedroom and sit down on the bed.

"Nothing." What else is the right answer?

If Mitchell were here, I'd make a gesture like a wildly chirp-
ing bird with my free hand. That's his code for Patrice. It's what

she looks like when she talks. Her head flops around on her neck like she's some kind of Muppet, her hair dancing wildly on her shoulders as she goes on and on about something amazing that just happened to her.

"Oh, my God. So the craziest thing just happened. This morning I woke up wanting a bagel, right? Totally craving one."

Patrice can't simply tell a story; she has to back up to the very beginning of time to make sure you're in her head space for whenever the craziness happens.

"Uh-huh. What kind?" I don't want to miss anything vital.

"Poppy seed."

I look down and notice a spot on my chest, just above the V of my T-shirt. It looks like it might be food, and I don't know how it got there. I rub at it, and it smudges a bit but doesn't go anywhere. It's a light blue color, and I can't even begin to guess what it could be.

As Patrice yammers on in my ear about running into a girl from her junior high in the checkout line, curiosity gets the best of me. I have to inspect further. I try leaning my head down to sniff the mark on my chest, because maybe it's some kind of makeup or toothpaste. But my neck won't reach where the spot is. It's closer to my breast, right on the edge of the cup of my bra. I raise my left breast with my hand to bring my chest closer to my nose. I sniff. It smells sweet. Could it be candy? I gingerly stretch out my tongue and give it a hesitant taste.

"I mean, wasn't I *just* talking about Lizzie three days ago?" Patrice asks, but I've got my tongue on my boob, so all I can give is a muffled "Uhnh."

Patrice can tell she's no longer the center of attention. She makes a clicking sound with her tongue and asks, "Are you eating something?"

I don't want Patrice to hear my laughter, so I double over, still clutching my breast, my head feeling like it's going to explode from keeping silent.

"Whatever," Patrice says, uninterested in hearing what I have to say. "Listen, about tonight."

Tonight!

"Oh."

"It's you, me, Myra, Tracy, and don't be mad, but I invited Georgia."

I can't do anything right. I've accidentally decided to leave my fiancé the same night as my bachelorette party.

"I'm not mad."

"Good. She'll be fun. We're going to Lucky's." That's Patrice's favorite place. I don't even know if I like jazz music. I think the fact that I called it "jazz music" and not simply "jazz" is proof enough I don't know anything.

I can't cancel this party because I'll have to tell her I'm leaving Mitchell, and if I tell her I'm leaving Mitchell, she'll try to talk me out of it. I tell Patrice I'll see her tonight and hang up the phone.

I dial Mitchell's number. I need to know what he was doing the day I left him.

"Mitchell Overton's office," he says, as if he's not Mitchell Overton. I bet Judy doesn't want to admit that means her son's an overprotective, controlling introvert who smells his socks before he throws them in the hamper.

"Sara King's apartment," I say back, mocking his tone. Except it's not my apartment for long.

"I was just thinking about you," Mitchell says, getting close to the phone with that little groan he makes before he tells me he was thinking about me in a sexy way. "In a sexy way."

"Oh, yeah? How?" I know all the ways to think about someone in a sexy way. Mitchell can't surprise me. I'm hoping this time it's a really weird way to think about me, like he's imagining me strapped naked to a windmill while he paints his toenails. That's what I'm capable of imagining. Can he top that?

"I don't know. I just was. Hey, are we still out of paper towels?"

Mitchell's sex drive comes in tiny waves. High tide doesn't come as often as it used to.

"I bought some yesterday."

"Would you do me a favor? I left a load of laundry in the wash. Would you move it to the dryer so it doesn't sit there wet all day?"

As soon as I move these whites to the dryer I'm going to leave Mitchell.

This will be the last time I touch his underwear. It's the last time I'll take his tube socks from the washer and toss them into the dryer. This is the last time I'll see his "Seniors '96" T-shirt, the one with the drunk raccoons dressed in pirate gear. I have washed this T-shirt hundreds of times over the years, and now it won't be in my life anymore. I'll never put it on after a hot bath. I'll never again use it as a pillowcase when the real ones are in the wash.

It was his idea to get married in the first place. Mitchell asked me because he always does the right thing. This time he did the right thing by finding the perfect ring and getting down on one knee at our favorite restaurant. Ladies at other tables were crying and an older couple bought us a bottle of champagne and everybody, absolutely everybody, tells me all the time that I must feel happy. Why does everyone assume every single second of being engaged is bliss? Mostly it's been hours searching the Internet for cheap caterers and going one hundred minutes over on my cell phone with a florist.

What does it mean that I haven't yet booked a photographer? I can't seem to figure out what flavor cake I want. I bought a dress, but I'm keeping it at Patrice's place. I'm afraid I'll put it on and it'll look wrong. Every decision has such weight to it. It's not just a cake flavor I'm deciding, it's the cake that begins our new life together. If the pictures aren't perfect, there's no way to prove the day was perfect, and that means the day wasn't perfect.

Before we hung up, Mitchell gave me some advice for tonight's bachelorette party. He said, "Don't do anything I wouldn't do." I wonder now if he said that on purpose, or if it was all of his fears and nervousness coming out in the worst advice he could possibly have given. His list of what he would do, or rather, of what he's done, is close to mind-boggling. I've met friends of his who were there during his college years, and they seem shocked that Mitchell is still alive. They all feel the need to tell me horror stories—times when Mitchell drank close to his weight in beer and then went skiing; the weeks when he went without showering because he had done so much cocaine he thought his skin was made of plastic and, therefore, waterproof; the women he slept with, sometimes three or four at a time, who never gave last names. They tell me these stories the way some people talk about someone who lost one hundred pounds. They want me to know I'm with the "After," and the "Before" was a very different person. They tell me these stories as if Mitchell's antics were not just legendary; they were the hallmark moments of those fraternity times.

His friends need me to know who Mitchell was back when Miles was still alive, when Mitchell was "Before." The cancer progressed very quickly, and Miles was gone before Mitchell had time to comprehend fully he was losing his best friend of twelve years. Nobody's supposed to die at twenty. That doesn't make any sense. You're supposed to have a big, scary hospital scene where people pace around the waiting room for hours wearing letterman jackets, pounding walls and wailing, gritting teeth and wiping eyes before finally falling asleep on each other's laps. Then the doctor's supposed to wake everyone by emerging from those double doors, pulling his surgical mask off his face with a triumphant yank. He's supposed to announce: "He's going to be okay." That's what's supposed to happen when your best friend is sick and only twenty years old.

Miles sent everyone out of the room so he could die without anyone watching. That's the story that every one of Mitchell's friends tells me, no matter who they are or when they tell me. Drunk or sober, that's the story they all tell. Miles sent his parents for a glass of water and told Mitchell to get a cup of coffee.

They were only gone for ten minutes, but when they came back he had died. His best friend didn't want him to be there in the last moments, when the body can squirm and make noises, twisting and twitching as life ends in a green, semisterile room. It says a lot about how people feel for Mitchell, the way they want to protect him from the bad stuff in life. But it says a lot more about how important he was to Miles.

Mitchell has been sober since that day, and I've never known him to be anything but calm, rational, and quietly amusing. Not that he's not funny, but he plans his moments. He won't take over a room, at least not as long as I've known him, as long as he's been the "After." He doesn't want all of the attention anymore. Mitchell's college friends tell of a night when he challenged an entire bar to a handstand contest. He apparently got everyone there to stand on their hands at the same time in order to win a free round of drinks from the bar owner. And the entire bar—girls in skirts included—dropped to their hands and hoisted their feet in the air as they counted to three in unison. I can't imagine. On the night of our engagement he was trembling like he was riding a roller coaster, all those people staring at him while he spoke rattled him to the core.

Watching that man shiver as he asked me to spend my life with him, I fell in love hard and heavy all over again, like the first time I looked across the bed at his sleeping face. That same breathless need. I wonder how I'm going to be without him. Will I always wish I were back here, in our unfinished bedroom, sleeping in the warm crook of his arm?

When I hear stories about Mitchell's wild past, I want to go back in time, back to New Orleans to meet Mitchell on a night when he's a magenta-faced combo of sunburn and beer buzz. I want to sit next to him at a bar and find out what he'd say about my white halter top or my slinky skirt. Would he still compliment my hair? He says it kills him the way my hair bounces when I look at him, how it bobs at my shoulders like I paid it to do that. He loves the way it smells, the way light bathes it in gold. There are times when he'll just hold some of my hair in his hand and look at it the way I sometimes catch myself staring at my diamond. I want to know if I'd still have been the perfect girl for him back when he was known as Super Mitchell—the guy who could do anything and get away with it. Would he even have noticed me? And would I have found him just as charming? More important: would I have given him my virginity back when there was no way we were ever going to get married? Was Mitchell the guy for the job no matter when in time I met him?

One of my favorite T-shirts is in the load of whites; I'll have to wait for the dryer to finish so I can take it with me. I don't want to have to come back here once I'm gone.

I stand in the middle of the living room and take three deep breaths. I'm starting to feel like I'm doing the wrong thing. I need it to be. It's time for me to learn how to do the wrong thing.

I'm the one who makes sure the thank-you notes are delivered, the bills are paid on time, and the milk is tossed before it spoils. I water the plants, fold the laundry, and report suspicious behavior to the neighborhood watch council. I recycle, use low-watt bulbs and fluorescents wherever possible, and keep an emergency supply kit in my garage.

If we're playing a game, I'm the one to keep score. I'm the banker, before and during the game. I'm the one who reads the directions and teaches everyone how to play. I'm in charge of the timer, doling out pencils, assigning teams. I clean up when we're all finished. I'm usually the winner.

If we're driving somewhere, I'm the one who mapped the route on-line. I pack the car with snacks and bottles of water. I fill up the tank. I get the oil changed every three thousand miles.

I set two alarm clocks next to my bed, spaced seven minutes apart.

I am the one people call to set up new electronic equipment, from VCRs to computers. I am the tech support for everybody's voice mail, wireless Internet connections, and TiVo.

I send paper invitations to my dinner parties. I don't wear white shoes after Labor Day. I manage to be both low-fat and low-carb. I have my manicures, haircuts, and facials scheduled every four weeks. I never miss my yearly visits to my dentist, optometrist, and gynecologist. I make my own mulch. I have ten years of day planners saved in a box next to seven years of tax receipts.

I am the one who people count on to get things done before they're due. I don't skimp or cut corners. I never get too drunk. I never make too much of a mess. If I'm your guest, I do your dishes, make my bed, and even wash the bathtub when I've finished my stay.

I send flowers from my own garden.

I make pies for housewarming parties.

I wanted to be good and ended up being perfect.

I thought if I did everything right, if I never left a single to-do item unchecked, I'd find peace. I assumed if I always did the right thing, I'd never have any regrets. I was wrong.

No more. No longer. This bird has flown.

It's time for me to make a mess.

I have to get out of this house. I have to leave Mitchell. Now.

I find my T-shirt inside the dampness of the dryer and toss it over my shoulder. I shove the letter into my purse. Mitchell shouldn't see it. It's wrong; it's not what I'm trying to say. I don't know the words because "Having the perfect marriage will throw me into endless depression" sounds certifiable.

Instead I write in black pen across the *TV Guide:* "I'm sorry. I can't." Right over Bill Cosby's face I've scrawled my final words to the man who thought he was going to be my husband.

The suitcase isn't as heavy as it should be. I packed before I realized all I was leaving behind. It's too late to stuff another knickknack in a pocket. My eyes linger at two picture frames on the wall. One is a baby picture of me—I'm eighteen months, and my mom's standing over me holding my hands as I walk on her feet. I'm sure Mitchell will send that to wherever my new address is. Why would he want it? No matter how sad you are after a breakup, you don't toss out someone's baby picture. You can't throw away a baby. Especially not when she's in the arms of her dead mommy.

The other photograph is of the two of us, Mitchell and me. We're standing at Alcatraz, and we're doing a touristy kiss. My arms are tight around Mitchell's shoulders. We're both in red T-shirts. My hair is crazy around my head from the wind, and we're both squinting as we kiss. What stops me now is what I've always loved about that photo. We're wearing these huge grins, like we've just won the entire city of San Francisco. It's a victory smile. If there were another picture in the series, we would be jumping in the air, fists over our heads in triumph.

I take the frame of Alcatraz off the wall and clutch it to my chest. I decide to take it.

I run into the kitchen and open the cabinet. I grab the flat sushi bowl and slide it into my purse.

Suitcase, purse, frame, makeup case, box of shoes.

She looks like she'd have a lot of baggage.

I ditch the shoes and makeup. I open the door and step out of the apartment.

For the last time, I close the door, putting my key in the lock and turning it.

Good-bye, Mitchell.

I can feel the deep cry swirling inside my stomach, ready to explode, but I don't want to draw any attention to myself as I head down the street to the bus stop. I keep taking deep breaths. If I'm too busy inhaling and exhaling, I can't get that moment necessary for the tears to take over. My eyes are wet as the bus arrives. My token has been positioned between my thumb and forefinger since I left my (not my, no longer my) front door. My arm is outstretched, waiting to drop the coin in the plastic box. I stand and climb the three steps, my head filled with the smells of gasoline and other people. My arm in front of me, I release my token, wishing it weren't this easy, waiting for the moment someone stops me and says, "It's time to wake up, Sara."

Nobody stops me. I take a seat next to a man holding an empty birdcage.

It was that easy.

My hand is trembling so hard as I sign the credit card receipt I don't recognize my own handwriting. My name looks like a wiggly *V.* I push the yellow slip back across the counter to the young clerk. It is disarming to me that I want to refer to him as a boy when I know he's probably in his early twenties, at the most a mere three or four years younger than I am. But his blond hair is dyed pink at the ends and is pulled severely to one side of his head in an intense, intentional comb-over. His eyebrow is pierced, with a purple bead resting on his skin. He looks down at the piece of paper and smiles, exposing a surprisingly beautiful white smile for all he's doing to make himself look unnerving. "This is your copy, Mrs. King."

"Miss," I instinctively correct him. It's the same tone I take when telemarketers ask for "Mr. Overton's wife." I used to take great pleasure in informing the intruding caller, "Mr. Overton doesn't have a wife."

But in telling this clerk here in the dark lobby of the Pathway Motel, admitting to this man-child whose name tag reads "Macho" that I am neither married nor getting married, it all feels suddenly very real. I rest against the counter on both forearms, the breath kicked out of me.

"You okay?" Macho asks. He touches me and then just as quickly pulls his hand back, unsure how to handle me. In his reaction I can see all of the late nights he's worked here dealing with the weirdest travelers America has to offer, from drunken prostitutes to hopped-up truckers.

"Yeah, sorry," I say, pushing myself back to standing. "I just left my fiancé." I expect the announcement to come with a flood of tears, but instead it triggers a giggle.

"Okay," Macho says. His body relaxes now that he knows he's dealing with only a regular old crazy lady, not some special crackhead, knife-brandishing crazy lady.

"I'll be in my room," I say to Macho as if I've checked into the Ritz-Carlton. Where's the busboy for my bags? When will the fresh flowers be delivered? What time is turndown service?

"The elevator's broken," Macho says, his head tilted toward the desk. He's deep in a paperback.

I climb three flights of stairs. I hear the hum of the fluorescents overhead. I follow the ugly purple patterned carpet down the seemingly infinite hallway to Room 309. I hear the door slam behind me and the lock click as I hit the mattress and curl into a ball and cry and cry and cry.

I've been engaged once before, right when I first started dating Mitchell. His name was Tomás and he was from Spain. We were going to get married so he could stay here and be with his boyfriend, his true love, my friend Andrew. I was sure I'd never find someone who would love me like Tomás loved my friend Andrew, and conversely, I didn't want to find someone who would remind me of once wanting to marry my parents.

Andrew and Tomás met at a Fourth of July picnic. Tomás was here on a work permit, and since it was running out, it only made sense he'd find his soul mate standing next to an open bag of Lay's potato chips. They started talking about something mundane—the perfect temperature for beer—and then quickly ditched the picnic and spent the next week in bed together. Drew was devastated this perfect man couldn't live here legally and had to go back to Spain in two weeks.

I don't remember who came up with the solution. I wanted to marry Tomás to keep Andrew this happy. He needed to be married more than I did. I never fantasized about my life as a wife. I pictured maybe one day having a partner, a companion, but it was never a necessity to have a husband.

"I think it's selfish," Mitchell had said when I told him our plan. I was sharing my fantasy of standing at City Hall, hearing "You may now kiss the bride," and stepping back to watch Tomás and Andrew kiss.

"How can this be selfish?" I asked. We had been dating for three months, and we were at the place where we were constantly testing the strength of our morals. Little things like whether to ask what someone wanted from the drive-through or if it was more important to already know what the other would order were becoming matters of life or death to us. One incompatible view on life could mean the end, and I had apparently just launched our biggest test.

"Because you're not doing this for Tomás and Drew, you're doing it because it makes you feel noble. It's like some kind of weird good-girl guilt."

As quickly as I knew that he was right, I vowed never to let him know.

"That's the most insulting thing you've ever said to me," I scoffed. We were in his car. I put my feet up on the dash because he hated it when I did that.

"What happens when we want to get married?" He had said it as if we'd been talking about marriage for a while, as if we'd been engaged for three years and then suddenly I decided to marry into a homosexual relationship instead. Like I was leaving him at the altar of intention.

"Then I'll divorce Tomás and then you and I can get hitched."

That was the first time I ever saw the face Mitchell makes at me when he thinks, *This woman is insane.* His eyes bug out as his eyebrows shoot down and meet above his nose. One corner of his lip curls just enough to show a sliver of his teeth.

Time was running out, as they had only two weeks to plan the entire ceremony. Five days before the three of us were to be married, Tomás and Andrew had a fight over how many guests were appropriate for their reception. Andrew was finally getting his dream wedding, and needed everybody to see it. He had even invited sworn enemies, just for the presents. While Tomás and I were busy researching the legalities of marrying for a green card, Andrew had become a rabid bride, planning his ceremony to the smallest detail, even demanding the hems on the sleeves of Tomás's tux be taken up by half a millimeter. He had begun spouting these sayings nobody had ever said before, like "No one loves a sloppy groom!" Tomás knew this was a glimpse into his future.

One day, while Andrew was busy choosing the stemware he wanted for the champagne toast, Tomás packed his things and moved back to Spain. He sent me a postcard. "Thank you for believing in love," it read. "You will make someone a happy husband someday."

I wake to the sound of my cell phone ringing. It takes a second to remember I'm in a motel room. I read the caller ID: it's Patrice.

"What is wrong with you?" is the first thing she says to me. No hello. This means Patrice is the kind of woman who gets things done. She doesn't do well with rules.

"Nothing," I say. I've been pulled inside out. It feels like my raw nerves and exposed tendons are resting on this scratchy bedspread.

"You don't sound like nothing," she says. I can hear a Prince song playing in the background.

"I'm fine."

"Good. I'll swing by and pick you up at seven."

"Don't," I say, imagining the scene where Patrice and Mitchell stand face-to-face, wondering what's really going on. "I'll meet you there."

"What? Why? Don't be crazy. I'm coming to get you."

I had to invoke the line I hate, the one I never do, but it was the only thing that was going to save me from this conversation. I say firmly, "It's what I want and I'm the bride."

"That's the spirit. Lucky's at seven. Wear something slutty."

"Men are going to behave like dogs as long as women keep treating them like puppies."

This is what Georgia is saying in my ear. Loudly. Repeatedly. She has said it three times in the past hour. You know the night has turned bad once someone can't stop repeating herself. We're deep into hour four of my bachelorette party, and the crowd at Lucky's has turned rowdy. One of the bands didn't show, and the missing hour has been filled with extra orders of booze, more stories told, and a swelling of anticipation that has to bubble up and go somewhere. My party has reached a drunken full tilt. It is important to note that I have also been drinking, and I rarely drink so when I do drink I can't hear things in the right order and I say things all wrong and I do things I shouldn't do. It's why I don't usually drink; it's why Patrice keeps ordering more.

Georgia's using her empty shot glass for emphasis, slamming it on the wooden bar, leaving sticky, wet rings like burst soap bubbles in a row. She's not looking where she's pounding. Her head's facing straight down. Her long, dangly earrings are sticking to her cheeks like silver war paint. I can see the muscles on her forearms working, her entire body concentrating on being here, staying coherent. It's fighting a losing battle.

"They're dogs," Georgia repeats.

Slam! I can feel my brain jostling from the vibrations on the wood.

"All dogs."

Slam! My vision blurs. I can see the sound waves rising from the shot glass. She's louder on this last part, turning to the rest of the crowd in the bar. "And men are going to behave like dogs as long as women keep treating them like puppies."

I bet she didn't even come up with this pithy statement. She probably heard it on talk radio on her way here.

I'm not the first to decide we've heard enough. It's Tracy, who has been single the longest, and therefore considers herself the expert on lonely. But Tracy prefers to tell you how it is one-on-one and wouldn't risk making a scene telling any of us in our current-condition why she's fed up. So Tracy doesn't say anything to Georgia, or even to me, for that matter. She just stands up, steadies herself on the bar with her left hand, making the sleeve of her pretty green dress trail in a beer circle on the wood. Then Tracy walks right out the front door.

"One down," Myra cheers, drink held high in the air. "We didn't need her anyway." Her eyes are sparkling with a mischievous air. All these ladies have crazy eyes going, and for a second I'm positive they've figured me out. They must know I've left Mitchell. It's why Tracy walked out, why Georgia's mad at men, and why Myra and Patrice have been giggling up next to each other all night.

When I stare at them really hard, as I need to do when I'm this inebriated, I realize I do not understand who these people are. I mean, I've known them for years, as we all went to college here in Kansas City together, but we didn't share classes, so our social lives have always stayed a little distant. We get together for parties and weddings, nights like tonight. But why tonight? Why did these women get so dressed up with their hair and their shoes that hurt? Why did they go to the ATM and pull out cash and drive here to celebrate my alleged impending marriage to Mitchell? What is this celebration truly about, anyway? Is tonight a send-off to my single years, or a congratulatory party for my married ones? Are they truly happy for me, or happy because they think I'm happy? Mitchell didn't go to college with us. He's older than we are by a couple of years. Do they look at him and think, *He's perfect for her*, or do they have absolutely no opinion?

I don't have girlfriends like other women do. These women get together to escape their lives, not celebrate them. They haven't asked a single question tonight about the ceremony, or even the reception. They're here for a night out, one that happens to be in my honor. I love these women, but tonight they feel like strangers.

"Pick your high school boyfriend," Georgia says, pleased with herself for coming up with a game. We've moved to a small table in a darkened corner, and Georgia has one finger pointing toward the back of the club. I follow her stare. I didn't see them enter, but now there's a group of thirty young boys in white shirts and black pants swarming the stage. Some of the boys are so young they couldn't be older than fourteen. Scrawny with big heads towering over their shoulders. Hands like paws at the ends of their lanky, tiny arms giving an indication of how big they'll grow up to be one day.

Men are going to behave like dogs as long as women keep treating them like puppies!

Georgia stands and points at the stage. "I got the one with the Mohawk."

"This is going to be awesome," Myra says as she hands me another beer. Her legs are dancing in her chair, and I can hear her heels clicking on the wooden floor like tiny firecrackers going off. She opens her denim purse, reaches in, and pulls out a lipstick. She does it without ever tearing her eyes from the stage, coating her mouth in a shade of purple that makes her look ten years older. I can't tell Myra this. I don't know how to talk to Myra at all anymore because she's getting a divorce the same month that I'm supposedly getting married and it makes me feel like I should apologize to her each and every day for my life going in a different direction than hers. She makes me feel guilty even though she's never said a word to me about how life is incredibly unfair.

Not that there's ever a great way to tell someone you're cheating on her, but Myra's idiot husband, Keith, could be nominated for some kind of asshole award. They were in bed, sleeping. He shook her awake, shaking like he'd had a bad dream. Myra went to put her arms around Keith, her instinct to soothe him back to slumber kicking in before she was even fully aware of where she was or what was happening. Keith pushed her back, a little too forcefully. "I have to go," he said to her. "I've been seeing another woman for a year. I don't love her, but I don't love you anymore, either." He then got out of bed, still in boxers, and left their apartment. Myra was sure Keith must have been talking from deep inside a bad dream and was worried he was sleepwalking all over the city. He wasn't. He went straight to his brother's house, where he stayed for another month. He wouldn't come to the door. He wouldn't answer the phone. Keith's brother threatened a restraining order against Myra if she came by the house one more time. Two weeks later, on the very day Mitchell proposed to me, Myra was served papers.

And now Myra's wearing deep purple lipstick and I'm wearing an engagement ring and it makes me feel like I robbed her of her marriage.

Myra stands up, looks from one side of the stage to the other. She sits back down slowly and gives us a cool grin. "I want Trumpet Boy."

"Which one?" Georgia asks.

"The blond."

"Ooh, he is hot."

"Yes, he is. And he's mine."

"How long have you been dating?" Georgia asks before she downs the rest of her drink.

"Just a month. He asked me to junior prom though."

Georgia punches Myra in the arm. "Lucky bitch."

It's easy to pick my high school boyfriend. He's the one looking in our direction, away from the rest of the jazz band, as if he just realized he'll be playing to an audience. He's sweaty around the hairline, cowlicks forcing his black hair into wild directions across his pale brow. He looks from left to right repeatedly, as if he's sure any moment someone will discover him, point at him with one bony, authoritative finger, and ask, "What the hell are you doing here?" He looks exactly like I feel.

Patrice picks the conductor. "He's the only one who looks legal," she says with an eye roll. "Y'all are disgusting." I see that crazy grin creep over Patrice's face, and I know she's in. "I bet my guy loves big asses."

Myra says, "You'd better hope, baby."

Patrice and Myra fall all over each other laughing as another round of beers arrives.

"So which one is he?" Myra asks me after she's attempted to compose herself.

I point at the wide-eyed boy who's clutching a trombone.

"I should have known." Myra squeezes my forearm so hard her acrylic nails dig into my flesh.

"He looks exactly like Mitchell," Patrice says with confusion.

"That's how you should have known!" Georgia shouts, already well into her laugh.

"Come on, Sara," Patrice says, full of disappointment. "It's supposed to be a fantasy." This coming from the girl who picked the adult conductor.

Now that I've left him, I wonder if Mitchell will become my fantasy.

"I dare you to go talk to him." It's Myra, nudging me with her elbow. Her pointy joint is digging under my rib. I lean away from her, shaking my head.

"What's the harm?" Georgia teases. "It's your last night to do something crazy."

"I say make that boy's year. Give him a big, wet kiss."

Myra's screeching with laughter. "I can just see her kissing that kid."

Before I have a chance to say anything, the band comes to life in its scattered, random method of birth. A horn here, a strum there. Clicks and notes and tones held for seconds at a time. Patrice's conductor turns and smiles at us.

"Hello, everybody. We're very excited to be here tonight at Lucky's. I'm Mike Blakeson, your conductor this evening. I'm the teacher of this talented group."

He adjusts his tie. Patrice sits a little taller. "Oh, yeah, I made the right call," she says.

"The Middletown High Jazz Ensemble is here all the way from Chicago," Mike continues. "We've got a big jazz competition on Saturday afternoon at the Music Hall, which we invite all of you to attend. But tonight we wanted to cut loose and play a little dirty, if you don't mind."

Myra's leaning over to me so close her breath feels wet on my ear. "Play a little dirty, Sara." She pushes me forward so hard my chair rattles. All three of them burst into inappropriately loud laughter.

"This is a Woody Herman piece," Mike says. "It's called 'Apple Honey.'"

Appreciative whoops and whistles come from the more informed jazz enthusiasts. Myra and Patrice clap loud and hard, their hands over their heads. The three of us together couldn't name ten jazz songs. I just like it when it's loud and fast.

That's exactly what happens next. We're engulfed in music. I can feel the sound of the horns pulsing in my chest, beating against my rib cage. The banging of the piano thumps underneath the soles of my feet, and my ears feel full of notes. Our high school boyfriends move as one living creature of frantic fingers, puffed-out cheeks, and swaying chests.

Then a solo: Myra's trumpet boy is standing alone, eyes squinted shut in equal parts concentration and inspiration. The rest of the band quiets slightly into an encouraging, constant throb. He finishes, taking his seat to thunderous applause.

My high school boyfriend stands on shaky legs, trombone glued to his hand as he gives one quick look around the room. I know deep in the most sober part of my brain that it's impossible, but for a moment I am positive he looks past the bright lights and right at me. I give him a big, dumb smile, convinced I've given him the encouragement to start his solo.

I'm screaming for him before he finishes putting instrument to lip. It's not long before the rest of the room joins me.

I'm breathless when the set ends, my skin cold from the goose bumps standing at attention against the back of my wet shirt.

"You should talk to him," Myra says, picking the conversation back up as if the entire room hadn't just rocked on its foundation, as if we hadn't had our minds jolted with sound.

"Yeah, go do that," Georgia says, standing up to stretch her legs while gesturing to the waitress for another drink. When will we be blessed with "last call"?

Patrice says so loudly I feel like the entire bar's listening: "I will pay you fifty bucks to go talk to him."

Georgia says, "He should know some old lady thinks he's talented."

"I'd like the fifty in cash, not a check," I say to Patrice as I walk away from the table. I don't turn around to see their reaction; the new Sara King doesn't do that.

My high school boyfriend is leaning against a wall next to a pay phone covered in white metal scratches. He could be waiting in line for the bathroom, but I feel like he's waiting for me.

He takes a drag off a cigarette. I stop in the middle of the hallway, not knowing where to go.

"'S up?" he asks, his head flicking back like he wants to get his hair out of his eyes. But his hair is stiff from gel, so the move looks like a nervous tic.

Up close I see how young he is, how he's only starting to learn how to be a man. He holds his cigarette loosely between his first and middle fingers, above the second knuckle. It juts out at an awkward angle, poised to fall to the ground at any moment. His skin is yellowish and dark under his eyes. There's acne around his lower lip that's glistening with sweat. He appears to be trying to grow a mustache that gave up somewhere along the way.

This is the part where I'm supposed to grab him and do something. I'm supposed to take him, press my body against him, pin his hands down by his sides, and kiss him. I feel like I'm spinning, twisting around my ankles, wringing myself out. I can taste beer and olives and pretzels, and the thought of this boy in my mouth is just too much.

"Excuse me," I say to him as I push my way past and enter the bathroom. I sprint the last three steps to the stall, hand clamped over my mouth. I make it to the toilet just in time.

* * *

It's very late when I get back to my motel room. Before my taxi pulled away from the bar, Patrice waved the driver to stop. "Take this with you," she said. "I can't keep it at my place anymore. My cats found it in the closet, and now they keep trying to turn it into their new pillow-top mattress. Besides, I can no longer resist the urge to put it on." At first I thought she was carrying a dead body in a heavy, white trash bag. It took a couple of seconds before I recognized the writing on the bag as the logo for a bridal boutique.

I take off my clothes, unleashing a dark musk of cigarettes and perfume. I stand in my underwear in the center of the small room. I can see the outline of myself in the mirror, the only light in the room coming from the bathroom. I can see why people call me a pretty girl; even here when I feel like less than nothing, I still have a glow to my skin. My hair looks full and healthy. My legs are firm.

I pull the heavy, zippered bag from the closet. In the tiny vanity area, the bathroom light illuminates the white linen like I'm holding a gift from an angel. I unzip slowly, as if not wanting to awaken what's inside.

I put on my wedding gown. I need to know what I would have looked like.

I can't get it to zip up the back. My arms aren't long enough. I look in the mirror and try to imagine what it'd be like if the front wasn't gaping around my chest, if the sides were flush with my waist, pulling me up and in. Without the zipper the strapless dress appears to be oozing down my body, like soggy whipped cream. It makes a swishy sound around my hips. I feel as if I'm standing behind the dress instead of wearing it.

I tuck the room key into my bra as I head down the three flights of stairs, holding the dress in not just both of my hands but heaping armfuls. I look like a sorority has hazed me, like I've come a close second in some kind of strange bridal shower game.

Macho looks up from his paperback and sees me. There is only the slightest lift of his eyebrow piercing. I can't believe he's still on duty this late in the night.

"Zip me up."

"I thought you weren't going to do this," he says, slowly placing his bookmark between the pages of Bukowski's *Hollywood*. I can't help but smirk at this punk using a placeholder, instead of dog-earing the page or tossing it aside, facedown. People are always full of surprises. They are never what they appear to be.

"I just want to see what I look like," I say. This is the longest day of my life. I know it's well into tomorrow now, today is tomorrow, but my eyelids feel raw from all of the tears I've been alternately shedding and holding back. My face is stretched tight like I'm wearing a mask made of mesh. Even my teeth feel rough and fuzzy, which is probably from the puking. The day has changed my chemical composition. I feel the thinness heartache causes, my muscles shrunken, hugging my bones, wanting to be comforted.

Macho leaps the front desk in a smooth, rehearsed motion. I turn to face the framed posters of sunsets and wolves. I smell wet ink and pencil erasers as he comes up behind me.

"What have we here?" he asks, his voice deeper than it's been. Perhaps Macho is as tired as I am. Maybe when his shift ends he'd rather come up to my room and spoon so we could sleep for days on end. I'd like that: Another body beside me as I sleep all of this off.

His hand touches the small of my back. I immediately stand up straighter, surprised by the feel of his warm fingers on my skin.

"Sorry," he says. "I need you to hold the dress up so I can pull the zipper."

I start to push the dress against me at my chest, but Macho corrects me, moving my hands down. I hold my hips like I'm about to give a stern lecture, pushing the fabric closer to my body. I look like Mary Poppins assessing a messy bedroom.

I hear the zipper slowly make its way up the trail of my spine.

"How'd you know how to do that?" I ask.

"Three sisters," he tells me. "There." He squeezes my right shoulder from behind. "You're all set to get hitched."

I turn back to him, and in the sudden quickening of his breath and the little twitch of his upper lip, I know I look beautiful.

"Thanks."

"A girl could get into a lot of trouble in that dress."

Macho might be closer to twenty-five. Maybe I was underestimating him at first glance. But now that I've seen his bookmark, heard his voice when it's tired and intrigued, felt his fingers when they decide to take advantage of a situation where they could brush a woman's naked body, I'm beginning to think he looks younger than he's lived.

"A girl's supposed to wear this dress precisely to get out of trouble," I say, but as I say it I know I've just agreed to something and now my night isn't anywhere close to being over.

"See those guys across the street?"

I turn and look through the glass doors of the lobby. I see a well-lit parking lot, half-filled with cars. There's an attendant booth, where two men appear to be playing a game of cards.

"Yeah."

"We play pranks on each other, just to keep the graveyard shift interesting."

"What kinds of pranks?"

"Oh, we order pizzas for each other, pretend someone famous has just checked into the hotel, stupid shit like that."

Macho's holding up a ring of keys; he's locked up his desk drawers. The paperback is tucked in the crook of his arm.

I don't say anything. I follow Macho. Other than the slithering sound of my dress's train sliding on the ugly carpet, the only thing I can hear is the pounding of my blood in my ears.

I'm supposed to ask these parking lot attendants how to get to Third Street. Since we're on Ninth, I'm going to look like an idiot, but Macho said these guys would gladly take the time to explain the way just to talk to a pretty girl for a few minutes.

The taller attendant smells strongly of musk and cigars. He wears a red vest over what used to be a white T-shirt. The collar is leaning to one side, smudged with dirt, the fabric exhausted. He is still holding three playing cards as he approaches me.

"Can I help you?"

I say exactly what Macho has told me to say. "I guess I'm lost."

The second attendant has now rushed to my side. He's about as tall as I am, with a patch of curly hair smack in the center of his forehead. The rest is damp and slicked back. I can't tell if it's intentional.

"You late for a wedding?" he asks, his accent throwing me off. The question sounds like one long word. "Where are you looking to go?"

"Third."

The attendants immediately point in two different directions, and I know Macho has told me the truth.

I play the confused damsel in distress for what feels like ten minutes. At one point the taller one gets brave, standing behind me and pointing my head in the proper direction, even raising my hand with his to show which direction he's talking about. We look like we're dancing.

The more lies I tell to these men, the easier it gets. I tell them I just got back from a costume party (thus the dress). I'm a schoolteacher and I'm in town for a conference. By the time I walk away, those men think that my name is Eustace, a single mother from Alabama trying to make a difference in the educational system. Just as Macho promised they would, they've given me thirty bucks to rent a room for the night, taking pity on this poor li'l lost girl from the sticks. I'm sad to leave Eustace behind as I walk back across the street to the motel.

"Happy wedding!" one of them shouts to me. People are

nicer to you when you're dressed like a bride. The dress means it's your special day. I have been in this gown long enough that it has ceased being cumbersome. It's as if I'm in a pair of jeans. The width of it is comforting. The bodice is sturdy like armor.

I pull the motel door handle and find that it is locked. The dead bolt clanks, the metal lock scraping against the frame. I yank again, rattling the glass.

I check the motel sign, as if I've somehow accidentally walked to the wrong place. I look around for a button to push that alerts Macho behind the front desk.

"Come on," I hear from behind me. I turn, ready to play Eustace again, a little pleased to continue the ruse. But instead I see Macho in a black Lexus, parked at the curb. He's leaning over to the open passenger window. He smiles that ultrawhite smile. "Get in," he says to me.

"Is this your car?" I ask. My gown is slippery on the leather seats. I pull and pull at the edges of my dress until I'm piled into the seat like a melting ice-cream cone.

The sunroof is open, and for the first few minutes I enjoy the sound of the wind whipping above our heads. I stare at the stars. Everything has seemed so bright until now. My eyes are aching.

"You look beautiful," he says.

I smile from behind my closed eyes. I'm in a car with a strange boy and we're driving to I-don't-know-where and he thinks I'm beautiful and I am beautiful and suddenly I am doing exactly what I wanted. I am free, a little dangerous, and nobody knows where I am. There are no expectations. I have no responsibilities. There's no map to print out, no reservations for two. All that has to be is right now. It's fantastic.

Macho slows down for a light, and I hear a clunking in the backseat. I turn around.

"Whoa!"

It's a mess. Empty beer bottles, wadded-up paper bags, spray paint cans, and fast-food wrappers are scattered everywhere.

"Macho, what did you do to your backseat?"

"I didn't do it."

"Well, your friends suck."

I reach back and find a spray paint can. "Midnight Black," it reads.

"Now you look like trouble," Macho says, turning the radio up. I don't recognize the song, but the pulse is constant. There are beeps and blips like computers having sex. I feel like someone else, someone who wears latex and hacks government computers in the middle of the night. Someone who drinks neon-colored drinks and pops pills and owns clothing that glows in the dark. The music, the car, and the spray paint are all part of this great plan, my transformation into a woman who doesn't own a day planner. A woman who doesn't need to check her front door three times to make sure it's really locked. Someone who answers the phone: "Talk to me."

Macho slows the car and pulls into an alley. We're parked in front of a billboard for a local mattress store. There's a picture of a couple lying on a bed, fully clothed, staring at each other in bliss. Mattress Mecca helped them find the right mattress, and now they can start their new lives together. The sign reads: "It Makes All the Difference."

"Go ahead," Macho says. "You know you want to."

When I was in the fifth grade, a stall in the girls' bathroom of my school suffered a month-long rash of graffiti. I was desperate to be a part of it.

Two tampons were walking down the street, read the first message scrawled in black marker. *They didn't talk to each other because they were stuck up cunts.*

Soon others joined in. The language would be awkward, testing out limits of both vulgarity and bravado. The handwriting would be loopy, swirling, with heart-dotted letters and flourishes of puffy clouds around some of the dirtiest words.

I hate Mrs. Alvarado's cockface.

When the recess bell rang, I'd run to the bathroom, even waiting in line sometimes just to sit on that toilet and read the latest manifesto. The messages could be conflicting and confusing.

Brenda McAdams eats shit and dies.

Then there was the continuing marker battle between two girls, each vying for door supremacy.

Math sucks, it read at the top.

So do you. That was scribbled just under it, in a different handwriting.

That's not what your boyfriend said, bitch. An arrow pointed to the earlier sentence, so as to avoid any confusion.

Fuck you, slut.

Then an addition: the other girl, applying two cleverly placed arrows, changed the last sentence to read *Fuck me, shit.*

Inspiration struck one day just as I had finished a spelling test. I turned my paper in at the teacher's desk and asked for a bathroom pass. My instrument of trouble was burning a hole in the front pocket of my overalls as I walked down the hallway. I was sure a teacher was going to be able to see the intent to commit vandalism on my face. I knew I looked guilty, pink-faced with the rush being intentionally bad can bring.

The bathroom was empty. I walked into the stall and locked the door. Sitting on the toilet, fully clothed, I read the latest message.

Everybody at this school is made of pussy and comes from pussy.

I dug my hand into my front pocket. I pulled out my pencil. I found an empty space at the bottom of the door, just under one of the words beginning with an *F.*

The pencil made a strange sound as it slid over the metal door. The line was too thin, too faint. I traced over my message until the gray lines were thick. I had committed my first crime. I had written a message to the next girl who sat down. That girl would know that Sara King had this to say:

Hi.

The bathroom door opened and I yelped, turning to flush the toilet in case it was my teacher looking for me. My pencil fell out of my hand and into the bowl, flushing away before I could save it.

I ran back to my classroom, terrified I'd be found out, called to the principal's office, my name read from a list of trouble-makers over the school's intercom. I wondered what else I'd get into now that I had started a life of trouble. I couldn't sleep that night, scared that the FBI would study my handwriting and determine I was one of the Bad Ones.

The next day, during a math test, I excused myself to the bathroom and erased my two-letter crime. At the time I had decided it wasn't worth the ulcer that was forming in my gut. I've never forgiven myself for backing out of being acceptably bad.

Macho is getting anxious in the driver's seat. "Now or never, pretty lady," he says.

I don't hold down the spray paint button for long. I don't need to. One swoop of paint, one swirl of my arm is all that's needed.

"Okay, Macho," I say, sitting back in the car. "What do you think?"

"Awesome!" Macho says, leaning over my lap to look at the sign. The couple on the bed are still smiling at each other, blissfully reclined on their new mattress. But now they're smiling because the man has his giant, black, spray paint penis pushing into the woman's crotch.

"Can you tell what he's doing?" I ask. I'm giving away my inexperience. Macho doesn't seem either to notice or to care.

"He's totally fucking her!" Macho says, laughing, pulling shut the passenger door. "That's hysterical," he says, and he turns the ignition and drives away.

I watch the billboard through the side-view mirror as it gets smaller and smaller behind us. I have committed my first real crime.

"Want more trouble?"

"Yes, please." Even my voice sounds dangerous, on edge. I'm shaking with elation. I can feel everything, every nerve in my body. Is this what I've been missing all these years? Why hasn't anyone told me about the dangerous thrill of not getting caught?

"Put out your hand and close your eyes and I'll give you a big surprise." He says it in singsong, like we're at recess.

Eyes closed, I hear the road under the tires, the wind over the open sunroof, other cars zipping past us. I feel a soft heaviness in my hands. I grip the round object with both hands. I look: it's a baseball bat.

"What's this for?" I ask, sounding every bit like the prude I'm trying to ditch.

"Roll down your window."

"There! Go! Go!"

He's picked a green, wooden mailbox. I lean out the window, bat raised, my arms feeling strong in the wind. My hair is whipping my face so hard I have to squint.

The jolt my arms suffer from the bat making contact makes my fillings rattle in my teeth. The mailbox seems to shatter around me, wooden chips flying up and back as we drive off faster than the damage can clatter to the ground. I hear Macho cheering from inside the car. I raise the bat again and spy the next target—a red bird-shaped atrocity begging to be put out of its misery.

Macho has told me to be careful to hit only the wooden ones at first, the ones that look weathered and weak. He says the metal ones can make too much noise for this hour.

I raise the bat, pulling my fists back behind my head like I'm waiting for the pitcher. I feel Macho hit the gas, and I swing.

The bird doesn't explode but instead knocks right off its post onto the ground. It's a little less festive, but the immediate plop of the big, red beast is so much more rewarding.

I fall back into my seat; I'm laughing so hard I'm silent.

"Awesome!" Macho says. He likes that word.

My wrists are still humming from the impact. I toss the bat into the backseat, feeling my stomach jumping around inside my body.

"I think I'm done," I say to Macho. I fold my arms in front of my chest and give him a satisfied grin. "Thank you." I feel really good, like I've stepped out of a steamy bath and into a cool room.

"Nah, you're not done," he says, digging one hand into his pocket. "You ain't no bad girl yet."

"You mean I have to start using double negatives and bad grammar?"

"Among other things." He hands me a joint, one that's half-smoked already. "Come on, Sara," he says. "Don't make me make a chicken sound. We're already encroaching on *After-School Special* territory as it is."

I don't know how to hold it. I pinch it between my middle two fingers and my thumb, like I'm making the sign of the devil horns while holding the illegal substance. It makes Macho laugh. He takes one hand off the wheel and positions the joint where it should feel natural. It doesn't. He starts to hand me the lighter, then thinks better of it.

"I'll get it started. You work on inhaling. It probably won't do anything for you, anyway. It's your first time."

He takes back the joint, lights it, and gives a deep inhale. He does that thing people in movies do when they smoke pot, how they barely open their lips so it makes that hissing sound like air seeping out of tires. His eyes even slant shut, like he's impersonating someone smoking a joint more than actually doing it. It looks so exaggerated. He hands me the joint, making that "'Ere!" sound, and I can't believe how this is all exactly how I thought it couldn't really be.

It tastes like wet dirt in my mouth, and I'm conscious of the fact that my lips are wrapped around paper soaked with Macho's spit. It's still red and glowing at the end and smells like burning grass, like cheap incense. Once I inhale, everything inside of me tries to stop what I'm doing. My throat closes up. My tongue swells and reaches the roof of my mouth. Even my teeth clamp shut. My lungs stop wanting to work, and my eyes water until they close. My body has stopped, waiting it out until I cease doing this terrible thing to myself. My mind might want to go bad, but the rest of me would much prefer an herbal tea.

I take one more inhale before I hand the joint back to Macho and hope I've smoked enough. When I finally stop coughing, he's moved on to something bigger.

We're parked in front of a duplex. Macho's staring at the front window, where there's a light coming from deep inside the building.

"Come on," he says to me. He opens the door and leaves.

In the three seconds of silence I have before following Macho, I wonder just how many days I've lived in these past sixteen hours. I can feel my bones creaking. My eyes feel like someone has soaked them in rubbing alcohol.

Macho's around the corner of the duplex, gesturing for me to follow him. This must be his place. He's climbing up a ladder that's leaning against the building. He motions for me to stay quiet as I approach. My head seems packed in gauze. I can't find my footing on the rungs, so I drop my petticoat from under my gown. Billows of tulle fall to my feet. It looks like I've hatched a cloud. Feeling much lighter, I follow Macho up the ladder, still holding the ends of my dress in one hand.

There's a tiny lounge on his roof, complete with a couch, a small table, and rows of planted flowers. The moon is full, and blue light pours onto everything, inviting us with an irresistible invitation to sit still for a long time.

I plop into the couch, the red velvet cushions comforting my heavy head.

"Mmm," I murmur. "This is nice. Macho, you have to feel this couch. It's amazing."

I run my hands over the soft, soft fabric. It's like a gigantic kitten, and I'm the luckiest girl in the world that I get to ride it. I can see the moonlight reflecting off my wedding gown like I'm under a black light. I am glowing, and everything feels so wonderful.

Macho sits next to me, and he just smells really great.

"Can I ask you a question?"

"Sure," I say, but it sounds as if my voice is coming from

somewhere else, somewhere on the other side of the couch. "Sure," I repeat, just to make sure I'm the one doing the talking.

"Why do you keep calling me Macho?"

His eyes are wild-bright from everything we've been doing, and the pink tips of his hair look purple in this light.

"Your hair is pretty," I tell him. He's styled it to look like it's moving, like it's running away from him. I finally understand all of it. The piercing, the Bukowski, the way he uses a bookmark, the way he needed me to be bad with him tonight. He's been sent here as a reward for the hard work I did today. How can I be with only one person when there are so many Machos out there, so many men who are willing to drop their lives in a nanosecond and go anywhere with me, share their worlds with me? How can marriage make sense in a world like that?

"Why do you keep calling me Macho?"

I take his hand, gently, wondering what kind of trick question this is. "That's what your name tag says," I say, confident that I've passed the test.

Macho laughs and swings a leg over my lap. He's sitting on me, pinning me to this soft, cushy couch. I want to touch his head but I might impale myself on his purple-pink spikes. "That's not my name," he says, and I can see his wet mouth, his eyebrow piercing shining blue and white above me. "I forgot I was wearing that. It's a joke."

I'm laughing, and then Macho's mouth is on mine. This dress feels like a cage. I'm bucking under him, trying to kick my legs so I can pull up my skirt because I want to feel his legs on mine, I want my skin on as much of his as possible. His tongue circles my teeth. My body goes mushy, wet and cold, but my face feels blood-hot. I can only hear my breath, hard and heavy, as I pull Macho tighter against me. His hands are under my dress and my underwear is between my knees and his fingers are on me and as soon as they enter me I'm sounding like a dog under the moon.

His free hand clamps over my mouth, and he stares me in the face, our eyes wide as his hand works on me, pushing in the right places, rubbing in the right spots. He has undone his pants and my hand is on him and we're moving together, hurried and grunting, as if we're trying to hurt each other.

"Can I be inside you?"

"No."

I lock up around him and the hard waves crash inside of me and seconds later his back is arched and he's making a sound like a morning stretch. He rests against my bare shoulder. I feel his breath on my skin.

It didn't feel better with Macho. It only felt different. Skinnier. Wetter. I could have had him be my second, but it wasn't going to prove anything. It wasn't going to make me better. It certainly wasn't going to make me badder.

"I need something for my hand," I say, holding it in the air. It's sticky and cold.

"Wipe it on the couch."

I drag my hand across the velvet, having to go against the nap to get clean.

Macho pushes himself up and barely hitches his pants around his waist before he's pacing the roof, fists pumped in the air. "Awesome!"

I yearn for a bath. My skin has a film to it, and my head has started to pulse at the base of my skull. I have been in this dress for too long; my sides are aching, and there's sweat pooled around my stomach.

"We go home now?" I say, talking like a baby for some reason, needing to process all of this in the safety of gallons of warm water and some bath salts.

Macho's holding two small plants, their terra-cotta bases balancing on each palm. "Let's roof-test some shit," he says.

"Roof-test?"

"See how they survive getting tossed off the roof."

"Those plants won't make it. They'll break."

"You don't know that."

I stand up and take one of the plants from him. It's a tiny fern with barely any leaves. "Yes, I do."

Macho tosses the plant over his shoulder. It falls out of our view off the roof. Seconds later there's a popping sound. "Awesome."

"Why did you do that?"

"Because it's fun." He grabs my wrist, and before I can stop it, the plant I'm holding flies out of my grip and over the edge of the roof, followed by the crash of planticide.

Macho is holding a folding lawn chair. "Ready?"

"You're crazy. You're ruining your stuff."

"I already told you that you could. That's barely being bad, if you've gotten permission."

I grab the chair from his hands and toss it over my head, not even looking to see where it heads. It drops right behind me, landing on the roof with a loud clatter. Macho shushes me and holds me tight to him for a second. He stops breathing and listens.

"Why are you shushing me?"

Macho doesn't answer. He walks to the couch and leans over the arm. "Roof-test the couch with me."

"I don't want to. This is stupid."

Macho tries to lift the couch by himself, but it's too heavy. He stares at me, hands on his hips. "Roof-test the couch with me and I'll take you back to the motel."

"Promise?"

"Hurry up."

The couch goes over in one push. Instead of a pop, there's a smashing sound, like the ground opened up.

"What the fuck?"

It's a woman's voice, and it's coming from below the roof. I knew we were going to hit someone. I knew this was stupid. My blood drops to ice, and I am rooted in complete fear.

"That's right!" Macho shouts, yelling to the woman below. "That's what I'm *talking* about!"

"I called the police."

I'm halfway down the ladder before she finishes the second syllable of that last word. I have to get out of here.

"You broke my heart, Christie. So I broke your couch."

"You're an asshole, Grant."

I'm running to the Lexus, and behind me I hear the argument that my brain is interpreting beyond my control. We're not at Macho's house, and his name isn't Macho. This is a girl's place, which explains the plants and nice couch where I gave a guy named Grant a hand job. I drop to my knees and begin wiping my hand in the grass, digging deep, coating my hand in dirt, wanting to erase everything.

More plants are shattering on the cement. The girl is running toward me. I hear her footsteps on the grass.

"Who the hell are you?"

Standing above me is a redhead in pajamas, a strap falling off one shoulder, her body tense with anger. She's so incredibly beautiful that my first impulse is to tell her. But I'm on my knees in her front yard plunging my hand into her mulch and I'm in a wedding gown and she's in her bare feet. There are no words for this situation.

Then there are sirens, and the police are really coming and my heartbeat screams: *Go-go! Go-go! Go-go! Go-go!*

Macho has the same idea and jumps into the Lexus. I pull open the door, but I'm still on my knees and I'm crawling into my seat.

"Whose car did you steal this time?" Christie asks as I slam the door shut and Macho stomps on the gas pedal and is it even worth putting on the seat belt at this point?

"You stole this car?" my voice is screeching, and my hands are clutching the dashboard. I can't breathe. I have to get out of this bodice.

"Why the fuck else do you think you were talking to those guys?" he asks, as he frantically checks the rearview mirror, side-view mirror, and then my mirror. His head is swiveling in all directions as the sirens behind us get louder.

"They're following us!" I shout.

"Duh!"

We've gone from "Awesome" to "Duh," and this is way too much for one day.

There's a light overhead, through the sunroof. I look up into the brightness of the sun, pure and white, burning my eyes. I want it to erase everything, rewind my life, back me up to before. It's loud, and behind us there are more lights, flashing blue, red, white.

"Fucking helicopters," Macho says as he pulls us onto the highway. "Fucking media!"

I can't believe the helicopters have already found us. Am I a hostage or an accomplice? I'm either going to die or going to spend the rest of my life rotting in jail.

I'm clutching my left hand in my right, rubbing my engagement ring with my thumb, wishing it was a magic stone that would transport me to Mitchell, to the safety of our unfinished bedroom with the perfect sheets, my face nuzzled next to his square of flawless chest hair. I want to go back to a world where the most important decision to make was whether or not to set about my task list in alphabetical order.

I shouldn't have left. I had no idea how great I had it, with a man who loves me in a healthy, happy home. Why wouldn't I want to be with Mitchell, and his normal sexual desires and his sweet, sober nature? This unpredictable life of being bad leads to being even worse, until there's nowhere to go but in the back of a police car. And I don't want to be in the back of a police car. I want to be on a couch with my fiancé. I want to run the risk of being bored on a Tuesday night. I want to get married and be a good wife. I want to be a mother who makes cookies and schedules playdates. I want the future that was right in front of me.

Of all the bad things I did tonight, the worst is losing the only life I've ever known.

There's a cell phone in the pile of trash at my feet. I lurch forward like I'm sick, but Macho is too busy trying to escape the cops. Somehow my life now includes the phrase *trying to escape the cops.*

I call home. Mitchell answers, "Hello?"

"It's me. I love you." Instinct dictates dialogue.

"You're on television!" is all Mitchell can say back.

"We're on television," I say to Macho like his nagging wife, as if he forgot to take out the trash and now the dogs have gotten into it.

"Awesome," he says, predictably.

"What's happening, Sara?" Mitchell asks. "You're on television. I see you in the car."

I stick my hand out the sunroof and wave.

"Hi, Sara!" he shouts back, and I can tell he's yelling at the television.

"Stop the car!" I'm screaming to Macho. I want to get out. "Are you okay?"

I'm crying now. "I'm really scared. I want to come home."

"Hang on, baby. I love you."

Macho takes the phone out of my hand, closes it, and jams it into his pocket.

The highway is empty in front of us, packed with approaching cars and sirens behind. Above us remains the steady helicopter beam. I can hear the police officers on their speakers, ordering us to pull over.

"What do you want to do?" I ask, trying to sound normal, trying to sound like we're wondering if we should pull over for gas or wait until the next rest stop.

Macho's eyes are different now, he's crossed a line somewhere—one where I wasn't invited. He looks at me, mouth slightly agape, as if he can't believe I'm still here.

"Are you scared?"

I nod. I worry that they're going to shoot out the windshield or they'll lay down spikes that will blow out the tires and the car will go skidding off a bridge and I'm going to die before I ever see Mitchell again.

"This is your special night. What do you want to do?"

"I want to go home."

"Which home?" He looks self-righteous, as if I'm admitting fault after an incredibly long argument.

"My real home. With Mitchell."

"That's his name?"

"Please let me marry him. Please let me go."

He's so surprised he takes his hands off the wheel and turns to me, as if he can stop driving at any time, like it's a video game. "You're not trapped here," he says, using a tone like I'm a little girl crying for her doll. I immediately grab the wheel and swerve us back into a lane.

Macho takes the steering wheel and shakes his head.

He stops the car, right there in the middle of the highway. Behind us, screeching closer, is the massive sound of the earth trying to stop its rotation.

In the tiny seconds before the world is screaming again, Macho takes my hand. He kisses it. "I'm sorry. I thought you wanted all of this."

He looks normal, like the boy I met in that lobby, the one who zipped me up and asked if I wanted to get into a little trouble tonight. Maybe this all got out of control for him, too. Being bad isn't something you can direct. You're good at being bad only when you know how to roll with it.

"I did," I say, hearing the officers outside. They're yelling for us to get out of the car with our hands up. This is the most trouble I've ever seen, and I can't believe how calm I am.

"Oh, good." He opens his door and steps out like he's simply running into a convenience store. He puts his hands over his head and drops to his knees. He's on the ground and pinned and my door opens and there are hands on me and my face is smashed onto surprisingly cold pavement. I hear the rapid clacking of guns drawn and aimed, pointed at me, the bad girl, the one who did something really, really wrong. The street glitters in the lights of the fleet of vehicles, dancing red, white, and blue all around. I hear the clicking of the cuffs and I know my dress is ruined and I'm in some serious fucking trouble, but all I can think of is how great it's going to be to go home and see Mitchell.

Grant tells them this was all his doing, all his idea. Christie, the owner of the place we trashed, tells them I looked like I was on something, disoriented and crazy, digging through her front lawn. The charges are dropped. I leave the station and walk into Mitchell's arms.

He holds me until he's crying.

"I'm okay," I say, and it sounds like my own voice. It's coming from this body.

"I thought I was going to lose you," he says. I don't know if he's talking about this morning or tonight. I don't know how much he knows. I don't think it matters anymore.

"I'm sorry," I want to say it over and over until my voice no longer works.

He takes my hand. He stares at my ring. "This is ten times worse than anything I've ever done. Not even counting the car, drugs, or vandalism. I mean, you were on a *police chase!*"

He's laughing, and for some reason I need him to take this more seriously. "There were guns pointed at my head!" I shriek. "It was scary!"

He loved me when I was perfect, and still wants me after I broke more than seven laws, including whatever perjury I committed to get the charges dropped. I am looking at the perfect man.

I kiss him, because it's the right thing and it's exactly what I want to do.

"It's bad luck for you to see me like this." My dress has an angry black streak from the chest down to my knees. It's torn in several places. There's black ink from when I was fingerprinted smeared across the waist. I look singed.

"You're beautiful."

"Can we please go home?"

"Absolutely."

"I'll drive."

Mitchell bites his lip, his eyebrows furrowing as he looks into me. "You don't have a license."

"I'd really like to drive."

"Do you know how?"

I stare at him until he says, "You'll figure it out."

He hands me the keys. The metal is warm from his pocket. I clutch them in my palm, ready to start my new life.

"I've got me an outlaw wife," Mitchell says, looking me up and down. "How cool is that?"

I drive us home, careful to obey the speed limit.

The Happiest Day of Your Life

Heather Swain

"So, you're engaged!" My aunt Agnes claps her hands together and grins idiotically at me. She and my cousin Patti have cornered me grill-side on my parents' back patio as we all go for a second bratwurst. (That's what I get for indulging in so many pork products on this trip.) The rest of my extended family mill around card tables and lounge about in lawn chairs on my parents' expansive backyard.

"How did he propose?" Patti asks eagerly.

I know that I will disappoint them because I have no story of Ben down on one knee in the middle of Central Park holding up a sparkling diamond while a skywriter chugged, WILL YOU MARRY ME, ANNIE? in puffy smoke letters overhead.

"We just sort of discussed it and decided that it was time to get married," I tell them.

Although this is true, I'm certain by the angle of their heads and the pitying looks on their faces they think either that I gave Ben an ultimatum or that I'm knocked up.

"Do you have a ring?" says Agnes, eyeing my naked left hand.

"We're getting matching bands. Nothing too fancy," I tell her. "I'm not into diamonds."

"When's the wedding?" Agnes asks, desperate to get at least one detail out of me.

"October Sixth," I say.

"Here?" Patti asks hopefully, meaning Colfax, the small town where I grew up and most of my family still lives.

"No." I squirt hearty brown mustard onto my brat and spoon diced onions on top. In New York, I would never eat like this, but put me back on Wisconsin soil and, suddenly, I'm a glutton. "We're planning a small ceremony in upstate New York."

"Oh," says Agnes, clearly disappointed. She turns away to busy herself with the relish.

Patti asks, "Is that where Ben is from?"

As she says Ben's name, I glance over at him. He sits on the edge of a picnic table bench. My father is across from him, hunched over a mound of baked beans. Next to him is my cousin Jeff, wearing a John Deere baseball cap high on his head. Jeff's hands are folded thoughtfully in front of his face. He seems to be considering something Ben is trying to explain.

Since Ben is a fluid mechanics engineer and Jeff *is* a mechanic, I imagine they're trying to find some common ground. Yet their exchange is probably more like two foreigners conversing in a shared second language than like a friendly discussion at an annual Fourth of July family picnic.

"Ben grew up in Boston," I tell Agnes and Patti. "We met upstate at an apple orchard, so we want to have the wedding there."

"At an orchard?" Patti asks, her voice creeping up an octave at the end of the question, as if to say, How very odd.

"Yep." I nod firmly. "The ceremony will be under the trees. The reception in a barn." I've learned that with my extended family, it's best not to offer too many explanations. Just state the facts as if they are steadfast and shouldn't be questioned. Otherwise, I end up reinforcing the notion that I do things just to be different and difficult.

"Heck," says Patti, "if you wanted to get married in a barn, why didn't you just do it here?"

Agnes laughs and I smile politely, then look out across the yard. Twenty-seven people are scattered between the house and the big shed where Dad keeps all his tools. Behind that, perfect rows of corn spread out for acres. At the edge of the field are the woods where my cousins, friends, and I used to build forts and shoot BB guns at wily squirrels.

"I remember every detail of my wedding." Agnes sighs wistfully and gazes toward my uncle Ed, who tosses horseshoes with some of my cousins' kids. I tossed horseshoes with my great-uncle Pete at this same cookout twenty years ago. Agnes looks back at me. "My wedding day was the happiest day of my life."

This has become one of the common refrains I've heard since Ben and I got engaged. But the more I hear it, the more I'm convinced that whoever claims her wedding day was the happiest day of her life either has been in a horrible boating accident that rendered her an amnesiac recently returned from a deserted island where she ate only fish and coconut for eight years or simply has a deep capacity for denial. In my aunt Agnes's case, it's denial.

I've heard stories of her wedding—how Uncle Ed was "kidnapped" by his groomsmen and taken to the local bar for a few drinks between the ceremony and the reception (a Wisconsin tradition) and only returned, shitfaced and stinking of pig manure, after the cake had been cut and most of the guests had given up on him and gone on home. Agnes had threatened to annul the wedding the next day. She even returned to my grandparents' house for a week until Ed redeemed himself in her eyes by purchasing a trailer for them to live in.

"But I'm sure your wedding will be wonderful wherever it is," says Patti kindly.

Personally, I think the amount of enthusiasm one imparts to her wedding memories is inversely proportional to how happy her marriage is. In other words, the crappier the marriage, the happier the memories of the wedding. Again, in my aunt Agnes's case, this is also true.

"Is everything pretty much set?" Agnes asks me just as my mother, Ingrid, saunters up to the grill in her latest Quacker Factory sequined American flag Stars and Stripes tunic. Mom snorts at the question, and I think I've been set up. Surely Agnes has been getting an earful from my mother for the past few months.

"Pretty much," I say. "There isn't a lot to do."

"It's going to be *small* and *simple*," says Mom, doing nothing to disguise her distress.

My mother is the queen of complicated theme parties: Greek Night complete with bedsheet togas, kalamata olives, and feta cheese; fifties sock hops with poodle skirts and cheeseburgers; character dinners in which everyone assumes another identity for the evening. This was great when I was a kid. Each year she outdid herself for my birthday: a make your own banana split party, a luau, and when I was seven an entire elaborate Cinderella ball. She loves the Fourth of July, with its built-in excuse for red, white, and blue bunting, flag waving, and Uncle Sam hats. Needless to say, my desire for a stripped-down, simple wedding is contrary to everything she loves about party planning.

"Only fifty people are invited," says Mom. "They aren't even having a cake."

"Why aren't you having a cake?" Patti asks, nearly aghast.

"They're expensive," I say. "And usually not very good."

My mom sniffs, then continues her assault. "And some stranger—Dirty Harry, Steamboat Jerry—what's his name?"

"Judge Larry," I remind her through a mouth full of sausage and bun.

"Right, *Judge Larry* is going to marry them. How did you find him anyway?" she asks. "Does he have a television show?"

"Ben found him over the Internet," I say with a laugh. Ben has only four tasks in the planning of our wedding—order the invitations, hire a band, buy a suit, and find an officiant. Because he's such a tech nerd, he's doing each of those things on the Web.

"And," my mother says, turning to Agnes again, "she won't even try on Granny's dress."

"Oh, Annie," Agnes gasps. "It's a lovely dress."

"I'm sure it is," I say, but for the record, it's not a lovely dress. In fact, it's a hideous dress, covered with frills and lace and strands of fake pearls like an ugly Victorian lampshade. It's the dress that my great-grandmother, my granny, and my mother all wore at their weddings. Now, it's supposed to be my turn, but I refuse.

"I've been thinking about her wedding since the day she was born," Mom says. Although that's surely an exaggeration, it's probably not by much. "But she won't take help from *anyone*."

It's not that I don't respect my mother's party-planning abilities or think she wouldn't be helpful. I readily admit, she's the consummate hostess. But I don't want the kind of wedding people usually have here. Weddings in Wisconsin tend to be big affairs with hundreds of guests and a legion of bridesmaids in tacky lavender taffeta and groomsmen in matching cummerbunds, followed by a prime rib buffet and the chicken dance at the local Elks' lodge. That's not my style.

Part of me understands my mother's preoccupation with my wedding. I am an only child, an oddity in these parts. I think she's embarrassed that I want to get married away from home, as if that reflects badly on our relationship. Or maybe she wants to make up for her own modest wedding—a quick ceremony at a small chapel with punch and mints afterward because my grandparents could afford to give her only a hundred dollars. Or maybe a wedding is just the ultimate theme party to plan, and I'm depriving her of her glory. Whatever it is, I am sorry to disappoint her, but not sorry enough to change my plans at this point.

Plus, it wouldn't be fair to drag Ben and his parents here. Their relationship is already strained enough. Their being out of place and outnumbered by my family would not help the situation. Besides, Ben and I agreed from the moment we got engaged that our wedding would consist of only our closest family and friends in a beautiful setting with good music and great food. That's all we want. So, before my mother can launch into her full diatribe about how I won't come home like a sensible daughter and let her help me plan the wedding of the year, I slink away.

At the edge of the yard, I skirt the rows of orange daylilies leaning toward the waning sun. They've grown here wild since I was a kid, and I used to pick huge armloads for my mother's late June birthday. (Now I send her Harry & David fruit baskets and gift certificates to Pottery Barn.) Further out in the woods are patches of wild blackberry bushes where my mom, granny, and I used to pick buckets full every July, then make jam and pie.

Gazing at the flowers and thinking of the berries makes me remember what I like about being in the Midwest. As a kid, I could walk down the road or through the woods and be to one of my uncles' or aunts' houses in a matter of minutes. If I rode my bike into town, I knew almost everyone I saw. Colfax was a cozy, safe place to grow up, where I never felt alone. Each year, when I come back for this picnic, I begin to think that I could be happy here again.

I turn and find Ben, surrounded by five men from my family, each of them bigger and blonder and more Germanic looking than the next. This is the first time Ben's come home with me for this picnic and met most of my extended family. His dark hair and slouchy posture stick out among all the upright Lutherans scattered around the property. In Brooklyn, where we live, my fair hair, pale skin, and five-eleven stature set me apart. But put me in khaki pants, white Keds, and T-shirt with the American flag, and here I'm just one of the gang. Except, that's not me. For example, I'm the only one wearing a black linen sundress and Chinese slippers today, or any day in Colfax for that matter. This is what reminds me that at some point in my life I felt more suffocated and stifled here than safe.

Ben catches my eye and excuses himself from the table. We meet under a willow tree where my old tire swing hangs neglected. I give it a push with my knee. It twirls in lazy circles. Someday, I imagine we'll bring our kids here, and they will love the simplicity of this place.

"How's it going?" I ask Ben and grimace, expecting the worst.

He runs his hands through the short, dark curls of his hair and sighs. "Well, no one has told any anti-Semitic jokes."

"Yet," I say.

"You remember that scene in *Annie Hall* when Woody Allen's character goes to visit Annie's family for the first time? The camera pans around the dinner table to each member of her family, happily eating, then it gets to Woody Allen, and he's dressed like a Hasid. That's basically how I feel."

I throw my arms around him and squeeze. "I'm sorry," I say, and I mean it. "Is it that bad?"

He laughs and rubs my lower back. "Nah," he says. "It's actually kind of cool. One of your cousins asked me if it hurt when I was circumcised at my bar mitzvah."

I squeeze my eyes shut. "That can't possibly be true."

"Seriously."

I look up at him. His dark eyebrows knit over deep-set eyes. "What'd you say?"

"I was so surprised anyone in your family knew what a bar mitzvah was that I was speechless. Then your uncle Jasper pulled up on that tractor thing and everyone got distracted."

"He is a farmer," I say by way of explaining how one's uncle could come to a cookout on a tractor. "And it is July." Ben looks at me blankly. "Never mind," I tell him. "Tomorrow we'll be back in New York."

As if on cue my great-uncle Pete walks up to us and shouts, "How's New York City treating you, Annie?" Uncle Pete has been going deaf for the past ten years, so that now a conversation with him is like sticking your head inside a bullhorn.

Ben and I instinctively take a step back. "Just fine, Uncle Pete," I shout. Pete inches forward so that he can hear my reply.

At this rate, we'll all be standing in the corn rows by the end of our talk.

My granny is right behind Pete. "I just don't know how you live there, honey," she says and shakes her head. "With all those terrorists. Aren't you scared?"

"There's no more to be afraid of in New York than there is here," I say.

"That's for sure," shouts Uncle Pete. "I keep telling the fellows down at the VFW Hall that the next place those terrorists are going to hit is a small industrial or agricultural base like Eau Claire." He rubs the gray stubble on his chin. "And we'll be ready for them. Yes sir."

I can only imagine what that means—Uncle Pete and his cronies with their hunting rifles and World War II grenades stockaded inside the VFW Hall, waiting on the terrorists. I'd be more scared of that than of any sort of attack.

"Statistically," Ben says, "we have no more chance of being involved in a terrorist attack in New York than you have of being caught in a tornado here."

I call this Ben's science brain, and normally I like his logical explanations of the world, only I know this won't go over well with Granny and Uncle Pete, so I interject, "Bad things happen everywhere. You just have to make your life."

"Well," says Gran. She shakes her head again. "I pray for you, honey. I pray for you every night."

"Thanks, Granny," I say and peck her on the cheek. Her skin is dry and papery. Since I left Wisconsin five years ago, she has shrunken down to a little old lady. Still, I'm always shocked that she's no longer my vigorous, youthful granny who took me mushroom hunting in the fall and ice skating in the winter. Who told ghost stories under the covers and always, no matter what, told me to be myself. "That's very sweet of you."

"You'll take good care of her, won't you?" Granny asks Ben.

He drapes his arm across my shoulders and says, "She takes pretty good care of herself."

This does not please my granny, who chews on her lower lip and jerks her head to the side. I feel the weight of Ben's arm on my shoulders, slumping and dejected. It's hard to imagine how Ben feels around my big, rowdy family. He has no relatives other than his parents. No siblings. No living grandparents. No aunts, uncles, or cousins. It's just him and his parents, and when I'm with the three of them, I feel claustrophobic.

I loop my arm around Ben's waist and give him a hug. "He takes real good care of me, Granny. We take care of each other."

"Well," she says and looks away. "I pray for you anyway."

At ten o'clock on Monday morning, my office phone rings, and Jane's number flashes on the caller ID screen. "So," she says when I pick up. "How was it?"

Of all the people in my life, Jane will understand. We've been best friends since fifth grade. We moved to New York together two years out of college, after Jane's boyfriend broke her heart and I was fired from my job as the marketing director for a farm implement company because I came in late, surly, and hungover a few too many times.

"It was tolerable," I say.

"Did anyone show up in white sheets to meet the *Jew* Annie is marrying?"

I laugh but say cautiously, "Everyone was very nice to Ben."

Jane giggles. "Howell was mortified the first time we went back. When Uncle Duane found out Howell is from New York, he actually called him a Yank. As if Wisconsin was in the Confederacy."

"Maybe he was talking baseball," I offer dryly.

"Yeah, maybe," Jane says sarcastically. "Anyway, guess who just called me."

"Uh, I don't know." I'm only half-listening to her as I look over new artwork for Fauntleroy.com, the website that I'm supposed to be designing. But when Jane says, "Your mother," she gets my full attention. "Oh no," I groan. I imagine my mother sitting at her kitchen table this morning making checklists of people to pester about my wedding. I'm certainly at the top of that list. "What did she want?"

Jane snorts. "What do you think she wanted? My recipe for lemon tea cookies?"

"I don't know what's gotten into her." I lean far back in my chair and put my feet on the edge of my desk. It makes me tired just thinking of reining in my mother. "It's like she's become obsessed."

"Welcome to the wonderful world of weddings!" Jane booms like a game-show announcer. "If you think for a minute that you're in control, you're seriously delusional. You have to remember, a wedding isn't for the bride or the groom. It's for the bride's mother."

"Your mom wasn't like this," I point out.

"Please," says Jane. "She'd already had three weddings of her own by the time I got married."

"How's your newest stepdad?" I ask.

"Apparently they're traveling a lot," she says and pauses. "On the NASCAR circuit. Which must explain why I didn't hear from mom on my birthday."

This is par for the course for Jane's mother, and it makes me feel worse about not embracing my own mother's help when I know she has only the best intentions.

I stare at the fluorescent lights overhead. "Well," I say with a resigned sigh. "I wish there was something my mom could do for my wedding, but everything is under control."

"As your maid of honor—" Jane starts to say, but I interrupt.

"This is a nontraditional wedding," I remind her. "I'm not having bridesmaids."

"What am I then?" Jane asks.

I think for a moment. "How about director of bridal services?"

"Fine. Whatever you want to call me, I have an idea that might appease your mom."

I drop my feet to the floor and sit up straight. "Kid," I say with mock enthusiasm, "if this works, I might just make you *executive* director of bridal services."

"Does that come with a raise?"

"Title only."

"I should hold out for something better, but in the interest of general happiness, I'll tell you anyway. Why don't I throw you a bridal shower in Colfax, but I'll let your mother be involved in the planning? That way she can feel useful and invite all her friends who aren't coming to the wedding, and you can still get married out here like you want."

I slump over my desk. "I don't know," I say wearily. I pick up my favorite picture of Ben from the corner of my desk. In it, he stands next to a five-foot-tall plastic cockroach we saw at a gas station in Utah. The cockroach is wearing Ben's Red Sox baseball hat, and Ben laughs as he squints into the sun. "We're not the kind of people who have bridal showers."

"It's a compromise, Annie," says Jane.

I consider this for a moment. The alternatives are letting my mom be more involved in the wedding planning or totally disappointing her, neither of which is a good option.

"Okay," I say. "But as executive director of bridal services, you have to promise to keep my mom in check. No stupid games, no paper plate hats covered with bows, no embarrassing PowerPoint presentations commemorating every date I've ever had."

"I can't promise about the paper plate hat," says Jane. "Simply because I'd love to see you look like such an ass."

"You've been demoted," I tell her. "You're now *assistant* director of bridal services."

"Fine by me," she says. "Better hours. Now I have to go. I have actual work to do."

"Actual work?" I shuffle papers from the Fauntleroy file on my desk. "I should try that, too." I turn back to my computer, irritated that I've become a person whose wedding has taken precedence over her job, exactly the situation I intend to avoid from now on.

The next morning, Ben and I walk to the subway station together, something we've done every morning since we moved into our apartment eight months ago. I assume someday we'll break this nicety. One of us will go to work at a different time, or be in a hurry one morning and rush off alone to save a few minutes. Then we'll never go back to our morning ritual. And this change will signal a shift in our relationship. The same as when we will no longer sleep intertwined in the center of the bed, or say "I love you" at the end of every phone call.

I know eventually things will change with us. Every relationship changes over time. (I look at Jane and Howell, who used to be so in love they couldn't stand to be apart. Now, they spend their time together taking little jabs at each other.) But I'll be sad when our relationship changes, because I want to believe that Ben and I will always be as in love and devoted to each other as we are right now, strolling along the tree-lined streets of Brooklyn Heights.

We bulldoze through the hordes of people crossing paths on their way to work—some descend into the subways, others come out, still more push through the doors of the court buildings surrounding Cadman Plaza. It's already hot and oppressive at 8:00 A.M. The humidity hangs heavy in the air, trapping the smells of too much humanity.

"Yick," I say and pull my tank top away from my skin. "I feel like I'm stuck inside an elevator with someone who has bad breath and B.O."

"I hope you're not describing me." Ben wipes beads of sweat from his upper lip.

I sniff at him and pronounce, "No, you smell like roses."

"You know, if everyone planted roses or trees or even grass on top of every building over ten stories high, the city would be about five degrees cooler on days like this."

I smile up at him. I love his scientific explanations of the world. As if everything is so easy and logical.

"By the way," says Ben. "We need to get a present for Alex Nessman."

"Who's Alex Nessman?" I ask. Pigeons scatter, then reconvene behind us to peck at muffin and bagel bits dropped by rushing commuters.

"My friend from prep school. His wedding is next month in Boston. Remember?"

"I totally forgot," I admit.

"We should book a hotel if we're going," says Ben.

"Why wouldn't we just stay with your parents?" I ask.

Ben frowns. "You want to spend the weekend with Saul and Miriam?"

As Ben says this, I imagine the stilted silence of his parents' house. The way they all tiptoe around one another and talk about only the most trivial details of their lives, never touching on anything remotely personal. As if exposing the smallest vulnerability would collapse their fragile façade of a happy family.

But I don't bring any of this up. Instead, I say, "Sure! Why not?" with far too much Pollyanna optimism.

"Because they're weird," says Ben.

"It'd be cheaper to stay with them," I say.

"I think we can afford a hundred dollars for a hotel," says Ben, and I roll my eyes. Money is a constant source of disagreement for us. Ben will hemorrhage his salary on electronic gadgets and fifteen-dollar-per-pound gourmet coffee while I happily drink deli sludge from a paper cup and shop only at discount stores like Century 21 or Loehmann's. We like to think this makes us a well-balanced couple, but sometimes it just makes us pissed off at each other.

"Regardless, I should get to know them better before our wedding," I say, trying to redirect the conversation.

"Suit yourself," Ben says with a shrug. "At least we'll see how other people put on a wedding if we go."

"You've been to other weddings," I point out.

"Yeah, but not when I was planning my own."

"Speaking of which . . ." I follow Ben through a line of sulking cars and trucks waiting to cross the Brooklyn Bridge. "Don't wait too long to find a band. The good ones get booked up early." I say this gingerly. Whenever I remind him of the four things he's agreed to do for our wedding, he gets testy.

"So are you going to let Jane do this bridal shower thing?" Ben asks, clearly ignoring what I've said. I let it go, not wanting to spark an argument this early in the morning.

"It sounds awful, doesn't it?" I ask.

"How bad could it be?"

"Bridal showers aren't like bachelor parties," I tell him. "Are you having one? A bachelor party, I mean."

"Are nerds allowed to have them?" Ben asks.

This makes me giggle because he truly is a nerd. On our first date, he took me to the Bronx Zoo and wore white socks with Teva sandals. I figured if that was all I could find wrong with him, he was a good catch.

"Can you see my geeky engineering buddies at a bachelor party? They wouldn't have a clue what to do."

"You'd have to get an inflatable hooker," I say.

Ben snickers. "Or a robot. They'd love that."

We step onto the escalator at the station and hear the rumble of a train. As we do most mornings, we immediately rush down the steps, leaving the loose ends of our conversation flapping behind us like coattails.

At work, my colleague Helen and I crowd behind my computer to discuss the designs for Fauntleroy.com. I change the font of the slogan, "For the Finest Things in Your Child's Life," from plain script to the fancier, more appropriately named Dauphin typeface.

"That looks good," says Helen. "It's sufficiently pretentious."

We scroll through the pages of gorgeous Italian linen baby clothes, eight-hundred-dollar Bugaboo strollers, miniature SUVs and Hummers for toddlers to drive, listings for multilingual au pairs who've graduated from elite boarding schools in Switzerland.

"I'm appalled that people would spend this kind of money on their children," I say. "My kids will be lucky to get a tire swing."

"You planning to have kids soon?" Helen asks.

Ben and I have had cursory discussions about kids. We both agree, in theory, that having a family someday would be a good thing, but we've never discussed details, like how many or when. "We're not in a hurry," I say.

I trim a photo of a three-story shake shingle tree house with a turret and a dumbwaiter, then drop it into the "Playhouses" page of the website.

"Jesus, that thing is nicer than my apartment," Helen says.

"Who has this stuff?" I ask.

"It's all those asshole Upper East Siders or stay-at-home mommies in the 'burbs, with their summer homes in the Hamptons," she sneers.

"Not everyone in the suburbs is like that," I say self-consciously, because personally, I can't imagine having kids in the city.

"I would shrivel up and die if I had to live in Westchester or Long Island."

As Helen says this, I realize that Ben and I have never seriously discussed leaving the city. Maybe he would hate it as much as Helen would. I look back at the website. "It wouldn't be so bad to leave," I say but wonder if someday I'll be raising urban babies while pining away for a large green lawn where my tots could frolic.

*　　*　　*

At the end of the week, Jane and I walk past the faux grungy bars and hipster hair salons of the East Village on our way to see Lenora Ng, the designer at a little boutique called Orange, where Jane had her wedding dress made a few years ago.

"I can't believe I let you talk me into this," I say. "After all the problems you had with Lenora."

"She wasn't that bad," says Jane.

"She gave your dress to someone else," I remind her. "Who left the state with it before she realized it wasn't hers. You didn't even get your dress back until six hours before you walked down the aisle."

"But I looked fabulous!" says Jane. She sidesteps a homeless guy eating lo mein from a discarded take-out container.

"Your dress was the best part of your wedding," I say.

"What's that supposed to mean?" Jane asks. "My wedding was great."

We pause at a light and wait for a line of cabs to pass, then we cross Avenue B. "Janey, Janey, what happened to you? You've become one of those people who selectively remembers her awful wedding as wonderful. Next you'll tell me that it was the happiest day of your life!"

"I wouldn't go that far, but there was nothing wrong with it."

"It was a catastrophe. A hell storm. Everything went wrong! The florist brought you pink roses not yellow, the caterer dropped the cake, and Howell got so drunk he threw up in the car on the way to the airport to leave for the honeymoon where it rained for six days straight."

"But my dress," says Jane sentimentally.

"Your dress was gorgeous," I admit, because I know it's a losing battle. "But I could probably find something just as nice off the rack for half the price."

"For God's sake," says Jane, completely out of patience with me. She stops short in the middle of the sidewalk, causing a kid on a skateboard to swerve and nearly hit a lamppost. "If you're going to be such a cheap ass, why don't you just wear your granny's dress?"

"Oh, God no!" I walk past her. "I've got to have some dignity."

She catches up to me again outside Lenora Ng's tiny shop, which is wedged between a vegan bakery and a tattoo parlor. "This better be worth it," I say to her as I swing open the door to Orange.

Inside, lengths of luxurious silks are draped over every surface, making the room feel like the most decadent inner sanctum of a harem. Lenora herself is a walking disaster, disheveled and perpetually mismatched in dots and stripes and plaids, with gold-tipped spikes of hair sticking out from her head like pineapple spurs and straight pins impaled all over her blouse.

She puts me on a pedestal in the center of the tiny shop and circles me, chewing on her lips and squinting. "I was born in Nha Trang. Vietnam, you know?" Lenora says. I've heard this story before. When I sat in the metal folding chair where Jane now sits smirking and Jane stood up here nervously. I have a feeling Lenora tells the same story to each new customer. "I was abandoned at Buddhist temple when I was six. My parents have too many kids. Want me to become nun. Ha! I look like nun to you?"

She stops in front of me, crosses her arms, and considers my body. Sweat prickles my underarms, and I want to flee. Go to Loehmann's, where I could find something decent for a few hundred dollars. But I stand still and remind myself why I'm here: this is my wedding dress, a dress that will be captured in photos and displayed for the rest of my life, a dress that will save my future daughter from the embarrassing fate of wearing Granny's monstrosity. It's an investment. A splurge.

Lenora circles again. "I never cut out for devout life," she says. "I run away. Work in sweatshop. Fourteen hours a day. No good. Never see sun." She stops by Jane, smacks her arm with the back of her hand, and says in a low voice, "Never see *men*."

How she got to New York is never made clear, but it seems to have something to do with an American businessman and a marriage and a quick divorce, leaving her with a chunk of change that she invested in her shop. Whatever the details, it doesn't matter. Lenora is a genius with needle and thread, and she understands a woman's body. Of mine she pronounces, "You have hips, you know?" She pokes my ass with her index finger. "But nice chest. Balanced. Yin and yang, ha ha ha! I make you something nice. What you want? Sexy? Slinky? Traditional?"

And then she's off, whizzing around her shop, picking up armloads of fabrics. "What color? Let's do something different. This is nice. Blue." She tosses it over my left shoulder. "Not many people choose. All American girls want white or off-white. What's the difference? How many kinds of white? In Asia white is for death. Red is for love. How about red? You like red?" She holds up a bolt of baboon-ass red silk. "Do something daring!" she admonishes. "You need strong color for your strong personality."

I shake my head. "My wedding is going to be very small and simple," I tell Lenora. "I think my dress should be that way, too."

She sighs. "I know what that means," she says gloomily. "White. Everybody same. White. White. White." She stomps to the rows of white silks in the back. "Come on." She waves me over. "Pick out what you want."

After an hour of poking and prodding, draping and pinning, we've come to some decisions. I will have an ivory sheath with a small swirl of fabric at the back and a slit up the front. Lenora will add fabric flowers and seed pearls across the bodice. It is simple, it is elegant, and it is costing me a thousand dollars. I find this appalling and could easily back out of it if it weren't for Jane and Lenora gushing over how fabulous I'll look.

"Now, when you need this again?" asks Lenora as she writes up the order and takes my deposit check for five hundred dollars.

"October sixth," I say.

She lifts her shoulders and flaps her lips. "That's fast. You come back for fitting in two weeks."

"All right," I say, uncertain what I'm getting myself into, but Jane gives me an excited look that says, It'll be worth it. I'm not so sure.

*   *   *

The next weekend, Jane and Howell come to our place to help us stuff and stamp our wedding invitations. We reward them by opening a couple decent bottles of red wine.

I sit on the couch with my feet nestled under Ben's thigh and our black pug, Lazlo, curled in my lap. Jane's got her long legs sprawled across the arms of Ben's leather recliner, while Howell perches on the edge of our puffy ottoman. This is where I'm happiest these days, in our cozy apartment with Ben, our best friends, and Lazlo by my side.

Sometimes I wonder how this happened. How I became such a homebody, barely interested in leaving Brooklyn at night. I used to make fun of my parents for having a social life that revolved around Aunt Agnes and Uncle Ed and the occasional trip to Eau Claire for dinner or a movie. But I suppose that's what love does to a person. It lulls one into contentment. I used to dread this kind of familiarity and predictability, because I thought it would mean that I had given up on living a fulfilling life. Then I met Ben and realized that fulfillment comes in many varieties.

"I don't understand this," Jane says. From the center of our cluttered coffee table, she picks up another wedding invitation, this one from our childhood friend Gracie MacMillan. It's a piece of handmade paper with dried flowers pressed into the edges around loopy calligraphy. "There is no groom?"

"That's right," I say as I pull labels off a sticky sheet and attach them to our envelopes.

"And it's not like there's another bride, right?" Howell asks.

He sips a glass of deep red Merlot. He's already dribbled a bit of wine on his blue oxford cloth shirt. I've never seen him without a blotch of something on his perpetually untucked shirts or rumpled khaki pants.

"Gracie didn't grow up to become a lesbian?" Jane asks.

"Not technically, no," I say. "But I suppose self-love could be called queer." I finish a stack of ten envelopes, then hand them to Ben for stamps.

"So, you're telling me that she's marrying herself?" Jane pokes at Gracie's invitation aggressively with her index finger. A strand of hair gets caught in her mouth, and she spits it out.

"That's right." I pick up another stack of ten envelopes.

"Can a person do this?" Jane demands. "Can a person legally marry herself?"

"I doubt the state will recognize it if there's a custody battle for her children," Ben answers with a smirk.

"But why? Why would someone do that?" Jane slumps back against the recliner. "Marriage isn't about yourself."

"What's it about, then?" I ask.

Jane snorts. "It's about the other jackass."

"You calling me a jackass?" Ben asks. He hands his stamped envelopes to Howell for stuffing.

"I believe she's calling me a jackass," says Howell as he puts our creamy white invites into the envelopes, then hands each one to Jane.

She runs her tongue over the glue and presses each flap down firmly. "Did you both really like this invitation?"

"Why?" I ask, immediately self-conscious about our plain

cards with their art deco script and simple border. "What's wrong with it?"

"Nothing's wrong with it," says Jane. "It just doesn't look like something either of you would choose."

"We couldn't agree," I say. "I wanted something understated."

"Cheap, she means," says Ben.

"Not cheap, but what's with all the different envelopes and pieces of tissue paper?" I ask.

"Just a silly tradition," says Jane.

"A silly tradition you had to have," Howell says with a snort.

"You didn't care," says Jane.

"I wasn't even allowed to comment," says Howell.

This time Jane is the one snorting. "You didn't give a rat's ass."

"I bet you ten bucks Ben doesn't either," says Howell. He picks up a piece of cheese off the platter on the coffee table, then tosses it to Lazlo.

I look at Ben. "Is that true?" I ask. "Do you care?"

"I suggested e-vites," says Ben.

I roll my eyes.

"They'd be cheap," he says.

"I believe the word is *tacky*," I say.

"Same difference," says Ben.

"Jackass," I mutter. We all chuckle, then go back to stuffing and stamping the invitations.

"Do you think Gracie'll change her name?" Jane asks.

We giggle meanly.

"She always was an odd bird," I say. "She loved to play house when we were kids. She had every conceivable plastic replica of domestic life in half-size proportions—a refrigerator, stove, sink, vacuum cleaner, groceries, and babies that shit and peed and cried like drowning kittens. My mom says there are like two hundred people invited to this wedding."

"Why do you suppose you got an invite and I didn't?" asks Jane.

"Did you actually want one?" asks Ben.

I turn to him. "Do you think we could get two hundred people to come to our wedding?"

"Would you want two hundred people at our wedding?" he asks.

"But it is a little weird, don't you think?" says Jane. "I mean, I grew up with her, too."

"I'm not saying I want two hundred people," I say to Ben. "I'm just asking if you think we *could* get two hundred people."

"Does this make any sense to you?" Ben asks Howell.

Howell holds up the empty bottle of Merlot. "I'll need more of this to understand." He rises and walks into the kitchen. Lazlo trots behind him.

"Don't you think it's odd that she's marrying *herself*, and two hundred people will come?" I ask.

"Just because she invites two hundred people—" Ben starts to say, but Jane interrupts.

"Who are these two hundred people?" she demands, "if I'm not one of them?"

"If we invited everyone we knew, from childhood, college,

and our combined years in New York, I bet we could get a pretty decent crowd," I tell Ben.

"Why does any of this matter?" he asks.

"It doesn't," I say, but that's not entirely true. Somehow, having all those people to invite seems to validate Gracie's weird scheme and makes me question the legitimacy of my own small wedding. Not that I'd actually admit any of this out loud.

"Are you going?" Jane asks me.

"We could," I say. "It's the same weekend as my shower. You could be my date."

"That would be hilarious!" Jane says.

Howell comes back with an open bottle of Shiraz. Lazlo follows, licking his chops happily. "For two people who left Wisconsin and claim to never want to go back, you're both awfully interested in what goes on there," he notes. He fills Ben's glass, then his own. Jane and I ignore him.

"You could get her a nice plastic replica of a toaster," says Jane. I laugh, nearly spewing my wine, which eggs Jane on. "Do you think she'll run from side to side during the exchange of vows?"

"You're awful," I say, clearly wanting her to continue.

"If she gets a date after the wedding, will that be considered cheating?"

I slap my thigh and cackle.

"Maybe you should send her a vibrator so she can consummate the marriage."

We both squeal happily.

Howell and Ben exchange looks as they stuff and stamp our

invitations, but then Howell pauses. "Hey, weird," he says as he studies one of the cards. "I thought the wedding is October Sixth."

Jane and I stop giggling. "It is," I say.

"This says October Sixteenth."

"Shut up, Howell," says Jane. "That's so immature."

"I'm not kidding." He holds the invitation out to me.

"Sure it does, Howell," I say as I snatch it from him. I look at it, and for once, Howell is serious. "Shit, shit, shit," I say.

"No way." Jane rips open the invite in front of her. "Oh, my God, Annie. Didn't you proofread it?"

I glare at Ben. "You had four things to do for this wedding!" I yell.

He shrinks beside me. "I glanced at it," he says lamely.

I pick up a throw pillow and beat him on the head as if I'm playing, but really I'm pissed. "Four measly things, and you couldn't get this one right?" I smoosh the pillow on his face.

Ben fends me off, laughing the whole time. He slings his arms around my waist to hug me, but I squirm away. "Sorry," he says. "I should've looked more closely."

I throw the invitation on the table. "What the hell are we going to do now?"

"We could Wite-Out the one," Ben suggests.

I sneer at him. "That's classy."

"You could change the wedding to the sixteenth," Howell suggests. Ben nods, a little too enthusiastically.

"Do you have any idea how hard it is to book a wedding in the first place and then try to change it this late?" Jane says.

"We could always check," says Ben.

"I don't want to get married on October Sixteenth!" I yell.

"What's the difference?" Ben asks.

"It's not the date we chose," I say.

"We only chose that date because the orchard was available," Mr. Science Brain points out.

"That's beside the point," I snap. Now I'm upset. Tears rim my eyes, which is embarrassing. I never thought something like this would matter to me, but it does. "This is awful," I moan. "It's our wedding. Something we'll only do once and it's fucked up."

Ben scoots closer to me. "Come on, Annie." He puts his arm around me, gently this time. "You're totally overreacting. We'll just order more and make it right."

"It's too late! These are going out late as it is. By the time we'd get more, the real wedding will be over."

"We can always do an e-vite," he says.

"You'd like it if we did everything over the Internet, including the actual ceremony, wouldn't you?" I say.

Ben doesn't take this as the insult I had planned. "A virtual wedding," he says, very logically, like a Vulcan.

"You're such a tech nerd," I say, then look to Jane for comfort.

"Okay, look," she says. "We could print up a nice little correction note and slip it inside the invitation. There are only twenty-five or thirty of them. It won't be hard. Then you can follow up with an e-mail making sure that everyone knows the real date is October Sixth."

"People will think we're the biggest idiots," I say.

"Who cares what people think?" Ben asks.

I fling the pillow at him, catching him the chest. "I care!" I yell.

Jane pats my leg. "Look at it this way, honey," she says. "Every wedding has something that goes terribly wrong. This will be your thing. From now on, it'll be smooth sailing."

"Someday it'll make a great story," Howell says as he fills my wineglass to the top. "This invite will be like a collector's edition of a flawed book."

Ben puts his arm around my shoulders again and kisses my cheek tenderly. "They're right," he says.

"You," I say angrily to him, "do not get to comment."

As soon as I walk into my office the next morning, Helen is at my desk. "Where have you been? Mitzi Davenport is already here," she says.

"Who's Mitzi Davenport?" I ask as I sling my bag over my chair and head for the coffee.

Helen grabs my arm. "No, you don't have time for coffee." She swings me around so we're facing the conference room. I glimpse a tiny, determined woman in a gray herringbone suit trailed by two red-faced little boys and a beleaguered nanny carrying a sobbing baby. "That's Mitzi Davenport, the creator of Fauntleroy.com."

"Shit!" I quickly open computer files to find the prototypes for pages and designs. "I was so preoccupied with my stupid wedding invitations last night that I totally forgot about this meeting."

"You better pull your head out of your ass then, because she already looks pissed," says Helen.

While we scramble to get everything together, Mitzi stops outside the conference room and points to a row of chairs. "Sit," she commands her children and her nanny. "And do not make a sound while Mummy is in her meeting."

"Why would she bring her kids with her?" I ask Helen with exasperation.

"So we can see the market demographic," Helen says sarcastically.

"I want chocolate!" the older boy wails.

Mitzi digs into her purse and pulls out a pink Fauchon box. She hands it to the nanny. "One each," she says firmly. The nanny opens the box, and the boys pounce on her, grabbing and stuffing as many chocolates into their mouths as possible. Mitzi ignores them, straightens her jacket, and walks boldly into the conference room.

"Yikes," I say as we head to the meeting. "If this is who we're supposed to cater to, we're going to be in trouble."

"Sorry about the kids," Mitzi says when we come in. "The cleaners are at our apartment this morning, and the au pair is new. She has no idea how to ride the subway with children. You know how it is."

Helen and I smile and nod (as if our cleaners and au pairs and children are just as troublesome) and lay out all the page proofs. With her tortoiseshell half-glasses, Mitzi peers down at each iteration of the logo, the slogan, the borders for the pages, mock-ups for the order form, and she scowls.

"I've had the idea for Fauntleroy since my first son, Ellis, was born," she tells us. I can see her kids through the large window behind her. Ellis has taken the Fauchon box and filled it with water from the watercooler. With a maniacal look on his face, he holds it over the head of his younger brother.

"I tried being a stay-at-home mom," Mitzi says. "And for a while it was working. I was on the beautification committee at our children's school. We were able to raise over twenty thousand dollars for new artwork."

Helen and I bob our heads like sycophants hanging on Mitzi's every utterance. Later, in the privacy of our cubicles, Helen will probably rip Mitzi to shreds, much to my delight.

"But then one day I looked around and I thought, I went to Yale. I'm not using my full potential. Sure being a mom is *wonderful*. There's nothing like it." She glances up at us. "Do either of you have children?" We both shake our heads no. "Well, you'll see someday what a joy children truly are."

As she says this, the younger of the boys retaliates against his brother-tormentor by kicking at the sopping Fauchon box. The nanny looks on with disdain.

"So I told my husband that I had an idea for this website. He thought it was brilliant. Just brilliant. We've really needed something like this, you know?"

Who's the *we*, I wonder? Would I become like Mitzi and her Upper East Side Bugaboo brigade if I had a family in New York?

Just then, the younger boy catches the dripping box of Fauchon with the tip of his toe, sending soggy cardboard and runny chocolate all over the nanny and the baby. A wail goes up, and Mitzi is out of her chair in an instant. We watch her fly out the door, grab each of the boys by their elbows, and stuff them back into the chairs. She bends over them, jabbing a finger in their faces, and speaks angrily through gritted teeth.

"Aah, motherhood," says Helen. "Such a joy."

I simply shake my head and hope to God I'll fare better someday.

On the first Friday in August, Jane and I fly home for my bridal shower—a brunch at my mother's house on Saturday morning. Jane completely ceded control after Mom started e-mailing her cheeseball recipes. This isn't necessarily a bad thing, though, because if Jane had been in charge of the food, we'd be eating Pop-Tarts and drinking Bloody Marys (not that I would have minded so much). Then again, if Jane had been in control, the entire downstairs of my parents' house wouldn't be covered with white netting and pink bows, crepe paper bells and strands of fake pearls.

Needless to say, my mother has gone all out. She's brought out the good china and fine crystal for her four egg dishes (quiche, frittata, sausage casserole, and curried deviled eggs), six kinds of muffins, an entire honey-baked ham, and two nut-crusted cheeseballs, not to mention fruit salad, fresh juice, and an assortment of cookies. She has also organized games: how many words can you make out of the letters in Anne Frances Olsen, twenty questions about Annie and Ben, and Bridal Bingo. The prizes were fake diamond rings and gift certificates to a card shop.

I've spent most of the time sitting on the couch, in the midst of thirty-seven people from my past, with a jaunty bow-covered paper plate on my head. I've repeatedly answered all the standard questions about my wedding without giving away that our invitations were screwed up and at my most recent fitting my dress was still a large sheet of white silk in the back of Lenora Ng's shop or that Ben has yet to find a band or a suit for himself.

Jane has found this all immensely amusing. When the party winds down, she plops beside me on the couch. "Nice lid," she says with a smirk.

"You've been enjoying yourself, haven't you?" I ask.

"More than you can imagine. But come on, it wasn't that bad, was it?"

I give her a look, but I admit, "Despite my stupid hat, it wasn't bad at all."

"At least Ingrid looks happy." Jane points to Mom, who is entirely in her element, refilling glasses, giving out recipe cards, and catching up on local gossip.

" . . . diagnosed with pancreatic cancer."

"You know how fast that goes."

"He'll be dead in two weeks."

" . . . couldn't even finish the semester and had to come home from school."

"They're thinking of trying rehab for her . . ."

" . . . twins, can you believe it?"

"Can they afford two more on what he makes?"

At one time, most details of my life were public domain. Who I was dating, what my grades were like, when and where I spent my time. It used to drive me crazy having so many people discussing my personal life. Now, as I listen in, I realize the talk isn't malicious as I had imagined when I was younger.

"Should one of us go to the hospital with her?"

"I can take them dinner on Tuesday."

"Can you do Wednesday?"

"My brother knows a doctor in Milwaukee who's an addiction specialist. He's very successful with teens . . ."

"I have so many baby clothes to give them."

How nice, I think as I listen, to have this group of people who've known me since my mother was pregnant. Who've followed my life and, even though they haven't seen me much in the past five years, have come to this party and given generously. I'm surrounded by towers of gifts. The stuff of a good domestic life. Towels and cookbooks. Coffee mugs and a bagel slicer. Sharp knives, nice linen napkins, photo albums to fill with the evidence of my life as a married woman. The assumption is that I will cook and clean and raise children in a tidy house, just as each of these women has done.

I think of Mitzi Davenport, the Fauntleroy.com maven. At one time I would've been envious of her—kids and a career in New York City. Now, as I sit here, I'm jealous of the lives these women have. Sometimes I think it would be so easy to come back here, set up a household down the street from my mom, and start another generation of Wisconsinites. It will never happen, though. When I chose to make my life with Ben, I knew that I was choosing to raise my children far away from the fields and forest and family of my childhood.

"Earth to Annie," Jane says.

I stare out the patio doors at the field behind my parents' house. The corn is getting high and starting to turn a dusty brown, ready for harvest. Some of the leaves in the woods have already changed to fiery red and orange. I pull my attention back into the room. "I always forget how pretty it is here in the late summer," I tell her.

"Yeah. Me too," she says.

"If you two came home more often . . ." Aunt Agnes suddenly inserts herself in our conversation, but then she stops and shrugs. "But, I know. It's hard. You have lives in New York."

"I like coming home," I say and hope I don't sound too defensive.

"Your mother loves having you," says Agnes. "We all do."

With that, my mother claps her hands and calls, "Woo-hoo! Woo-hoo!" until the group quiets down. I glance at Jane, who hides behind her hand, suppressing giggles. What could my mother have up her sleeve now? A photo montage or surprise visits from my old boyfriends?

But my mom simply raises her glass of orange juice and says, "A toast, to Annie." Everyone follows her lead. "May her marriage to Ben be as happy and loving as her life has been here!"

I smile at her as I clink my glass against Agnes's, then Jane's cup. Despite all my bitching, I know I'm fortunate to have a mother who loves me enough to do these things for me. "Thank you," I mouth.

"You're welcome," she says and beams.

*　　*　　*

That evening, after everyone is long gone and all the wrapping paper and bows have been stuffed into garbage bags, my mother rushes through the house, putting her earrings on. "You're sure you don't want to come? The MacMillans would be happy to have you."

"No," I tell her. "I'd rather spend some time with Granny than go to Gracie's wedding."

"What's Jane doing tonight?"

"Dinner with her mom and her new stepdad," I say.

"Poor Janey." My mom shakes her head. "It must be hard for her to come home."

She says this, and I think she's right. It's totally different for Jane to come back home than it is for me. Her mother has been married and divorced four times since Jane was seven. They moved to a new house almost every year when Jane was growing up. This is the only place I've ever lived, and whenever I return I know exactly what to expect. I used to think that was boring. Now I find it reassuring.

My father stands at the back door, impatiently twirling his keys. Mom grabs her purse and stands beside him. "How do we look?" she asks as she straightens his tie.

They're the classic handsome couple in the color-coordinated clothes. My mother wears a dark pink suit with a flowered blouse beneath—the perfect thing for an evening wedding. My father has on a blue pin-striped suit with a pink floral tie. "Someday, very soon," I tell them, "you'll be wearing matching satin jackets."

"Oh, hush," says my mother.

Will Ben and I ever do this? I certainly hope not, but then again, would my parents have guessed that someday they'd be coordinating their outfits? "You look very nice," I tell them. "Do you want me to take your picture?"

"No," says my father firmly. "We're late as it is." He puts his hand on the small of my mother's back and gently prods her toward the door. I watch them go and hope that, even if Ben and I can avoid dressing alike, we'll at least stay as happy with each other as my parents have.

I drive my mother's Cadillac to my granny's house, which is less than a mile away, a distance I would easily walk in Brooklyn, but here I'd have to cut across two cow pastures and through the woods, something I'm not eager to do in the dark. It's a pretty drive, though. The sun has turned orange as it sinks behind the trees. A V of Canada geese fly overhead, honking their way south.

When I walk in Granny's back door, the familiar smell of lemon cleaner, bleach, and roasting meat immediately transports me back to the excitement I felt every time I came here as a kid. I never knew what kind of project Granny would have for us to do. Planting flowers, picking tomatoes, icing cookies. Even the mundane chores, like cutting the grass and washing windows, seemed more fun at her house.

Granny is at the kitchen sink, scrubbing potatoes while the farm report blares from her little AM radio on the windowsill, something my grandfather listened to every evening when he was alive.

"Hey, Gran," I say and peck her on the cheek, which makes her jump.

"You scared me, Annie," she says, but she laughs.

"Sorry. Thought you heard me come in."

She flicks off the radio. "My hearing," she says but doesn't finish.

"What're you making?" I lean against the countertop and watch her peel a potato with quick swipes of a paring knife.

"I've got a pork roast in the oven," she says. Then she looks at me. "You still eat pork?"

"Sure," I say. "Why wouldn't I?" I grab a baby carrot from the colander in the sink. "I'm not a vegetarian."

"You're marrying a Jew," she says.

I pop the carrot in my mouth. "Ben eats pork," I say between crunches.

"I thought Jews didn't."

"He's not very Jewish," I tell her.

"Think he'll convert?" She gathers the potato skins and tosses them into an empty milk carton along with all the other food scraps from the day.

"To Christianity?" I ask and laugh. "I doubt it. He's not very religious in general."

"You're not going to convert, are you?" she asks.

"I'm not planning on it."

She cuts the peeled potatoes into quarters and drops them in a pot full of water. "What about your kids?" she asks. "What will they be?"

I shrug. "I don't know. Whatever we are, I guess."

"Confused, sounds like it."

I laugh but then stop because I'm not sure she's joking.

"You going to keep working when you have kids?"

I think of Mitzi Davenport and her three hellions again. Would I become as disgruntled as she is if I quit my job and tried to stay home full-time? "That's a long way away," I tell Granny.

"Hmph" is all she says as she takes off her apron. "I found something I thought you might like." I tag along behind her to the living room.

A box of old albums sits next to the couch, and loose pictures are scattered over the coffee table. "What are these?" I ask.

"Wedding pictures." She sinks down into the couch. I sit on the floor beside her and hunch over the table to examine the black-and-white photos. "Mine, my mother's, my sister's, your mother's, Agnes's." Granny picks up an old sepia-toned picture and hands it to me. "This is my mother," she says.

A proud, tall woman with the same nose as my granny, mother, and me poses in front of an altar in the Dress.

"Is this one you?" I ask, picking out a black-and-white picture of a young bride, staring seriously into the camera. "That's my sister Alice," she says. "This one is me."

She hands me another picture, and I see the Dress again. I hold her wedding photo next to her mother's. Somehow in these old photos the Dress doesn't look quite as hideous as I remember it. In fact, both my great-grandmother and Granny are quite stunning in the lace and finery.

"Where's Mom's picture?" I ask. Of course, I've seen her

wedding photos dozens of times, but never alongside Granny's.

She shifts through the pictures on the table until she finds the color shot of my parents, young and vibrant, smiling unabashedly from behind a reception table. Again, the Dress. Again, it's not quite as bad as I thought.

"Are you upset that I'm not going to wear the dress?" I ask.

Granny laughs and says, "No, why would I be?"

"Mom wants me to wear it."

"She's sentimental about things like that. I'm not. I think you should wear what you want to wear."

"I'm spending too much money on my dress," I tell her.

She shrugs. "You only get married once. Or at least you hope so."

I lay the pictures side by side on the table. "You all look alike," I say. "Do you think I look like the rest of you?"

Granny studies me for a moment, then she says, "No, you're much prettier than any of us ever were. I'm sure you'll make a lovely bride."

"Thanks, Gran." I look over the other pictures and imagine my own photos added to this box.

She sighs. "Just wish I'd be there to see it."

I look up at her, alarmed. "Why wouldn't you be there?"

"Oh, honey, I'm too old to come to New York City," she says.

"The wedding isn't in the city," I tell her. "It's upstate, at an orchard. You'll like it there."

She shakes her head. "I'd have to fly into New York, and I just can't do that. If you'd had the wedding here . . ."

"But, Gran," I say.

"Oh, honey," she says and pats me on the back. "You won't miss me a bit."

I'm flummoxed. Getting married while my grandmother sits at home in Colfax is unthinkable, and suddenly I'm reeling. Have I been horribly selfish by planning my wedding out East? Maybe I should have it here, like my mother, and apparently my grandmother, want. After all, Jane said that the wedding isn't for me or for Ben. Before I can figure out how to say any of this to my grandmother, the timer goes off and she stands up.

"Now how about some pork roast?" she asks, heading back into the kitchen.

Granny and I eat dinner over a strange, formal conversation full of long pauses and polite exchanges. I'm too hurt to bring up her refusal to come to my wedding without blubbering like a fool, and if there is one thing my grandmother hates, it's a blubbering fool. I help her with the dishes, then head back to my parents' earlier than I had planned.

On the drive, I dial Jane on my cell phone, hoping she'll be able to make sense of Granny's decision not to come to my wedding. When Jane answers, I hear a muffled din of voices and bad country music in the background. "Where are you?" I ask.

"Oh, Christ," Jane says, slightly slurry. "Mom and Leonard insisted on taking me to some unendurable supper club out in the sticks that serves nothing but fried crappie and hush puppies. Thank God for bourbon. Where are you?"

"Driving home from Granny's."

"I love your granny," she says with a sentimental sigh.

"She says she's not coming to my wedding," I blurt out, but a sudden swell of cheering and booing behind Jane obscures my voice.

"God, this is pathetic," she grumbles. "You'd think the Packers were kicking some Vikings ass, but it's only my new daddy whooping the bartender in darts."

"Did you hear me?" I ask. "Granny says—"

"Can we get a flight back to New York tonight?" Jane asks.

"We'll be back tomorrow," I tell her.

"Shit, Annie," Jane yells over the growing ruckus. "I can't hear you. I'll have to talk to you in the morning."

As soon as I hang up, Ben's *Star Wars* theme rings on my phone. "Hey, baby love," I coo into the phone. "I'm cruising in my mama's Caddy, missing you."

"Cadillacs are egregious gas guzzlers," he tells me.

"I wish you were here so we could go parking and make out in the back," I say.

"Are the seats leather?" he asks.

"Yep."

"Nice," he says. "I've never done it on leather seats. Or in a gas guzzler, for that matter."

"Have you ever done it in a car?" I ask him.

"Yes," he says, a bit indignant.

"God, I miss you," I tell him.

"How's it going?"

"The shower was okay, but now my granny is pulling some bullshit, saying she won't come to the wedding."

"It's not surprising," says Ben.

"Yes, it is," I insist. "She's been at every major event in my life. I have no idea why—"

"Annie." Ben cuts me off. "You're marrying a Jew."

"Granny doesn't care about that," I snap. I turn down my parents' road. The moon shimmers through a canopy of giant elm trees and dances on the shiny hood of the car. I wonder if he's right.

"I got some bad news from Judge Larry today," Ben says, changing the subject.

"Has he been arrested for impersonating a real judge?" I ask.

"He double-booked himself and has to do a sweat lodge the day of our wedding."

"A sweat lodge is more important than our wedding?"

"Apparently to Judge Larry it is."

"What are we supposed to do?" I ask.

"It's not a big deal," says Ben. "I can find somebody else."

"Just like you're finding a band?" I say and immediately regret it when Ben inhales, then exhales loudly, a clear sign of his annoyance with me.

"Technically any fool can marry us. All you have to do is get ordained on-line."

I pull into my parents' driveway and kill the engine. "This is really starting to suck," I say with a derisive laugh. "My grandmother is boycotting New York. You think she's a closeted anti-Semite. Our invitations are wrong. A Web-ordained fool will marry us. And we have no music. This is not how I envisioned our wedding."

"You're not turning into a kvetch, are you?" Ben asks.

"What's a kvetch?" I ask, figuring it's not something flattering.

"You know, a nag. A bridezilla. One of those women who gets completely obsessed about every detail of her wedding and makes everyone around her miserable."

I snort and sputter. "No. God. I can't even believe you'd say that. I was only joking." I say this, but I know it's not true. I am upset.

"Good," Ben says. "Because I think I'd have to call the wedding off if you got like that."

I take the keys out of the ignition and climb out into the cool evening air. "Jesus, Ben. Just because I give a rat's ass—"

"I was joking," Ben says. "Can you calm down?"

I take a deep breath and smell hay and mown grass and manure. "It wasn't funny."

"Sorry," he mumbles.

"When I get back, we're getting serious and finishing all the plans for this wedding, because it's driving me nuts."

"All right, Ingrid," he says.

"You're not funny," I say.

"See you tomorrow," he says.

"I love you," I mutter and hang up.

By the time my parents pull into the driveway, I'm standing at the kitchen counter with a spoon, a half-finished quart of Chunky Monkey ice cream, an open bottle of Maker's Mark whiskey, and I'm totally in a funk.

"How was the 'wedding'?" I ask and frame my fingers in quotes around the word when my parents come in the back door.

"Actually," says Mom, "it was very nice." She takes off her earrings, the first thing she does whenever she comes in the house.

"Oh, come on." I sneer. "Gracie married herself. How could that be anything but weird?" I shovel more ice cream in my mouth.

"It was more like a commitment ceremony to herself than a real wedding," says my dad.

"A *commitment ceremony*," I repeat. "To *herself*?"

My mother opens the silverware drawer and takes out a spoon. "Gracie's been through some hard times lately," she says as she digs into the carton beside me.

"What? She couldn't get a date?" I laugh, sip the whiskey, then take another bite of ice cream. It's a yummy combination.

"You're being awfully hard on her," says Dad.

"She had to move back home for a while until she got straightened out," my mom adds. I picture Gracie as an adult, living in her miniature playhouse behind the MacMillans' split-level ranch. "The minister did a lovely job," Mom continues. "She was a Unitarian. She talked a lot about honoring oneself and loving oneself as the first step in a lifetime of contentment and happiness."

I roll my eyes and nearly huff with irritation. "Even if the minister's hokum were true," I ask, jabbing my spoon in the air for emphasis, "why does Gracie MacMillan get to make everyone witness her life commitment to herself, then give her presents? Shouldn't she learn to love herself behind closed doors in a shrink's office like the rest of us?"

Mom and Dad look at each other. My father discreetly puts the cap on the whiskey and carries it to the cabinet.

"You never really liked Gracie, did you?" Mom asks. My cheeks grow warm, and I'm a little embarrassed by how childish I'm being. "She always wanted to be friends with you and Jane so badly," says Mom. "But neither of you were very nice to her."

Mom's right. I've been unfriendly to Gracie all my life, and now, even as an adult, I can't find a way to be happy for her. Maybe it's because Gracie represents everything I've tried so hard not to be. She stayed behind and made her small life in the small town where we grew up, and she seemed to be happy with that choice. When I heard that she wasn't actually happy, that she had dropped out of community college and become an OxyContin fiend and a lush, I felt vindicated. As if her failure to be happy in Colfax validated my choice to go far away. But now, here I am far away with a wedding unraveling at my feet. And here's Gracie, back at home, happily married to herself.

"Is there something else bothering you?" Mom asks.

I want to tell them that Judge Larry has backed out and Ben still hasn't found a band. That the invitations are wrong and Lenora's made no progress on my dress. That I have no idea what I should do—move the wedding to Wisconsin, where my mom can take care of all the loose ends that are starting to strangle me, or try to make things work in New York with or without Steamboat Jerry and my grandmother in attendance.

But I can't because that will be admitting that I shouldn't have tried to plan the wedding by myself in the first place. So in order to avoid all of this, I say, "Since when did Granny become an anti-Semite?"

They're both quiet.

"Did you already know that?" I demand.

"What brought this on?" asks my dad.

"She's not coming to my wedding," I say, and my nose tickles as if I'm going to cry.

"Oh dear," says Mom. "And you think that's because of Ben?"

"What else could it be?" I ask. "She was asking me all these questions about who was converting and how I'm going to raise my kids."

"Honey," says Mom. "She likes Ben a great deal."

"Then how can she not come?" I whine.

"A lot of people out here feel like New York isn't safe anymore," my mom explains.

I roll my eyes incredulously. "That was so long ago," I say.

"She and Uncle Pete still talk about Pearl Harbor," says Dad.

"I guess this is what I get for falling in love with someone who isn't a white Christian farmer from Wisconsin, then planning my wedding halfway across the country."

"Annie," says my mother. "You're being ridiculous."

I jab my spoon into the ice cream. My wedding was supposed to be simple and hassle-free. I never intended to spend this much time or energy fretting over it. "Maybe we'll elope," I mutter.

"Don't worry," says my mom. "We'll figure something out to get Granny there."

"Maybe if we drive . . . ," says my dad.

On the weekend of Alex Nessman's wedding, Ben and I drive to Boston through a gigantic thunder and lightning storm. At times the rain is so heavy that we can't see and Ben has to pull over on the side of the highway until things let up. All I can think is that if we die on our way to some stranger's wedding before I have my own, I'm going to be really pissed.

We make it to the synagogue halfway through the ceremony and slip into the back. I sit self-consciously next to Ben and look around at everyone who mumbles Hebrew scripture together. Can they tell that I'm a shiksa? Ben knows when to stand up and sit down, but he doesn't join any of the prayers.

Soon enough we're at the reception, where the only difference between the other guests and me is the amount of alcohol we've consumed at the open bar. I'm still nursing my first glass of wine, while most everyone else, including the wedding party, is sloshed. Ben assumed that other old acquaintances from his prep school would be here, but he was wrong. He knows no one but the groom. So we conveniently tuck ourselves away at a small corner table close to the exit, where we don't have to socialize with anyone. We plan to stay at the reception for a polite half hour, then congratulate Alex and his bride, and bow out, claiming the long car ride back to New York as our excuse for leaving. This is a lie, of course. We're simply hoping to buy some time alone between the wedding and the rest of the weekend at Ben's parents' house in Newton.

Our plan falters when Alex spots us from the bar and stumbles over to our table, shouting, "Ben! Benji! Benjamin Weisberg! I'd recognize you anywhere, man!"

Ben tries to stand to greet Alex, but when he's halfway out of his seat, Alex throws his arm around Ben's shoulders and leans heavily against him, squishing him down again.

"You are so fucking awesome for coming to my wedding!" Alex shouts. "All the way from New York City, man. New York Fucking City! Woo-hoo!"

"Sure, we wouldn't miss—" Ben starts to say, but Alex has already slid off his shoulders and draped himself over me. "And who's this?" he yells in my ear. "Is this your girlfriend? Does little Benji Weisberg have a girlfriend?" He slaps Ben on the back. "Man, Ben and I were total dorks together," Alex says to me.

"I can't even imagine," I deadpan, which makes Ben smile.

"We never thought we'd get dates," says Alex. "And now look!" He holds his arms out wide, then thumps himself on the chest, splattering his white tux shirt with beer. "I'm a married man! Can you believe it? Can you fucking believe it?"

"Your wife seems like—" Ben starts to say, but Alex drops to a squat between our chairs and steadies himself with one hand on Ben's shoulder while the other cradles his drink.

"How the hell are you, man? Thanks for coming." Ben nods, tries to speak, but Alex holds up his hand to stop him. "No really, man. It means so much to me and Katya. So much."

And here Alex becomes weepy. "So fucking much. I mean,

who are all these people?" He makes a grand, sweeping gesture toward the crowded ballroom. "Who are they? I don't even know them. Who is that?" He points to a random woman carrying two vodka tonics away from the bar. "Who are you!" he yells at the woman as she walks by. She startles, and her drinks splash on the front of her dress. "I've never seen her in my life," Alex says to us. "Am I related to her? Is she someone's friend? I don't know. But you!" He thumps Ben on the chest with the back of his hand. "You are one of my oldest friends in the world, Benji. I mean, I know we don't exactly hang out anymore, but you're like an old friend. An old, old friend. Someone who knew me way back when. Back in the day. You know? Ben fucking Weisberg. Wow. Thanks for being here, man. Thanks."

"Sure," says Ben, and as he opens his mouth to say something else ("Congratulations" perhaps, maybe "It's good to see you, too" or possibly "You're a drunken fool"), the groomsmen rush over to Alex, grab him by the arms, and pull him away toward the dance floor.

"See?" Ben says to me as he straightens his tie. "That's what happens when you pad the guest list."

"We're just having the people we like," I assure him.

"We don't have to invite my parents then?" Ben asks.

"You love your parents," I say.

"Love, yes. Like?" He shrugs.

I know he's only half-joking, but sometimes I think he's too harsh on his parents. "They're not that bad," I say.

He looks at me with an eyebrow raised skeptically. "Since when did you become a fan of Saul and Miriam?"

"I think it's important that we get along with each other's parents," I tell him seriously.

Ben shakes his head. "Just because we're getting married, you don't have to suddenly adore my parents."

"You like my parents," I say.

"That's different. They aren't so weird."

I leave it at that, not wanting to dig into Ben's strained relationship with Saul and Miriam, especially because I suspect that I add to that strain.

Ben gathers our things from the table. "Let's get out of here before something else happens."

Ben and Katya and their families are gathered on the dance floor. "Shouldn't we wait to say good-bye? We haven't even said congratulations."

"Are you joking?" asks Ben. "They're so stinking drunk that neither of them is going to remember cutting the cake, let alone whether dorky Benji Weisberg and his girlfriend said congratulations."

As we leave the ballroom, I glance back to see Alex and Katya being paraded through the ballroom on chairs as the guests dance in circles, clapping, dancing, and singing.

"Wow, look at that," I say. "Maybe we should do that at our reception."

"Sure," Ben says sarcastically. "And while we're at it, why don't we throw some Hindu ritual and a sweat lodge in there, too?"

"Maybe we could get Judge Larry back," I say cattily, but Ben doesn't take the bait.

*   *   *

By the time we leave the reception, the storm has died out, but most of the side streets are holding water. We drive slowly through giant puddles to Ben's parents' large, white Victorian house with multiple roof peaks. Tree branches are scattered across the yard. We pull into the driveway and sit in the car, staring at the yellow lights glowing from the black-shuttered windows.

"What do you suppose they're doing?" I ask.

"Sitting quietly," he says.

"Do you think they like me?"

"Sure," says Ben.

"How do you know?" There are no outward signs. Not like my parents, who go overboard to make Ben feel like a part of our family. My mom throws her arms around Ben, leaves lipstick prints on his cheek, buys him Christmas presents but wraps them in Hanukkah paper. My father stays up late with Ben, discussing religion, politics, and life. Even Granny, whatever her politics, is always friendly to him.

"They treat you like they treat me, and I know that they like me," Ben reasons.

"But do you think they wish I was Jewish?"

"I think they wish *I* was Jewish," says Ben. He opens his car door. "Let's go in."

As we come in the front door, Mrs. Weisberg extends her hand and welcomes me with a tepid handshake and a dry little kiss to the cheek. Mr. Weisberg keeps a good arm's length away as he shakes my hand, then immediately shoves his hands back in his pockets, as if he is embarrassed by our contact. He was raised Orthodox, and touching a woman other than his wife never seems to settle right with him, even though he long ago left the strictures of his religion.

"I've put fresh sheets in the den downstairs," Mrs. Weisberg tells me. It's common knowledge that Ben and I have been shacking up for the better part of a year, but the Weisbergs have never acknowledged it.

Ben walks past her with our bags. "We'll both crash in my room," he says nonchalantly and heads for the stairs.

I stand, awkwardly, not sure which way to go. Should I follow Ben, asserting my independence with my future in-laws, or should I defer to his mother, setting a precedent that I am malleable? I have no idea which way to go. Mrs. Weisberg saves me the trouble of having to choose sides. She shrugs and turns away, effectively giving me the okay to follow her son. Which I do. Quickly.

"Why'd you do that?" I whisper to Ben when we're safely behind the door of his bedroom.

"Do what?"

"Obviously she's uncomfortable with us sleeping together."

"That's stupid," says Ben. "We live together and we're getting married in a few weeks."

"Now she probably really hates me."

Ben rolls his eyes. "She's fine. Let's go downstairs. I need a snack."

* * *

Mr. and Mrs. Weisberg sit quietly, side by side on the couch, Mr. Weisberg hidden behind the pages of *Investor's Business Daily,* Mrs. Weisberg's head bowed over an Allegra Goodman novel. As Ben and I walk through the living room toward the kitchen, Mrs. Weisberg looks up momentarily.

"There's cheese in the fridge," she says. "Crackers in the pantry. We have apples."

Ben stops. I skitter behind him, trip, and bang into his back. We stand still as "We have apples" hangs in the air between us and them. Is it the start of a conversation? I have no idea how these people operate. I am sweating despite the after-storm chill in the air.

Finally, I say, "I love apples," and feel like a moron. It isn't even true. I prefer other fruits. Orange, fleshy fruits. Peaches, apricots, cantaloupe. Plums even. No one replies. I hate this silence. I feel so midwestern. So Christian in my need to blather on about something, anything. "What kind of apples?" I ask, because I just can't help it.

Mrs. Weisberg looks at Mr. Weisberg. "What kind of apples are they, Saul?"

Mr. Weisberg ruffles the paper and lowers it so the top half of his face appears. "Gala," he says.

I nod, eagerly. Too eagerly. Like a small lapdog. "Gala are good," I say. "My mother bakes pies." I wince. I shouldn't have said that. Does it sound like a judgment? Like I expect Mrs. Weisberg to bake me a pie? The conversation is insane. A series of near non sequiturs. I should shut up, but I can't, because Ben stays put. Doesn't move. Doesn't speak. The silence is oppressive.

"Ben and I met because of apples. Did you know that?" I ask, almost breathless from the effort of not talking.

Mrs. Weisberg cocks her head to one side. Mr. Weisberg raises his eyebrows. Is it a sign? Do they want me to continue?

"At an orchard. Upstate. You knew that, right?"

"No," says Mr. Weisberg. "I didn't know that. Did you know how they met, Miriam?"

Mrs. Weisberg shakes her head. "I thought you worked together."

"Ben was asleep under a Fuji tree. It was the only one with any fruit left on it and I wanted some." I look at Ben for encouragement. He gazes at me like his parents do, and I keep talking, just to fill up the space among us all.

"So I started picking the apples. Then I dropped one on him and he woke up. He thought it was funny, but his girlfriend came back and got all mad. She said I should give her the apples that I had picked because Ben was supposed to be saving the tree. She called me an apple thief."

"Were you stealing?" Mr. Weisberg asks.

I'm not sure how to answer. Is he testing my morals? Did I believe I was stealing? Is there a right answer? "Yes," I say tentatively. "I suppose in a way I was."

"She didn't give the apples back, though," Ben says proudly.

Mrs. Weisberg grins. Then she laughs. "That's why you're having the wedding at an orchard," she says.

"Yes!" I almost yell it. I want to run over and plop down on the couch beside her. "Let's talk!" I want to scream. "Let's get to know each other." I could tell them more about Ben and me.

How I left the orchard that day thinking I had a funny story for Jane and Howell, but then two weeks later, while I waited for Jane in a bar on the Lower East Side, the bartender handed me a bright green apple-tini and said, "It's from that guy." I looked down the bar, expecting to see some big loser sending me a loser drink, but there was Ben, smiling shyly, holding up his own electric green apple martini.

"Hmm," says Mr. Weisberg. "I never knew that." Then he lifts his paper again, effectively ending that part of our conversation.

But I'm not ready to let go yet. "How did the two of you meet?" I ask, and everyone looks at me strangely.

"Well," says Mrs. Weisberg slowly. "We met at temple."

Mr. Weisberg ruffles the paper, clears his throat, and says, "There were very few women my age who went to Friday night services. I thought she was pretty."

Mrs. Weisberg's cheeks warm just a bit. "I smiled at him for seven straight Fridays before he even said hello."

Mr. Weisberg peeks over the paper a bit more. "I was shy then. I wasn't used to talking to girls."

I glance at Ben. He looks genuinely interested, like he's never heard this story.

"My parents wanted me to marry a family friend," says Mrs. Weisberg. "A man named Morris Weintraub. He was a tailor, and I thought he smelled like gefilte fish." She giggles.

This is great, I think. Now we're getting somewhere. Breaking through walls. "Did you have a big wedding?" I ask.

"No, it was just us, the rabbi, and two friends. What were

their names?" Mrs. Weisberg touches her fingers to her forehead as she thinks. "Do you remember who they were, Saul? The Feinsteins? The Finkelsteins?"

Mr. Weisberg thinks for a second, then says, "I don't remember."

"Were your parents mad that you were marrying . . ." I pause. I've never called Mr. Weisberg Saul, but it would sound stupid to say "Mr. Weisberg," so I say, "him," and motion to Ben's dad.

Mrs. Weisberg looks down at her hands. "Our parents had died by the time we were married," she says.

Good Christ, I think and wish I could slip into one of the cracks in the wood floor. What a thing to bring up. The conversation has died. The air is dead.

Ben tugs on my arm. "Let's have some cheese," he says.

I shuffle after him, demoralized and certain that the Weisbergs will never really like me.

Later, when Ben and I lie in his teenage water bed, making waves, I ask, "How much sex have you had in this bed?" I undulate my body. The water sloshes beneath us.

"I was a nerd, remember?" he says and wraps his arms tightly around me.

"No sex for nerds?" I ask.

"Not when I lived here anyway."

I know Ben's history. His first real girlfriend was in college, when being a tech nerd had some cachet. "But didn't you ever bring what's her face, from the apple orchard, here?"

"Nope."

"How many girls have you brought home to Mom and Dad?" I ask, even though I already know the answer.

"One," he says.

"Only little ol' me?"

"Yep."

I roll away from Ben and look at the glow-in-the-dark stick-on stars stuck to his ceiling. I have to smile at the thought of Ben as a little kid reaching up to create a night sky above his bed. It's such a hopeful act. I sigh and think of his parents tonight. How his mother looked down at her hands when I asked about her parents.

"Do you think your parents are sad because they're Jewish?" I ask and immediately know that I sound stupid.

"I don't think they have a problem being Jewish," Ben says.

"No, that's not what I meant. It came out wrong. It's just that when I'm around them I feel so shallow. As if nothing bad has ever happened to me and all my grousing about silly little things is unwarranted. And here they are. Living their lives. No family but you."

"What's any of that have to do with them being Jewish?"

I turn over and lean on my elbow. The bed ripples beneath us. "Genocide," I say, but then I giggle because a wave knocks me back. It's hard to have a serious conversation when one is buoyant.

Ben stares at me with a perplexed look on his face. "I have no idea what you're talking about, Annie. No one in my family died in the Holocaust."

"I know, but maybe being so alone feels different when you're Jewish." I turn and look at him. "Do you like being Jewish?"

"Do you like being Lutheran?" he asks me.

"I'm not really Lutheran."

"I'm not really Jewish, then."

I roll toward him. "But being Jewish isn't like being Lutheran. You can't not be Jewish."

"Why the sudden obsession with me being Jewish? This was never an issue before," he says.

I touch his chest with my left hand. "Sometimes I'm afraid you'll have some crisis in life and realize that being Jewish is actually really important to you."

"Or maybe I'll become a Jehovah's Witness," says Ben.

"Oh, Lord, I hope not. I'll be embarrassed if you start going door to door to spread the good news."

Ben laughs softly. "I have no more intention of becoming a practicing Jew again than you do of moving back to Wisconsin and becoming the deacon of a Lutheran church."

I'm quiet when Ben says this. "Would that be so bad?" I ask sincerely.

He wraps his arms around my torso and pulls me close. "What are you afraid of, Annie?" he asks me.

I lie in Ben's arms and think of my family. How robust and cheery they all are. How nothing bad ever happens to us. There have been no horrible accidents or murders. No tragic stories. People die when they are old in my family. No one has ever gone insane. My family seems almost silly next to Ben's.

"What if someday I do want to go back to Wisconsin?"

"I thought you loved living in New York."

"I do, but I don't know that I'll want to forever. Especially if we have kids."

"We could find a place that suits both of us. The only two choices aren't living in Colfax like good Lutherans or moving to Newton and becoming kosher."

I think about how different our two families are. I try to imagine them all mixing at the wedding. My relatives will surround Ben's parents, slap them on the back, tell jokes and stories, and ask them questions that they'd rather not answer. Mr. and Mrs. Weisberg will be miserable. I groan and smash a pillow over my head.

"What's wrong now, Annie?" Ben asks.

I lift the pillow from my face. "I'm thinking of my family and your family together."

This amuses Ben. "That'll be a sight."

I try to sit up, but a swell of water knocks me over. "Maybe we shouldn't have the wedding," I say from my back.

"We can do whatever you want to do," he says.

I sit up and steady myself against the wooden rail of the bed. "Do you even want to get married?" I ask, the alarm in my voice is clear. "Sometimes I don't think you do."

"Why would you say that?" he asks calmly.

"Because, everything I've asked you to do for the wedding, you've done half-assed. The invitations, Judge Larry, the band you've never found. You don't even have a suit yet. How can you explain all of that?" I search his face in the dark. His features are a grayish blur, but I can see that he has his hands behind his head and his eyes are open.

After a few moments, he says, "The details of a wedding aren't very important to me. But that's different than not wanting to get married."

I lie down and try to accept what he's said. "You sure?" I ask.

"Of course I'm sure," he says resolutely.

"Okay," I say, but I'm not convinced. Even if what he said is true, his reluctance to take our wedding seriously doesn't bode well for our future. "What else isn't all that important to you that I should know about?" I ask. "Will you misspell our kids' names on their birth certificates? Will you procrastinate on mortgage papers? Forget preschool applications? Will you remember our anniversary?"

"Is that what's really most important to you, Annie?" he asks me in the dark. "Dates, papers, certificates? Because if it is, then you're marrying the wrong guy."

"That's not fair," I say. "Those things aren't *most* important to me, but they *are* important. They're a part of life."

Ben finds my hand. He weaves his fingers through mine and brings my knuckles to his lips. "I'll make mistakes, I'll forget things, but that's not a reflection on how I feel about you. I love you, Annie. That's the best I can offer."

I'm chastised by his words.

"But if it'll make you happy, I'll program a reminder of our anniversary in my PalmPilot," he tells me with a laugh.

"You'd need a reminder?" I ask.

He pulls me down to his chest and hugs me tight against his body. "Let's go to sleep now, Annie," he says dreamily.

Lying with Ben, listening to him breathe, used to be enough to calm my niggling worries about the world. But tonight I stare at the greenish glowing stars overhead while his breath deepens to even sighs, and I mull over all the small problems that seem to be mounting.

The next day, when Ben and I are driving home on the pretty, tree-lined Henry Hudson Parkway, he turns to me and asks, "What did you think of Alex's wedding?"

"It was fine," I say. "Did you notice they had a band *and* a cake?" I smile at Ben so he knows I'm joking, or at least half-joking. He smirks back at me. "Honestly, I liked some of the religious stuff. Maybe we should do something Jewish. We could get married under a hula."

Ben stares at me for a moment, then blinks. "A what?"

"A hula. You know. That tent thingy they held over the bride's and groom's heads."

Ben barks a short laugh.

"What?" I ask. "Why is that funny?"

"It's called a chuppah," he tells me as he continues to snicker.

"Hula, chuppah, whatever," I say, and he cracks up. My face grows warm.

"Come on, Annie." He squeezes my thigh. "You have to admit that was funny."

I cross my arms and tuck my chin against my chest, like a perfect pouting five-year-old. "I'll have a much better sense of humor when everything for our wedding is done."

"Okay," says Ben, slowly, carefully, as if he's merely trying to appease me. "Let's make a list. What do we need to do?"

"For one thing, if we're not having a cake, what are we having for dessert?"

"Do we need something?"

"Of course we need something. How can you have a wedding without some sort of celebratory dessert? Or a reception without any music? Even the Amish have cakes and music."

"Actually—" he starts to say.

"You know what I mean," I snap.

"Seems to me we can have anything we want at our wedding," says Ben.

I shake my head. "You just don't get it, do you?"

"We don't have to go overboard," he says.

"A cake and a band are not going overboard," I insist. "And believe me, compared to most people, we're not even remotely going overboard."

"We don't have to compare ourselves to anybody else. A wedding is not a contest," says Mr. Science Brain.

"To other people it is, though," I say. "They'll leave our wedding and they'll say, 'Oh, that wasn't nearly as nice as Bob and Sally's wedding,' or 'That was one of the best weddings I've been to in a long time.' You just did it yourself, asking me what I thought of Alex's wedding."

"When did all this stuff start to matter to you?"

"I don't know when it started to matter, but it does. And we need a cake," I tell him. "And someone to marry us. And a band. Which you're supposed to be in charge of, but clearly—"

He holds up his hand. "Don't," he says.

"Don't tell me 'don't,'" I snap at him.

He rolls his eyes and I'm silent. He's never done that to me. Rolled his eyes. Told me *don't* as if I'm an annoying child.

"I'm sick of you nagging me," he says.

I'm dumbfounded when he calls me a nag. It's so unlike us to fight like this. I stare out the window at the trees whizzing by the car. Vines grow up most of the trunks, making it seem like we're driving through the middle of a verdant forest rather than heading back into the city. I miss Wisconsin just then, and I can't help but wonder what kind of life I would have had if I had stayed. Would I already be married by now? Would I have kids? And would it have been easier than this? Would there have been so many compromises to make? So many differences to take into account?

"Why has all this petty little shit become so important to you all of a sudden?" Ben asks.

"It's not petty shit!" I explode.

"You've become obsessed with a band," says Ben. "And a cake. For God's sake, Annie. A band? A cake?"

"That's not it!" I yell back at him. "None of that really matters to me."

"Then what is it?" Ben asks, exasperated.

"It's everything else that we never talked about," I tell him, and my heart pounds because I realize that all my inane worries about this wedding have been red herrings. "How did we forget to have a discussion about where we'd live and how we'd raise our kids and why we spend money so differently? Or even that you're from Boston and I'm from Colfax. And what about the most fundamental difference between us, I'm a Christian and you're a Jew?"

My palms are prickly as I watch Ben stare forward at the road, then turn slowly to me. "What have we been talking about for the past few years?" I ask him.

"I don't know," says Ben. "Politics. Ideas. What we'd have for dinner. Things that mattered."

"You don't think kids, money, religion, and where we'll live matter?"

"I thought we'd figure those things out as we went along."

"Maybe I want to figure some of them out now," I say.

His eyes are narrow, as if he is squinting to see me clearly. "You used to have opinions about the world, Annie. We could have an interesting conversation. At least before we got engaged. Now all you can talk about is this goddamned stupid wedding and how we're supposed to spend our lives for the next twenty-seven years."

"You think the wedding is stupid?" I ask.

Ben tightens his grip on the steering wheel. "That's not what I said."

"You said, and I quote, 'this goddamned stupid wedding.'"

"I was referring to your level of engrossment in its planning," Ben says as if he's parsing an equation.

I turn away, too angry to look at him anymore. We're in the city now. The traffic has become thick, and we're puny beneath the gray and brown buildings of Manhattan. After several minutes of hard silence, I ask, "So you don't want to discuss this anymore?"

"Not right now I don't," he says coldly.

When we get home, we're not talking. We move around our apartment in a strange, unfriendly hush, giving each other wide berth. Poor Lazlo, attention starved after only a few visits and walks with Howell since we've been gone, trots back and forth between us, cocking his head to the side and wagging his small, curly tail as if to ask, What's wrong with you people?

In the bedroom, I push the button on our answering machine and listen to messages as I unpack my overnight bag. Jane. My mother. I'll call them later. Then a stranger's voice fills the room. "Hi, uh, this is Ken, the manager up here at O'Connor's Orchard, and we have a bit of a problem."

I stop with my hands full of underwear and socks.

"We had a big storm up here over the weekend, and well, why don't you give me a call as soon as you can?"

Ben stands in the doorway with his arms crossed. We look at each other uncertainly. "I'll call," he says finally.

I lie on the bed with Lazlo curled in a ball beside me as Ben talks. "Yes. Uh-huh. I see. A tornado. And the barn? Completely destroyed? What about the trees? Any chance? No? Okay. What do you suggest?" He's quiet, then he says, "I see. Can I get the number there?"

I stare at the ceiling fan. It's dusty. I should clean it. That's all I can think about at the moment because I'm tired of problems and obstacles and judges named Larry and crazy Vietnamese seamstresses and big storms that can knock down barns weeks before my wedding. And most of all, I'm tired of myself caring so much and being irritated with Ben.

He turns to me. "Well," he says, and I think, *What an odd word. Well,* as in "all is well"? Or *well,* as in a deep, dark hole that we can't get out of?

"How bad?" I ask.

"This is the perfect opportunity to call it off, if you want."

My chest is heavy, my stomach churns. "Is that what you want?" I whisper.

"It's up to you," he says.

"Do we have a place for a wedding?"

"The Elks' lodge up the road from the orchard is available on the sixth if we want it."

I lose it then and laugh from deep in my gut. "God," I say with my hands over my face. "Serves me right, doesn't it?"

"What does?" Ben asks.

I peek at him from between my fingers. "I spend all this time trying to avoid a big Wisconsin wedding, but I'll end up at the Elks' lodge after all."

"If that's not what you want," Ben says.

"What do you want?" I ask.

"I want whatever makes you happy."

I reach for his hand. "You make me happy," I say.

"But do you want to get married?"

"Yes," I say resolutely.

"What about, you know, all the other stuff?"

I wave the question away. "Let's just book the Elks' lodge and forget about everything else," I say, because at this point another small obstacle to our wedding is so much easier to deal with than the giant issues of money, kids, and religion that will define our marriage.

On the evening of my fifth fitting, which is exactly three weeks before our wedding, I walk over to Orange after work. We've spent the week tracking down a deejay (because every decent band was booked), finding a new caterer since the orchard's kitchen was destroyed (we're having duck, but we still have no dessert), and shopping for Ben's suit and our wedding rings.

When I get to Orange, the door is locked. The place is dark. I press my face up against the windows and peer in. The room is empty, and my stomach sinks. I dig my cell phone out of my purse and call Jane.

"Something's wrong," I say to her as soon as she answers. "I think Lenora skipped town."

"She wouldn't do that," Jane says.

"The place is locked up. Everything is gone." As I say this, my stomach curdles, my chin quivers, sweat prickles beneath my clothes. Of course Lenora is gone. Why would I assume that even the most basic thing like my wedding dress would work out at this point?

"Don't move," says Jane. "I'll be there in fifteen minutes."

By the time Jane arrives, I've gotten the story out of the tattoo guy next door. Jimbo tells me that Lenora got deported. "Major visa violations," he says. "It happened real quick. Those government bastards don't mess around anymore after 9/11. Civil liberties are going to hell." He shakes his head sadly. "Fucking Patriot Act."

Jane steps out of a cab and rushes to the sidewalk where I stand with Jimbo.

"What now?" I ask her.

She stares at the empty shop and says, "We need a drink."

Jane and I go to a bar down the street. "Don't worry, Annie," she tells me after our second round. "There are plenty of great wedding dresses out there. We'll find you one."

"I'm going to end up in my granny's dress at an Elks' lodge with a deejay playing the chicken dance record over and over and over," I say and finish my beer in one long drink. "And my mom will be standing in the back of the room, shaking her head, saying, 'I told you so. I told you so.'"

"No, no, no," says Jane. "We won't let that happen. We will find you a dress."

"Dress, schmess," I say. "That's not even the half of it." I dig my cell phone out of my purse. "I'm calling my granny."

"No!" Jane smacks at my hand while I dial. "I won't let you give up this easily."

"I'm not going to wear her dress," I say and push Jane away from me. "I'm finding out why she's not coming to my wedding."

"You're drunk," says Jane as she motions the bartender for another round.

My granny answers the phone on the first ring. "Granny, it's Annie," I say, then I giggle because I rhymed.

"Where are you?" she asks suspiciously.

"At a synagogue," I say and elbow Jane. She rolls her eyes and puts a fresh beer in front of me.

"Have you been drinking?" Granny asks.

"Which would be worse?" I ask and lift the beer to my lips. "If I was a drunk or if I was a Jew?"

"Anne Frances Olsen, what has gotten into you?" Granny demands.

I wipe the foam from my mouth with the back of my hand. "Do you like Ben?"

"For heaven's sake, Annie, of course I like him. What's this all about?"

"I don't understand why you won't come to my wedding." I sniff, suddenly a mushy, sappy mess. "You've been at every major event in my life—dance recitals, school plays, graduation ceremonies—and now you won't come to the most important one."

"You think that has something to do with Ben?" she asks.

"Because he's Jewish," I spew.

Granny is quiet. This scares me, because I realize then that I don't want to know if she's an anti-Semite. It would ruin our relationship. I drink more beer.

"I thought you knew me better than this," Granny says.

"I thought I did, too," I say meekly.

"Annie, I don't care if Ben is a one-armed paper hanger from St. Louis who worships cucumbers. If you love him and he's good to you, then I'm happy for you."

I let go a little sob, mostly from relief. "Thank you, Granny," I say. "Thank you so much for saying that."

"But," she adds, and I swallow hard. "I'm just too old to get on a plane and fly to New York City."

"What if Mom and Dad drove and you didn't have to come into Manhattan?" I ask quickly.

"Oh, dear," she says. "Is it really that important to you?"

"Yes," I plead. "I need you here. I can't get married without you."

Granny sighs. "All right, then. We'll work something out."

"Thank you, Granny!" I blather drunkenly into the phone. "I love you. I love you so much! I can't wait to see you and to get married and to live happily ever after."

"Anne Frances," my grandmother says seriously.

"Yes."

"Stop drinking," she says.

"Yes, Granny," I say, then finish off my beer.

When I hang up, Jane is gathering her jacket and purse. "Come on," she says. "I called the boys. We're going for sushi at Tomoe."

"Oh, goody!" I jump off my stool and stumble out of the bar behind her.

After stuffing my drunken face with sushi, I'm feeling much better. Of course, I'm more drunk, too. As we walk slowly through the West Village, toward the subway station, I try my best to focus on my triumph with Granny tonight and to forget about my dress and the five hundred dollars that have vanished with Lenora Ng's unfortunate departure. But I know that, once I slow down, all the other problems with the wedding will hit me and I'll be a basket case.

"Let's not go home yet," I say to Jane.

She turns to Howell and Ben, who lag behind, and says, "Annie wants to stay out."

"I know what we should do then," Howell says. He grabs Jane by the hand and pulls her forward. "Follow me!" Ben intertwines his arm in mine, and we hurry behind them.

Howell makes a few turns, and it's not long before I'm lost. The Village has never made sense to me, with its roads that intersect themselves, but Howell lived down here for years before he married Jane and moved to Brooklyn, and he knows all the little nooks and crannies. He turns one more corner and points to a long line of people outside a tiny bakery.

Jane claps her hands like a greedy little kid. "Howell," she says, nearly jumping up and down. "You're a fucking genius. We haven't done this in so long."

"What is it?" I ask.

"Magnolia cupcakes," they say and join the back of the line.

A young, beleaguered guy guards the door. He has flour in his hair and chocolate smears across his white apron. Every few minutes two or three people come bursting out the door, babbling happily, carrying their cupcakes triumphantly, then the guy lets a few more people in.

"I hope this is worth standing in line at ten-thirty on a Friday night," says Ben.

Howell wraps his arms around Jane's waist. "Trust me," he says.

"Are you even hungry?" I ask.

Jane and Howell shake their heads at us. "You don't get it," says Jane. "These are Magnolia cupcakes." She kisses Howell on the cheek. "He brought me here after our first date." She kisses him on the mouth.

"God, you two," I say, feigning disgust at their affection. Really, I'm relieved to see them so happy, because it gives me hope that Ben and I can get married and stay goofily in love. That is, if the wedding doesn't kill us first.

After twenty minutes we've got our cupcakes. Chocolate with chocolate frosting for Howell (who has frosting on his cuffs before he even takes a bite). White with chocolate frosting for Jane. White with buttercream frosting and sprinkles for Ben and me. We walk across the street to a little park that's full of couples and people with dogs and teenagers making out on the benches.

"Oh my God," I say as I take my first bite. "This is seriously the best cupcake I've ever had in my life." The buttercream frosting is soft and delicate but not too sweet. The top of the cupcake has just the tiniest crunch, but the bottom is airy and light. I take another bite and another.

"I don't even really like cupcakes," says Ben. He has frosting on the tip of his nose. "But this is ridiculously good."

Jane sits on Howell's knee and happily eats her cupcake. "You guys should have these at your wedding."

I lick my fingers and the paper wrapper. "I would," I say.

"Hell yeah," says Ben. He puts the last bite in his mouth.

"Seriously?" I ask.

"Sure," says Ben. "I think cupcakes would be cool."

"Well, hellfire and damnation!" I hoot and slur through my fog of beer, raw fish, and sugar. "We'll have the best fucked-up wedding ever with these cupcakes. Howell, you are a fucking genius after all!"

"Thanks," says Howell as he licks icing off his shirt.

"Hey," says Ben. "I have a great idea."

"Let's hear it!" I say far too loudly, but I don't care. Screw all the other people in the world. I'm wallowing in my unfortunate wedding tonight.

"Since Howell has saved our wedding, he should get ordained on-line and marry us!" says Ben. It's the first time I've heard him be remotely enthusiastic about our wedding.

"Would you do that, Howell?" I ask.

Howell looks at Jane. She nods eagerly. He shrugs and says, "Sure, why the hell not?"

We all cheer. "This is the best night ever!" I holler and stand up to make my point. Then I vomit in the bushes.

"T minus two weeks," I say to Ben as I gather my Fauntleroy.com files from the coffee table and shove them into my briefcase.

"Until what?" he asks. I look sharply at him, and he smiles. "Kidding," he says. He puts Lazlo on his lap on the couch and rubs behind his ears.

I chug the rest of my cold coffee and take one more bite out of a stale bagel, then do a final sweep of the living room to make sure I haven't forgotten anything for my early meeting with Mitzi Davenport.

"Don't forget we're meeting at six to look at rings," I say.

"It's in my PalmPilot," he says.

I lean down over him. "I'll miss walking to the subway with you."

"It's just one morning," he says.

"I know," I say. "But it's the first time."

I kiss him briefly on the mouth, and he pats my hip, then goes back to reading the paper. We've been cautious with each other since we got back from Boston. Although he's helped me get things done and I've tried not to nag, our easy banter is missing. Sometimes I think it's just the mounting stress of the wedding. Other times I worry this wariness stems from questions about our fundamental differences lurking below the surface of our interactions. Whatever it is, we've simply ducked our heads and barreled forward with wedding plans on faith that we'll work out the details as we go along.

At 8:56, my office phone rings. I see Ben's cell number flash on the caller ID screen. "Hey," I say. "I've got this meeting in four minutes, what's up?"

"Caterer called. There's a problem with the entrée. The price of duck went up, and she has to either charge us more or she can do chicken."

"Figures," I say with complete resignation. "Why doesn't she roast up some hot dogs and open a bag of chips?"

"Fine by me," Ben says.

I hear a truck screech past him. "Where are you?" I ask.

"Almost to the subway," he says.

"I have to go." I put all the Fauntleroy.com design sheets in a portfolio and see Mitzi marching into the conference room behind Helen. She already looks pissed, but at least this time she is without children.

"Good luck," says Ben.

Helen waves frantically to me. Neither of us wants to be in the room alone with Mitzi for a second longer than we have to.

"And Annie," says Ben, "don't worry about the duck. Everything will be fine."

I snort because the notion of everything being fine at this point is ridiculous. "See you at six," I say and hang up.

Mitzi is still a pain in the ass. Every design we've done, she wants something slightly different. Helen has even gone to print some old logos that we had already decided against. I'm about ready to tell Mitzi to stick it up her ass when the door to the conference room opens. I look up at the clock. It's only 9:30, but I feel like we've been trapped in here for hours. I hope Helen has found something that will please this woman so we can get out of here and I can track the caterer down before my next meeting.

Helen stands at the door. "Annie," she says. Something is wrong with her. Her face is ashen.

"What's wrong?" I ask.

She stares at me. Her eyes are shiny, her skin is mottled.

Maybe she's sick. Or has a fever. I excuse myself and leave the room. "Are you okay?" I ask her in the hall.

She puts her arms around my shoulders and pulls me close. She must be delirious. "Hey," I say softly. "Let's sit down." I'll call her a cab. Make sure she gets home safely. Deal with Mitzi on my own, then deal with the caterer. Or not. Maybe I'll let it go.

"There was a bomb." Helen breathes these words into my hair.

"A what, honey?" I say. I push back and look at her. I smile gently. She is delirious.

"A bomb," she says again. "The subway."

As I glance quickly around the office, I know it's true. People are huddled at computers. People are frantically dialing phones. One of the secretaries has told Mitzi, who's gathered her things and run out the door. There is an urgency and a hush over everything. I remember this. This is how it was the last time. We scurried. We hurried. We tried to understand what had happened, but it was impossible because nothing like it had ever happened before.

"What line?" I ask. It comes out quiet.

Helen looks at me. She blinks and blinks and blinks. Tears stream down her face. She tries. Her mouth moves.

"Not the A," I say simply.

"Penn" is all she can utter.

"Penn Station?" I ask. I grab her arm. I need her to tell me what she knows. I need to steady myself. "A bomb at Penn Station? Which line?" She stands, mute. I push her aside and rush to the first row of desks. "What happened? Someone tell me what happened!" I am yelling. I am surprised by how loud I am. I'm making a scene. I'm being dramatic. I should lower my voice, but I can't. "Which fucking line!" I yell.

Everyone turns. We are all scared. "We're not sure," Bill from accounting says. He turns from his computer. On the screen is a live news report from CNN. There is chaos behind him. Sirens scream. Humanity jostles. People yell. I squint and look for Ben. "It may have been on an A train coming into Penn Station. But the reports are all different. It could have been the two or the three."

I don't know what to do. I don't know how to react. I am frozen. I am planted. "Ben," I squeak.

"I'm sure he's . . ." someone starts to say.

"I just talked to him. Less than half an hour ago." I'm whispering now. "He had just gotten to the train." They all look at me. They all wait.

"He's fine," someone else says.

"The chances are so slim . . ."

Helen is behind me. She has her hands on my arms. She is holding me up. I turn to her. "I just talked to him. He said everything would be fine . . ." I trail off.

She puts me in a chair. I sit with one arm wrapped tightly around my stomach, my elbow resting on my fist, my other fist pressed against my mouth. I press and press until my lip is numb. I can't take my hand away from my mouth. I sit, quietly. Nothing. There is nothing I can do.

Everything. Everything will change. The last time, I was at

my old apartment. Ben was with me. Why were we home on a weekday? It was a beautiful fall day. Why weren't we at work? The sky was purely blue, no clouds, and it was warm. We were in the garden. Had we both taken the day off? We were putting chicken wire over a hole in the fence so Lazlo couldn't escape. He was just a puppy. Ben had given him to me for my birthday. I remember standing in the garden, working beside Ben. I remember handing him tools. Wire clippers. I remember that I was happy.

When we were finished, I went inside to check my e-mail. I saw the headline on my start page. An airplane had crashed into one of the World Trade towers. I thought it was a joke. A sick and stupid joke. Someone had hacked into the news site and was putting up false headlines. That was the worst I could imagine. Ben walked through the house. The knees of his jeans were dirty from kneeling in the dirt. Lazlo trotted behind him.

"Look at this," I told him.

He frowned. In the kitchen, he turned on the radio. No one understood yet. It had just happened. Maybe it was a Cessna.

"Let's go to the roof and look," Ben said. He wiped his dirty hands on the back of his jeans.

We climbed the stairs. Four of our neighbors were already there. We all faced the city. We all speculated. We couldn't even come close to guessing what had happened as we watched dark smoke waft up from the towers.

Afterward, it took a long time to remember how to feel safe. If you couldn't, you left. If you could, you stayed. We stayed, but it took a long time. We all had our fears. The ones we kept inside and wouldn't say. Mine was the Brooklyn Bridge. For months, every time we drove across it, my palms would sweat, my head pound, my heart crawl into my throat. I would imagine it over and over. On the bridge, beside Ben, looking west at the gaping hole where that funeral pyre had burned for so long. Where so many people had incinerated. So many that it was unreal. And I was afraid that the bridge would fall next. That Ben and I would die on the bridge.

Then slowly, I forgot to be afraid when I was on the bridge. I forgot to look up every time I heard a low-flying plane. We all learned how to walk around the city again like the fearless assholes we always were. So blindly confident that we would be okay. If you stayed, then you learned to ignore the orange codes and vague warnings. I scoffed at my family's fears. Attacks were like tornadoes or muggings or spontaneous combustions, I told them. Possible, but not likely. You couldn't worry about it. You had to make your life.

But now. Now. I sit. I sit and I wait with my fist pressed against my lip until both throb and my teeth feel numb. I don't know where Ben is. Every time I dial his cell phone, I get a busy signal. The Web is slow, the reporters are unclear. It's been ten minutes and nobody knows anything except a subway train blew up in a tunnel outside of Penn Station. All we know is that it could've been worse. That if it had been planned, then someone botched it, because surely it should've gone off later, in the station. And if it wasn't planned, then something horrible has gone wrong.

I sit. I know nothing except that I'm sickened at the

thought of Ben surrounded by strangers, in pain, or something worse that I can't allow myself to consider. It can't be him, I tell myself. He's too special. He has too much to offer. His logic, his science brain, the way he sees the world and how he makes it a better place to be. Twenty minutes have passed. Ben can't have been on that train, because if he was, then everything is over. Everything is done. It took me so long to find him. To know that he was the one I wanted to try to spend the rest of my life with. Without him, nothing will ever be the same and I will die. If he is gone, then I will die with him.

I think this, and then I know that it's not true. I won't die. I'll keep going, but not here. I will be one of the people who has to give up and leave. Where will I go? Back home? Trailing this story behind me in and out of rooms. Whispered behind hands. "Her fiancé . . . two weeks before their wedding . . ."

A half an hour has passed. I try over and over to call his phone. The circuits are jammed. Too many people trying at once. Helen sits beside me. She dials her cell over and over. I dial my cell. An urgent busy signal is the only response. I press my fist against my teeth.

In these minutes, I realize that everything in my life has been frivolous. I've focused on e-vites and cupcakes and how much a single dress would cost. I've fretted over whether Ben and I could spend money in the same way or find a place to live or what holiday our children would celebrate in December. I nearly laugh at the stupidity of it all. I would give anything, all of it, every single happy moment of my life I would trade to know right now, at this minute, that Ben is okay. That he is safe and that I will see him. That I will touch him again. The phone is busy. Over and over. I cannot move.

"Annie?" Someone's voice behind me. Choked and soft. I don't want to turn around. I don't want to know. "Annie?" I turn slowly, and I see Ben.

He is covered in gray dust. His hair sticks up at odd angles. I gulp air because I can't say anything.

"Annie?" he says again and holds out his arms.

I am out of my seat. I am in his arms. We are on the floor. We crash onto the carpet. We are on our knees.

"You, you, you," I sob into his chest.

"I'm fine. I'm fine. I'm fine," he chants this mantra.

"I thought . . ."

"Annie." He says my name, clearly this time. His familiar voice stops me. "I'm fine," he says again. I breathe. Slump to the side. "I was on the train just ahead," he says to me. "But I'm okay. I got out and everything is fine."

Ben and I hold hands on the airplane as we idle on the tarmac at JFK. The FASTEN SEAT BELT sign glows. The flight attendants have cross-checked and disappeared.

"What about your mom?" Ben says to me.

I lay my head on his shoulder. "What about her?" I ask.

"She'll be disappointed."

"We'll make it up to her later," I say and close my eyes. With my forefinger, I trace a pattern on his thigh. It's been a week, and still, every time I'm with him, I have to touch him. I have to feel the weight of his existence beneath my fingers.

"And your granny?" he says.

"She'd never come now anyway."

"What about a dress? You really wanted a great dress."

"I don't care," I say, because I don't.

"Will you regret it someday?" Ben asks me. "Will you look back and wish we had done this differently?"

"We can still have a party," I tell him. "Everyone can come. Or not. It doesn't matter."

None of it matters anymore. I'm a good Lutheran girl from Wisconsin who will always be torn between two places. He's a nice Jewish boy from Boston who finds God in science. I am thrifty, he is wasteful. And we don't value all the same things. So what? The only thing that matters is that one day we found each other in an apple orchard and then we met again. And we fell in love. It didn't take that long. It wasn't monumental. We just slipped into a life together that we both wanted now and in the future.

So now he and I sit here together. We are lucky in this. I am acutely aware. Too many people were unlucky. Too many people lost everything important to them, and somehow we escaped that fate. So who cares about judges and caterers and rings and dresses? Budgets and geography and whose God got it right? I don't anymore.

"You know this won't change anything," says Ben. "You know that, right? We still live here. We still have to come back here, where it happened."

"I'm not trying to change anything," I tell him. "I just want this, right now."

Ben looks at me. He has amusement in his eyes. They sparkle with his hidden laugh. "But eloping to Las Vegas? It's so unlike you. I figured you'd want to go home and do this in a little chapel somewhere in the middle of cornfields with all your family around. Where you'd feel safe."

I bite at my bottom lip and consider this. "I'm not looking for safety," I tell him. "Because you never know when you'll lose everything." And this is the truest thing I can think of. In an instant, in an explosion, in the most remote possibility, everything could change, and no amount of sanctity or planning will ever save me from it.

"I want something frivolous, Ben. Don't you see?" I turn in my seat to face him fully. "Because I got it wrong, all along. I thought love and marriage should be this serious thing. But they're not. They're frivolous. And our wedding should reflect that."

The plane begins to taxi, and I know that this is what I want. I want the speed. I want the liftoff and the leaving. I think of the people I know who are married. My parents with their small, ordinary wedding. My aunt Agnes and uncle Ed's disaster. Gracie MacMillan marrying herself. Alex Nessman's drunken celebration. Mr. and Mrs. Weisberg's lonely little ceremony. Jane and Howell's wedding mishaps. It's one day in a life. People choose to make their own memories of that day, and I'm sure I'll do the same.

"I want the quickest, tackiest, stupidest, most frivolous wedding in the world," I say to Ben. "I'm not looking for anything special anymore." I pull his face to mine, and I kiss him as the plane lifts into the air. "I've already had the happiest day of my life, and that is enough."

Emily & Jules

Lisa Tucker

– Outside World Crisis –

Emily's brother's wedding was the occasion for her OWC, but Jules was the reason for it. Jules, who she liked more than any guy she'd ever met, even though she'd never met him.

It all started when she joined the group. From the beginning, she wondered if she really belonged there. She didn't have the panic attacks other people described; she never felt even a little nervous when she went to get groceries or rent a movie. But there had to be something wrong with her, or why was she spending hour after hour, day after day, a virtual prisoner in the house she'd grown up in? Why was she unwilling to consider looking for another job, no matter how tired she'd grown of waiting for the words to come, hoping she could find yet another way to express some feeling she didn't feel?

Emily was a freelancer at Perfectwords.com, a greeting card company. The website announced: *For all of life's occasions— from your heart to theirs.* As if there was no middleman at all, no Emily-level person struggling to find some new way to Welcome the New Baby or offer Congratulations to the Happy Couple on the Occasion of Their Engagement.

Her brother David had been one of the first to receive her newest, Happy Couple Number 197H. Unfortunately, a card wasn't what he was looking for. David expected her to come to the wedding, and he pulled out all the stops to get her to agree. "Don't you think Mom and Dad would want you to be there?" he said. "And what about Clara? She's hoping you'll be a bridesmaid. She's been trying to call you about it."

Clara was David's fiancée, and Emily had been avoiding her calls. She would have avoided this one too, but the caller ID had come up "unavailable." Even if it had shown his number, she probably wouldn't have recognized it. She hadn't called her brother once since he moved to Santa Fe after their parents died.

Thank God for the agoraphobia group. Since they rarely left their homes, there was always someone online, even at midnight, when David had decided to call. Rude as always, Emily thought, knowing it was only ten o'clock where he was. "You're a night owl," he explained. "I knew you'd be up." It was true, but it still infuriated her. "You don't know me at all anymore," she snapped. This was also true, and Emily felt a little better when her brother's voice became sad.

The group had a special message thread for this kind of thing: the OWC. Emily posted the usual Help! on top of the news about the wedding, then proceeded to bask in the warm outrage of her fellow group members, who COULD NOT BE-LIEVE (most of them used caps, unashamed to be shouting) how insensitive Emily's brother was about her problem.

David was insensitive, no doubt about that. He'd left all the funeral arrangements to Emily because he was on a fellowship at some biological research center in the middle of the ocean, studying something absurd like the sex lives of salmon. "I can't make it back right now," he said. Actually, he didn't say it, because he didn't call. He used Western Union, which Emily didn't even know still existed.

> I'm so sorry. Stop. Please do whatever you need
> to do with their house and things. Stop. I love
> you, little sis. Stop. Be good to yourself. Stop.

The stops weren't really there, but Emily had seen them in movies so many times, she heard them anyway. Later, when she told Jules about the Western Union message, she inserted them before remembering she'd only imagined that part.

Jules wasn't online the night of Emily's OWC, but then he rarely was anymore. He'd told Emily he didn't need the agoraphobia board, now that he had her. Every day for the last few months, they'd spent hours instant messaging each other and on the phone. They talked about everything from art and music to what they were eating and what they were watching on television. Actually, they spent more time together than most couples—ignoring the little detail that they'd never really been together at all.

How many times had Emily written a card with the word *friend*? Counting drafts that weren't produced, it had to be in the thousands. And yet, until she met him, she wasn't sure she'd ever had a true friend. He was her Jules Verne, a name he used as a joke, given that he never went anywhere, but Emily thought it fit him perfectly. He was always discovering something to share with her. Thanks to Jules, she'd seen the sunset at Maui and the first bloom of flowers on the mountains of Peru. She'd listened to the London Philharmonic live and gone up to the top of the Eiffel Tower and even been to see the Pope. Of course the Pope couldn't see her, because it was a virtual experience, not real. But Emily didn't mind. "We cherish the memories," she told Jules, quoting from one of her Perfectwords bereavement cards. Then she tried to explain, "If we never did something but clearly remembered doing it, would there really be any difference?"

Jules had laughed as he always did when Emily made excuses for them. Whenever she praised him for one of his internet discoveries, he reminded her that reality was a thousand times richer than anything you could find on the web.

"Maybe someday we'll see for ourselves," Emily would say, about Maui or France or Peru.

"Maybe," Jules repeated, but Emily could hear the doubt in his voice. She remembered something she'd read about agoraphobia being rarer in men and possibly much more intractable, much more serious.

Emily had been in the group for about four months when Jules joined. She noticed him immediately because he lived in Ardmore, Pennsylvania, only about forty miles from where she was, in New Hope. His first question to the board was a practical one about finding dentists who make house calls and grocery stores that deliver. The response of the group was sympathetic but worried that he seemed more interested in adjusting to his situation than in getting the help he needed. They expressed their hopes that he had some family to assist him and especially a good therapist.

Since Emily herself had neither therapist nor family (except her brother David, who she felt didn't count), she emailed Jules privately to tell him she understood and she'd be glad to help with anything she could in their area. Not that she knew much, other than that the clerks at her own Acme would have howled with laughter if she'd asked them to deliver. But when he emailed back, he only asked her how she'd ended up in New Hope. Was this a choice or circumstances? Was it as peaceful as he'd always heard?

For obvious reasons, questions about the towns where members lived were rare on the board. If anything, the group tended to ignore the world completely except when that world threatened to push them into an action they weren't ready for. No one had ever said the word *peaceful* about the Outside World. Emily figured it would be like telling a bunch of infertile people about an adorable baby.

But to continue with the analogy, Jules himself was also infertile. So shouldn't saying this make him feel worse too?

Shouldn't his second email to her, with photos of fall in Pennsylvania, photos he'd spent hours searching for and downloading, choosing the best from among the hundreds available online, have been a painful reminder to him of what he couldn't have?

Emily's greeting card job had turned her into someone who was just dying to be blunt in some part of her life. She wrote back to him, "Aren't you worried you're making me feel like shit with these?" His reply was simple, not defensive at all. He said he would be more worried if she didn't see them, adding, "Don't you hear your mind crying out for beautiful things?"

The truth was no. In fact, Emily had barely bothered to look at the photos Jules had sent her. She'd grown up in Pennsylvania; she'd seen plenty of falls before. For the first month or so, everything Jules emailed to her was of so little interest that Emily found herself wondering if her agoraphobia was caused by some kind of premature aging of her soul. "I can't understand why everything seems so pointless to me," she admitted to him. "It's like I'm too tired to care anymore." Then, because she was embarrassed, she added, "Poor me, tiny violins. Tired, yeah right. I sleep twelve hours a day and pretty much never leave my chair."

She couldn't resist putting her phone number at the end of that email. By this point, she knew he was a real person; she'd found his name and address on the web. He really lived in Ardmore. She'd also found him listed as an alumnus of some college in New York, in the same year he'd said he'd graduated, only two years before she herself had graduated from Penn State.

He wrote her back: a sympathetic reply, complete with a list of weblinks on the meaning of existence—but no mention of calling. Maybe he was afraid of the phone, she thought. A lot of the people on the board were. She forced herself to wait a few days before she broke down and asked if she could call him. When he said yes, and included the number she'd already written on a piece of paper by her computer, she paced the room and sang scales for almost an hour to get the frog out of her throat, then picked up the phone.

His voice was exactly like she knew it would be: low, musical, unmistakably caring. Everything he said was so thoughtful; even his pauses seemed thoughtful to her. He talked like they'd known each other for years, and when she finally asked him why, he said because knowing someone was a lot simpler than most people think. The trick to knowing someone, Jules said, was asking just two questions: "What do you believe is beautiful? And how do you feel about witnessing its destruction?"

Emily was confused. "But I already told you nothing is beautiful to me."

"You told me everything is pointless to you. That isn't the same at all." He inhaled and took a drink of something. She wondered what it was, what his cup looked like, and most of all what he looked like.

"Maybe you've just seen too much destruction," he said.

"Maybe," she said, but she didn't believe it. Her life was hardly a tragedy. True, her parents had died in a car accident, but she was already a grown-up at the time. The word *orphan* was reserved for children who still needed their parents, not adults who hadn't even bothered to visit them except on holidays.

Her friends thought she'd moved into her parents' house to punish herself for not being there more when they were alive, but it wasn't true. She'd moved into their house because she thought it was a good time to quit her crappy job as a bank management trainee and figure out what she wanted to do with the rest of her life. And it wasn't like New Hope was the end of the earth. Most of her friends lived in Center City Philly; she could drive into town and party with them whenever she wanted. This was back when she was assuming she would want to party with them, once the grief wasn't so fresh, maybe in a month or two. She also thought she would want to continue seeing Peter, her boyfriend, who stayed by her side at the funeral and squeezed her shoulder and was really nice about what happened, except for the time he spent outside the church, talking about some skiing trip on his cell phone.

Why she cut herself off from everyone, she still didn't totally understand. It wasn't a decision; it was just a process of saying "next time" and "later" until the offers stopped coming. Peter let her go first, less than a month after the funeral. Her friends tried harder, but even they gave up surprisingly quickly, proving what Emily had begun to believe in college: that people had become as interchangeable as clothes or CDs. Even though everyone had to have some people in their lives, they no longer needed any particular person. Maybe there wasn't even such a thing as a particular person anymore.

In the kitchen of her parents' house, the house she grew up

in, was a framed needlework her mom had bought in the Pennsylvania Dutch country. "Human beings are like snowflakes: each unique, one of a kind, miraculous." When she was a little kid, she'd liked the pretty blue thread. When she was about ten, the saying bugged her: "Unique *is* one of a kind, Mom." After that, she forgot about it. But during the long winter alone after her parents died, sitting at the kitchen table, eating soup straight from the pot, she decided it should say: "Human beings are like greeting cards, each one pawning itself off as though it's unique when really we're all mass-produced imitations."

Emily joined the group because she was afraid the hollowness inside of her was getting worse, threatening to become permanent. And it helped, even if she found herself unable to agree with the premise stated at the top of the agoraphobia website: that their condition was holding them back from a much better life.

It wasn't until she became friends with Jules that Emily began to think maybe it was true, maybe there was something better beyond this house, beyond her neighborhood, beyond her own mind. He almost never talked about himself, and yet he seemed like the most individual person she'd ever met. Here was the real thing, she thought: a particular person. A genuine snowflake.

What he saw in her, she honestly didn't know. Sometimes she tried to find things to show him, but she never came up with anything even half as good as the things he routinely gave to her. He really was an explorer, able to uncover the strangest places on the internet, the most wonderful pictures of mountains and lakes and stars and especially the way people lived. After a while, Emily couldn't remember what she'd meant when she'd said everything was pointless. Nothing was pointless through Jules's eyes. There was so much beauty, looking through Jules's eyes, that Emily woke up every morning with a sense of anticipation even the stupidest Perfectwords assignment couldn't change.

Plus, there was always the possibility Jules would IM or call and interrupt that assignment. Or she could call him, with another of her jokes.

Her dumb jokes about agoraphobia were the only things she had that he didn't. She always told them over the phone; she loved to hear him laughing.

What do you get when you cross an agoraphobic with a flea? A housebound louse.

Why did the agoraphobic cross the road? I don't know, but the question makes me nervous.

A priest, a rabbi, and an agoraphobic walk into a bar— "Hold on a minute," the agoraphobic says. "The towel bar I get, but why are that priest and rabbi in my bathroom?"

After she told a new joke to Jules, she would often post it on the board for the group. She liked all the responding LOLs and tee-hees. Of course everyone knew it was all in good fun, because Emily had been there since last spring. She was one of the veterans now.

She never meant to deceive them. When everything changed for her on that December day, she would happily have told them exactly what had happened—but then she would have had to tell Jules.

The odd part was that it was Jules himself who had caused her to change on that day, when he sent her a picture. Actually, two pictures. The first was of a snow-covered bridge in Bucks County, a lovely photograph, but they were all lovely to her now. What really got to her was what Jules had written:

> I found this picture when I was searching the area where you live. I think it's only about five miles from your house. I like to imagine that you went there as a child. I like to imagine that someday you'll be standing there again.

He was right, the bridge was nearby, but Emily didn't remember ever going there as a child. Still, what he said stopped her heart. She suddenly felt like she had to try to get to this place, for him.

As she climbed into her Toyota, she thought of the group telling her that the grocery store and the movie rental place were in what they called her "personal safety zone," and she braced herself for what would happen when she went farther away. She had a shaky moment or two as she drove by the grocery parking lot, but within a few blocks, she was absolutely fine. The road was busy, but she'd always been a good driver. The traffic didn't make her nervous. Being at the bridge didn't make her nervous. Getting out of her car and walking for probably a mile up the river, and then back, inhaling the cold winter air, feeling the wind on her cheeks—none of it made her nervous. She felt a little silly, for believing it was so inevitable, when she'd never had panic attacks before. Never in her life.

She spent the rest of the day out in the world, doing things she'd put off, like replacing her phone, and things she used to enjoy, like swimming at the Y. By the time she got home—late, because she'd gone out to eat and to see a movie; still testing herself, wanting to be absolutely sure—she knew she didn't have agoraphobia. The last year was a glitch in her life, and now she was over it. The sense of freedom amazed her. She hadn't known the weight of her prison until she felt this freedom.

She'd stayed gone so long that it was too late to call Jules to tell him about her day, though she was dying to. She did log on to the net, intending to send him an email of all the details. But first she had to open all the emails from him—fourteen of them, all with attached pictures, as usual. She smiled as she went through the field of daisies, the Navajo sculpture, the microscopic shot of a raindrop exploding on the pavement. She smiled through the first thirteen pictures, wishing she'd been here to receive all this, and then she got to the fourteenth, which was actually the second one sent that morning, right after the covered bridge. She felt her breath catch when she realized what it was, the last thing she expected on that day, a photograph of Jules himself.

She'd sent him a picture of herself back in October, wanting to get it over with, terrified he'd find her unattractive but more terrified of letting this friendship go on, not knowing what he'd think. He'd replied with a poem about the compassion of her eyes, the kindness of her mouth, the "goodness that took shape, becoming her face." She'd cried when she read it—the first tears she'd shed since the funeral. But when she asked if he'd send her his photo, he said he wasn't ready. She told him she could wait as long as necessary. She really believed that no matter what he looked like, even if he was a wart-covered troll, her feelings for him wouldn't change.

But she was wrong. Her feelings did change when she saw his picture. She didn't want it to be true, but it was. His pale skin and enormous dark eyes, very dark hair, long face, obvious intelligence—he looked exactly like the boys she'd always wished she could date in college, if only she'd been part of a different crowd. A poet herself, or a painter. A passionate scientist. Something, anything, other than a business school finance major or, just as bad, what she was now: a cheesy greeting card writer.

All the compassion he saw in her face was actually in his own. This was what confused Emily, as she sat motionless at her computer, staring at the blowup of Jules on her screen. Why did he assume she was anywhere close to as sensitive as he was? Why, when all she ever had to offer was a collection of stupid jokes?

Later she thought the answer was obvious, but she also knew why she'd let herself forget. For the first time in over a year, she'd spent a whole day out of her house. For the first time in eight months, she hadn't even checked in with the other people on the board.

Before she turned off her computer she did check in with them, and she did send Jules an email. She talked about the other photographs, and she told him how honored she was that he'd trusted her with his picture, finally. She said something vague but positive about the way he looked. Before, she would have gushed about how much she loved his face, but now her feelings for him had changed, and she was too shy.

Of course she had to give him some reason why she hadn't answered any of his emails for twelve hours—or the phone, since she knew from caller ID that he'd called three times—and so she gave him a reason: she said she'd been in bed with a bad flu and she'd turned off her phone. As she expected, he called her the next morning, worried, checking to see if she was all right.

"We have to look out for each other," he said. His voice grew soft. "In our situation."

In our situation. She didn't mean to deceive him, but she just couldn't stand giving up that shared plural.

By the time she found out about David's wedding, it was February and she was used to her double life. It wasn't like she went all that many places anyway. She could do her daily swimming at the Y before Jules was awake. She could shovel the driveway or go out in the backyard; the phone reception was great all the way back to the fence. She could make it to the library and back in forty-five minutes—as long as she decided what she wanted before she left and used the online catalog to reserve a copy. If Jules called while she was gone, she told him she was in the shower. When she really took a shower, she took the phone in with her. She'd had to walk around with shampoo drying in her hair only a couple of times.

Her brother's wedding, though, was a real crisis. How on earth would she do it? Even if she got a cell phone and tried to act like she was still home, she'd be out of commission for at least six hours during the flight to Santa Fe and six more on the flight back. Jules might get so worried about her he'd call the police.

The day after her OWC post, while she was explaining to him who Clara was and why the wedding was such a big deal (since Clara was Emily's friend; Clara had been at the funeral and held Emily's hand and even offered to stay with her as long as it took, until she felt better), Emily suddenly found herself wishing more than anything that Jules could go with her to Santa Fe. She'd been there before; she knew he'd love the hillside adobes with pink and blue shutters, the mountains covered in shrubs and valleys in hyssop and especially the enormous, brilliant sky.

Having him with her wasn't an option. Even telling him she was going wasn't an option. There were no options at all, Emily thought, as she wished for the hundredth time that she could just drive to his house, bang on the door, and yell "I'm cured." He wouldn't answer, she was sure, since everyone on the board had trouble with visitors. Her sudden arrival would upset him, and it might even make his own agoraphobia worse.

She felt a wave of desperation and closed her eyes, so at least she wouldn't have to see the stupid draft she was supposed to be working on. It was for the "no occasion" line of cards, or BLISS, as they were called at Perfectwords. "For no other reason than *Because Life IS Sweet*." Right before Jules called, she'd crossed out everything she'd come up with today but the first seven words. "Whenever I think of you, I wish . . ."

Her eyes snapped open when, all of a sudden, in the middle

of something Jules was talking about, she heard the words she'd been dying to say to him, tumbling out of her mouth.

"I wish I could kiss you."

And then, before she could backtrack or laugh it off, he said, "I feel the same way."

The burst of happiness propelled her from her office chair and onto the wood floor, where she twirled around in her socks, smiling at every wall of the quiet house. It wasn't until later that night, alone in her bed, that she remembered she still had the crisis. The wish couldn't do anything about that. Of course not. There was no genie here. The wish couldn't even get her a kiss.

– In-Between Man –

Even as Jules made his plan to help Emily go to her brother's wedding, he wondered how he could possibly pull it off. If he somehow managed all the phone calls, he'd still have to deal with leaving the apartment.

The last time he'd gone anywhere was months ago. When he needed food, he ordered pizza or Chinese. When he needed soap or shaving cream, he got it from a nearby store that was happy to deliver, as long as he was willing to pay an extra fifteen percent.

His parents called what he was doing "taking a break," as though he'd just stepped out for coffee instead of exiting his life. He told them he'd quit his job at the advertising agency, which wasn't untrue: he had quit, because his boss decided it was the best way to handle what happened. "Julian Reed was too good to let this destroy his future," as Stan, the boss, put it to Jules. Stan always talked to his employees using the third person and their full names. Everyone knew this about Stan; it was acceptably odd, unlike what Jules did, which was so unacceptable that he was not only asked to resign but escorted out of the building. Of course he'd been in his office for nine days at that point. If they hadn't escorted him out, he might never have left.

Pulling an all-nighter in the office for an account deadline was normal; staying in the office for nine days and nights doing nothing was not. Jules hadn't showered or shaved or even eaten anything beyond the food his assistant kept forcing on him. Her eyes were filled with sympathy when Stan finally stormed past all her excuses and found Jules huddled in the corner underneath the window. "What the fuck is he doing?" Stan said. Jules looked like hell, but worse, his desk was cleared of all the papers and pens and files that indicated work was being done. Even his computer was shut down.

Jules couldn't answer Stan's question. Until two weeks before, he'd been a successful creative director with several national clients. He'd spent his time going all over the country to present campaigns, always first class: flights, restaurants, hotels. His parents back in Kansas loved to brag about their big-shot son. He was the first of his family to finish college, and here he was, not even thirty and already making six figures.

And then he just stopped. It was that sudden, that inexplicable—at least to Stan and Jules's assistant Heather and all the other people on his team. To Jules himself it was also a mystery, though later, he realized there had been signs he was having problems. He had trouble sleeping, for one thing. He sometimes felt like he couldn't breathe, especially when he woke in the middle of the night in a strange city. He had his first panic attack—though he didn't know the name for it at the time—when he was staying on the forty-fourth floor of a fancy hotel in Chicago. He'd never been afraid of heights or a fire, but that night, he was terrified of both. He couldn't even ask for another room because he couldn't trust his voice enough to pick up the phone. The next day, the whole incident seemed more ridiculous than frightening. He even mentioned it to his girlfriend Liz, and she laughed, which he decided was the reaction he wanted. What would happen if she took it seriously?

Jules didn't consider himself sensitive. Hardly. Sensitive people don't get promoted in a cutthroat business like advertising. True, he'd been an art major in college, but he'd grown up and out of his dream of being a photographer. As the company recruiter told him during his first interview, most photographers end up in places like Kmart, shooting pictures of drooling, screaming babies. He couldn't let that happen to him, not after all the money his parents had spent sending him to college—money they really didn't have. His father worked on the assembly line of a potato chip factory; his mother was a nurse's aide. They'd mortgaged their three-bedroom ranch house to pay tuition. Jules was relieved when he could pay that mortgage off for them.

That was two years into his job, after one promotion but before the others. He was so good at his work that he became a little arrogant, and then more arrogant, until he didn't hesitate to tell the people he worked with exactly why their ideas were "unworkable," "uninspired," even stupid. Most of those people were afraid of him, and though Jules sometimes felt bad about that, he also knew it gave him more power.

Power and money: the American dream. Great apartment, attractive girlfriend, even a job most people would consider creative—though Jules knew it wasn't, since he'd been promoted past the point where he got to do anything but approve and present the creative work of everybody else. Whenever he asked himself what more he could want, he couldn't come up with an answer. And yet, sometimes he felt afraid that his life had turned into something he couldn't even recognize. His girlfriend Liz seemed to be primarily interested in shopping and parties and gossip. He only saw his parents on Thanksgiving and Christmas, if that. He had a camera that cost ten times what his camera cost in college, but he never had time to use it.

Still, he would gladly have stayed where he was. He would never have chosen to have a panic attack on that ordinary morning, riding the elevator up to his office. He certainly wouldn't have chosen the breakdown that followed: the nine days during which he couldn't think of going anywhere without having the panic start all over again. Nine days when he couldn't sleep or work or do anything but crawl around his office floor and wonder if he was dying. Naturally he was afraid he'd gone insane—that was why he refused to let Stan call an ambulance to take him to a psychiatric hospital: he was terrified he'd never get out. He left Stan no choice but to fire him. He left Liz no choice but to break up with him, when he wouldn't come out of his apartment or tell her what was going on. He left his landlord no choice but to start eviction proceedings, when he neglected to pay rent for three months. And finally, he left himself no choice but to leave New York, when he couldn't think of any reason to stay.

The apartment in Ardmore, Pennsylvania, fell in his lap after an old college friend got transferred overseas. It was already furnished, and the rent was paid for two months: Jules didn't have to do anything but get there. Even that proved so difficult he ended up packing only his computer and camera and one suitcase of clothes, and then taking a cab from Manhattan, 117 miles. But fine, he'd saved enough he could afford it. He had enough money to last for a while, especially now that he had nothing he wanted to spend it on. The other thing he had plenty of, for a change, was time.

He was too nervous to read and he quickly got bored with television. Originally, he turned to the internet the same way he used to when he lived in New York: to scan the news, to surf for something mindless to distract himself. It took a few days before he thought to check out the art photography sites, and after he did, he couldn't get enough. The web was full of amazing pictures, but what really stunned him was how clearly he could see things now, so much more clearly than when he'd been looking at real things out in the world. How had he missed all this? Why hadn't he seen the beauty? And the question that most made him want to weep: why hadn't he been taking photographs every minute when he had the chance, photos of everything and anything—of oceans and mountains and buildings and cracks in the sidewalk and slumped old women and drooling, screaming babies?

In art school he'd had two questions tacked on the bulletin board above his desk: "What do you believe is beautiful? How do you feel about witnessing its destruction?" He loved these questions because they seemed to express the central truth of being an artist, the responsibility not only to create but to refuse to be part of anything that destroyed. But after he left college, he managed to forget that truth so thoroughly he forgot he ever knew it. Now he'd remembered, and that was something. He remembered, and he knew he'd never let himself forget again . . . even if the only beauty he could experience was trapped inside his computer screen.

Trapped, just like he himself was—because unfortunately none of his realizations made any difference; he still couldn't walk to the door of his apartment building without starting to panic. Of course he was incredibly lonely, living with only the accusing silence of his failures. On the rare occasions when he felt brave enough to call someone other than his parents, he tried making contact with one of his friends or co-workers in New York, but the conversations were so strained he always felt worse when he hung up. It wasn't just the awkwardness of their questions about how he was feeling or their avoidance of any mention of what he was doing and whether he would ever work again. They were waiting for him to talk like he used to when he was in advertising; they expected the kind of clever banter he'd been so good at back then. Now the things he came up with were invariably more earnest than ironic, more serious than sarcastic. Half the time, he found himself unable to come up with anything at all.

The first time Emily called, he worried he'd have nothing to say to her either. In emails, he could express himself to her perfectly, but that was because he never had to talk about himself but instead could focus on the things he cared about now, the beauty that was everywhere. He expected Emily might have some conversational problems of her own, being another agoraphobic, and he wouldn't have been surprised if they had hung on the line until both of them blurted out an awkward good-bye. That it didn't happen that way continued to surprise him day after day, phone call after phone call, until he finally accepted that Emily was unlike any woman he'd ever known. When he told her so, she laughed, but he could tell she was touched.

He could always tell how she felt because she didn't try to hide it, the way most people did. She wasn't concerned with how her feelings made her look, but only with the truth of them. When she told jokes, they weren't at anyone's expense but her own. She seemed incapable of cruelty, incapable of being other than who she was. Her eyes, her mouth, even the shape of her face spoke of this directness and lack of pretense. Admittedly, she was also very pretty, and Jules spent almost as much time looking at her picture as he did searching the web. Sometimes he spent so much time staring at her that he was surprised when he looked in the dresser mirror and caught a glimpse of himself.

By the time she started asking him personal questions, he was no longer afraid to discover the answers. "Do you remember what caused your panic attack in the elevator?" she said. He'd never known what caused it, but he agreed to try to think about that morning trip to work. (Initially, she'd been very surprised he'd been a director at an ad agency. "That wasn't right for you at all," she said. He couldn't argue with that.)

"Were you worried about anything?" she said.

"I doubt it. I didn't worry very much then."

"Do you remember what were you thinking about?"

"No. Probably a campaign."

"Did anything unusual happen in the elevator?"

"Not that I remember. It didn't stop or break, if that's what you mean."

"Okay," she said and paused for a moment. Then she asked if there were any sick people on the elevator. Anyone upset or crying. Anyone who reminded him of a relative. Anyone who made him feel afraid. Maybe ten more questions like that, and he said no to them all. Finally she said, "Guess no big trauma then?"

"Guess not," he said, but strangely, he did feel a little anxious. He wasn't having trouble breathing yet, but his heart had sped up. When he told Emily, she said she was going to change the subject. "Unless you don't want me to," she added.

"New subject," he said. He might have been willing to have an attack on the phone with Emily—if he'd been willing to have an attack at all. But nothing would ever make him willingly go back there. It was the most profound fear he'd ever known. It was like everything around him was being swallowed up into a void, like there was nothing left on earth but the deafening sound of his own betraying heart.

Of course Emily came up with another subject, as promised. It was another thing he liked about her: how she seemed to have a thousand things to talk about. If she felt like being light, she could make fun of her "dumb job" at the greeting card company. And it wasn't a ploy to get him to tell her it wasn't true, though sometimes he did because he liked the cards she wrote, so full of words and tangible sentiments, not really profound or poetic but hinting at the true feelings people had for one another, the ones they wished they could name. If she was in a serious mood, she could talk about her parents or her brother or (her favorite topic) something he'd sent her from the internet. Her reaction to the photographs he found made him remember how he used to feel in art school. As though what he saw could be communicated. As though if he worked hard, he might someday take a photo that would crack open the world's heart.

Because Emily saw what he saw, it freed him to see more. As they continued talking about his past, he eventually remembered what he'd been worried about before his attack in the elevator that morning, which really wasn't anything, yet it still upset him whenever he thought about it. A friend of his, Rob, had started at the company a few months before. Rob was a nice guy, a former midwesterner, like Jules himself. He wanted to be a cartoonist; he ended up at the agency because his infant son had medical problems and Rob needed the insurance. On that particular morning, Jules was thinking about what to do about Rob's performance, which was consistently falling short of the team's standards. The last week had been a disaster, because Rob had questioned Jules in front of the CEO of a big account. Jules was dreading the damage control and especially dealing with Rob, who didn't mean any harm. That was the problem with Rob: he was weirdly innocent, like a lamb thrown into a tank of sharks.

"Anyone who had to deal with this would get upset," Emily said. "It sounds like a mess."

"Upset, yes. Almost losing consciousness, no."

"The more compassionate, the more upset."

He smiled; she was always making excuses for him. "I think the compassionate thing would have been to figure out a way to help Rob improve."

"You would have done that if you'd stayed. You would have helped him."

He didn't say anything, but he doubted it was true. He couldn't remember ever helping anyone at work, unless by helping he could enhance his own position. But he wished he'd been the type to help people, and he was glad he had a second chance to be that way now—with Emily.

At first he tried to talk her out of caring so much about her brother's wedding. He hated to see her being so hard on herself for not being able to go. When that didn't work, he began researching agoraphobia with an energy he'd never had when he was trying to figure out his own situation. During one late-night internet session, he finally found the website that gave him the idea of Fred. He might have surfed on if the site hadn't specifically mentioned a way agoraphobics could travel out of their safety zones, even travel on planes.

He spent the next day pacing his apartment, gathering courage. First, he had to find a doctor who would document he was agoraphobic, because of course he was going to act like he was the one traveling. He found a website with a "panic assessment" test that went on for pages, and he spent several hours answering all the questions. When the option to email it to a doctor came up, he typed in the information for a psychiatrist in downtown Philadelphia, a Dr. Wilson he'd found online. A few days later, Jules called Dr. Wilson's office, to ask him if he would provide a letter stating Jules had agoraphobia. He didn't want to share anything else with Dr. Wilson, and he certainly didn't want to start therapy. When the doctor insisted he do something to begin treatment, Jules agreed to try medication.

He wasn't planning to take the two drugs, but Dr. Wilson said he wouldn't send the letter until Jules picked up the prescriptions. The nearest pharmacy was a full two blocks away. Jules called them hoping they would deliver, but the pharmacist said no, not to a new customer. Maybe they would have changed their minds if Jules had pushed them, but he couldn't. He'd already hung up so he could breathe deeply and try not to think about walking those blocks.

In the end it was the idea of kissing Emily, not helping her, that allowed him to make it. That and drinking both bottles of Michelob that had been left in the refrigerator by his old college friend. He timed it so he'd arrive at exactly 9:00 A.M., when they opened; he knew he couldn't handle it if the store was crowded.

He didn't have a panic attack, but he came so close he had no desire ever to repeat the experience. But he had the meds, and when the doctor checked, the pharmacy would tell him so.

That night, as he thought about making all the phone calls that came next, it occurred to him these drugs could make it easier. He wasn't antimedicine, even if he didn't believe it would solve anything in the long run. He swallowed both pills and called Emily, to listen to her talk. About an hour later, she said he sounded tired, but it wasn't exactly true. He felt like he was floating in the space between wakefulness and sleep, and all he wanted was to stay right there and not have to choose.

"I think I love you," said the in-between man. He floated on, not even realizing Emily hadn't said anything until she started to cry.

"I can't stand this," she stammered. He couldn't remember if he'd asked her what was wrong; he hoped so.

"It's going to end soon," he said, thinking of his plan. He couldn't say why, but he always felt positive that what he was going to do would not only let Emily travel to her brother's wedding but also cure her. The idea made him sad sometimes, because he knew once she was out, he wouldn't have her anymore. Even if he got his own Fred, he would still be trapped inside his illness. Hers was somehow temporary, he was sure, while his was unfortunately permanent.

Still, the medicine made him calmer, and he needed to be calm to do all this, so he kept taking it. A few weeks and dozens of phone calls later, he'd found a place in the Philly area that trained service dogs for physical and psychiatric disabilities. He was glad they agreed to find him a golden retriever, because he knew Emily had had a golden retriever throughout her childhood. Emily's dog had been named Fred, and he told the woman at the training center he planned to call the new dog Fred also. She said that wasn't possible, the new dog would already have a name. All of the dogs they dealt with were old enough to have been trained for basic service: obeying commands, possessing public access skills, being responsive to humans. "Your dog will be trained to alert to anxiety," she said. "Then we'll have to train you to handle the dog." She paused for a moment. "In your case, that can be done at home."

But it still had to be done, and Jules was dreading it. He couldn't give the new Fred to Emily until the training was finished, but in the meantime, he'd have to care for it. A dog had to be walked every day and fed something other than Chinese. And what if the dog got sick? The responsibility was overwhelming.

The dog's name was Alicia, and she was a beautiful animal: white fur tinged with brown, fluffy ears, big padded feet, classic retriever snout and eyes. Perfect for Emily, Jules thought, although naturally he went along with the trainer's assumption that he would be the final owner. The trainer, Kelvin, was a huge man, patient, kind, with obvious experience dealing with agoraphobics. He told Jules he'd take Alicia home until Jules felt up to dealing with her daily needs by himself.

Jules wondered if that would ever happen—and then a few weeks later, it did. It was a Thursday; he'd talked to Emily for hours that morning while he was waiting for Kelvin and Alicia to arrive. One of Emily's favorite things to do was to pretend they were going somewhere exotic and then look at the pictures he found of the place as though they were already there. That morning it was Vienna, because he already had good bookmarks for Vienna and he was too distracted to search for a new place.

He and Emily were inside one of Beethoven's houses, turned into a museum, when he thought he heard a van pull up outside. Kelvin might be early. He told her he had to go.

"Is something wrong?" She sounded genuinely worried, and he wished he could tell her the truth. But he knew what she'd say if he did—the same thing he would have said if someone tried to get a service dog for him: I appreciate the gesture, but it will never work. She might even tell him not to go any further with the training, which would depress him, given all he'd done already, but more important, it would make it impossible for her to go to the wedding.

He told her he was fine. Before he hung up, he told her they could go wherever she wanted for dinner tonight: San Francisco, Madrid, Paris.

The most difficult thing Jules had to do each day was take Alicia for a walk. It was always a short walk, because Kelvin said Jules could call it off whenever he wished, and he always called it off before they'd made it halfway down the street. He wasn't panicking, but he wasn't ready to risk it. He told Kelvin not yet but soon. Tomorrow. The next day at the latest.

That Thursday, he had no intention of going any farther than usual. It was a beautiful spring day, but he hadn't slept much the night before, and he wondered if the meds were already losing the uphill battle against his anxiety. He could tell Kelvin was disappointed when he insisted on turning around in front of the green house only four doors down from his own building. "Sorry," Jules said, looking down at the sidewalk. He felt bad for Alicia, too. She'd been panting excitedly but turned around instantly when he pulled the leash.

They'd just started walking back when they heard the siren. The sound came from a police car across the street and was so sudden and loud even Kelvin jumped a little. For Jules, though, the earsplitting screech began the familiar, terrible process of an attack. Loud noises had never been a problem for him before his breakdown, but now he couldn't bear them. He even kept his TV turned low, so the sudden volume of the commercials wouldn't startle him.

The police car had barely turned the corner, but Jules's heart was already beating twice as fast as usual and his breath was coming in short, desperate gasps. He wanted to tell Kelvin what was happening, but he couldn't even get enough air to form words. He braced his hands on his knees and leaned his head down, yet he couldn't make it stop.

His only thought about Alicia was to make sure he closed his sweaty hand tightly around her leash. Of course he knew she'd been trained to help him. The brochures from the service dog organization had explained how it worked: when people are anxious, they release a pheromone dogs can sense. Alicia was supposed to stave off a panic attack by focusing on her owner, offering tactile stimulation, even bracing him up if the dizziness got bad. But everything Jules had read hadn't prepared him for how it would feel to have Alicia rubbing her snout against his face, whimpering softly, and leaning her body against his. It felt as if she really understood what he was going through, but not as an outsider would, no matter how sympathetic. As if she could see into his heart and his mind, and she was saying it was all right: nothing he had ever done made him deserve this.

Later, he thought it was Alicia's lack of judgment that freed him to stop judging himself long enough to think about what had happened. That morning, before he got in the elevator, before his panic attack, he was planning how to get rid of Rob. Emily had called it a "mess," but all he'd been thinking about was the best way to do it. He was going to destroy a person who counted him as a friend, simply because that friend had dared to question him in public. The only thing that mattered to him back then was his own status, his own position. In other words, Jules had turned into something he hated. No wonder his heart had rebelled.

As he stood on the sidewalk, trying to breathe, he knew there was no way to know for sure. Maybe all this had nothing to do with his breakdown that morning; maybe it was bad chemistry or bad genes or just bad luck. But still, he felt sure this dog was offering him forgiveness. All he had to do was accept.

Alicia wagged her tail when Jules looked up. His heart was still racing, but he was able to take a deep breath and then another. He wanted to laugh when he saw that Alicia was panting like she was trying to show him how it was done. Kelvin asked if he was all right, and he nodded and scratched Alicia behind her ears. When his heartbeat finally settled, Alicia licked his face as though she was congratulating him for making it through this one.

He was still shaky, but he made the entire fifteen-minute walk Kelvin wanted him to. When they got back to the apartment, Kelvin asked if he felt up to having Alicia stay with him tonight. He said yes, but he tried not to be too excited. The wedding was only a month away now, and he wouldn't be able to keep Alicia with him much longer. He had to give Emily time to adjust to her new dog.

– View, Shared –

Emily wondered if Jules was starting to suspect she wasn't really agoraphobic. Why else would he have asked her if she ever got nervous when she answered her door? Why else would he have insisted on returning to that question—after she'd managed to distract him—saying that he wanted to know?

No, she finally admitted, answering the door is no problem for me. She knew she didn't have a choice: she was running out of time for her double life.

The wedding was only weeks away, and she'd made up her mind that before she left, she was going to tell Jules the truth. They were closer than ever, but it was too hard, caring so deeply for a man she couldn't touch or even see. She felt sure he wouldn't dump her once he knew. In fact, she was almost positive he'd want her to come over. Of course he would, the sooner the better.

She felt so confident about this that she decided to buy him a birthday present. If he didn't want to see her, she could always mail it to him, but she didn't dwell on that possibility. On Thursday, she got a call from the camera store that her order had arrived. The store was down in Center City, but since his birthday was Monday, she decided to drive to pick it up.

Emily knew how badly Jules missed taking pictures. The camera she picked, called a "view camera," seemed old-fashioned at first, but all the experts she'd consulted assured her that any serious photographer would love it. More important, it had to be used with a so-called focusing cloth. The focusing cloth was intended to help the photographer see better by blocking out the light, but Emily wanted it for Jules for another reason entirely. It covered up the photographer's face. He could leave the house and still be hidden from the world.

She didn't tell Jules where she was going that day, but it wasn't a problem. They almost never talked in the early afternoon, since they'd usually talked for hours in the morning, including that one. She figured she'd be back by four at the latest, and she was. As she drove up to her house, she was thinking how happy Jules would be when she gave him the present—and how happy she would be, standing in his apartment with him.

When she first saw a man on her front porch, sitting in the rocking chair, the chair that had been her mother's, she was so stunned she almost plowed right into the neighbor's truck. By the time she got into her driveway, though, all she felt was thrilled. How it happened she had no idea, but there he was. Jules was at her house!

She was already out of the Toyota and running up the front walk when she saw that he had a dog with him. A golden retriever, just like her childhood dog Fred.

"What are you doing here?" she said, smiling. She was only a few feet away now, and she saw that he was even cuter than his picture. Those gorgeous dark eyes. When he stood up, she realized he was tall, too. She smiled wider and had to resist the impulse to grab him in her arms.

"I came to introduce you to Alicia," he said, nodding at the dog. He wasn't smiling. His tone was clipped and tight in a way that it never was on the phone.

"How did you get here?" she said. She still had her keys in her hand. She pointed at the door. "Come in."

"I don't think so," he said. He rubbed his hand across his forehead. She watched it drop back down to his side and noticed his fingers were trembling.

"I know this had to be tough." She felt so bad for him. She wanted to hold his hand, but she was afraid of making it worse. "I'm really glad you came here."

"It was tough," he said slowly. "The hardest part was when the cab had already dropped me off and I realized you weren't home."

She gulped. "Have you been waiting a long time?"

"I think so. I don't have my watch, but I think it's been an hour and a half, maybe more." He paused; then he looked at

Emily before reaching down and petting his dog. She knew what he was thinking even before he said the words.

"You don't have agoraphobia."

Not a question, but she nodded.

"Did you ever have it?" His voice was soft now.

"No. I mean, I thought I did." She spoke quickly, hoping he would process it all at once. "I was staying in the house most of the time, and I wasn't sure. I knew I could leave, but I never wanted to, so I figured there was something wrong. I joined the online group because I thought it fit me. But then I realized I didn't belong."

"When?"

She tried to catch his eye. "When what?"

"When did you realize that?"

If only she could have said last week, or at least last month. But she'd vowed to stop lying about this. "December," she said, looking past him to where the tulips were blooming in her front yard.

He blinked, trying to adjust to this news. She knew he had to be thinking about all the hundreds of conversations and emails they'd had since December. All the times she'd let him assume they were the same.

She clutched her hands together. "I wanted to tell you this before, Jules, really. I just—"

"Lied to me instead?" The words were angry, but his voice was just hurt. "Lied to all the people on the board? Why, because you were having fun with the freaks?"

"No." She said quietly. "Because I liked you."

He knelt down and put his arm around Alicia. The dog nuzzled his chin, and Emily wanted to cry.

"So you lied to me?" He was talking into the dog's fur, more to himself than to her. "I can't believe I thought you were the most honest person I'd ever known."

She was so surprised, she blurted out, "I never said I was honest."

"No, you didn't," he mumbled. "I guess that's one thing you didn't lie about." He finally took a deep breath and glanced at her. "Is your brother really getting married? Or did you make that up too?"

"No. David is marrying Clara."

"But you're going to the wedding, right? You were always going."

She nodded and slumped down in the rocker. "I'm leaving a week from Wednesday. I have to go early; I'm a bridesmaid."

"Great." He laughed then, but it was a harsh laugh. "Do you want to know why I came here today?"

"You said you wanted to introduce me to your dog?"

"That's right. This is Alicia. She's a service dog who helps people with psychiatric disabilities. I had her trained to work with agoraphobia, so she could help you travel." He shook his head. "I guess that seems incredibly stupid to you."

Emily did start to cry then, soundless tears. She wanted to tell him that it wasn't stupid at all; it was the sweetest thing anyone had ever done for her. Before she could find the words, he said, "Will you please just call me a cab?"

"But I can drive you home. I really—"

"No." He closed his eyes and took several deep breaths in quick succession. "Just the cab."

She hesitated for a moment, then went inside and did as he asked. Before she came back out, she blew her nose several times and wiped her eyes, trying to calm down. She knew she had to say one more thing to him. It was her only hope.

He was already off the porch, sitting huddled on her front steps, looking at the road. Alicia was facing him, with her paws on his knees.

"Jules," she said. He didn't turn back, so she walked around to face him. "Jules, the thing is I—"

His expression when he looked at her stopped her cold. It wasn't cruel or mean; it was just empty. As if he were looking at a stranger. Which in a way he was.

She wasn't the same as Jules, that was the truth. She'd always known it, since the day she saw his picture. The agoraphobia connection had made him think she was like him, but she wasn't. She wrote cheesy greeting cards and swam a lot, while he had imagination and compassion and a love for nature and poetry and music and especially photographs. He loved photographs the way she had never loved anything but him.

She stood in her yard, a few feet away, waiting for the cab. It was turning cool, but she didn't go back inside to get her jacket. She wanted to be with him every minute, in case he changed his mind.

He didn't. The cab arrived, and the only thing he said was "Thanks" when she ran to her car and grabbed the large, wrapped present, and then pressed it into his hands, insisting he take it.

"It's for your birthday. I hope you like it."

He was breathing more rapidly as he got into the cab. She felt like her heart would break, thinking of what he went through to bring her Alicia. Thinking of how much he'd cared about her to do this.

She spent the rest of the night checking and rechecking her email, still unable to stop hoping that something would change his mind. Maybe the present would convince him she did understand agoraphobia. (Unless it convinced him of the opposite, which it also might—how could she be sure?) Maybe he would find himself wanting a good laugh and call to hear her latest joke. (Doubtful, she knew, since the jokes were about agoraphobia. If he thought of them at all, he'd probably think she was an even bigger fake.) Maybe he would just feel like sharing a photo with her. (More likely he'd be angry all over again every time he thought of how she pretended to need the pictures, when she could have had the real world any old time.)

Before she went to bed, she tried to IM him good night, but he wasn't there. She tried again in the morning and every few hours for the next several days, and it was always the same. "JulesReed04 is not signed on." Whenever she tried to call, she got his answering machine. She didn't leave a message. Everything she could think of to say was much too late.

In the weeks Jules and Alicia had been together, they'd developed a routine. Every morning they walked into downtown

Ardmore, so he could have coffee and read the newspaper. Every evening, they walked the other way, to Bryn Mawr, where Jules picked up dog food or milk or fruit or a movie.

He wished he could believe that he was getting over his agoraphobia, now that he could go out every day without panicking, but he knew it wasn't true. His trip to Emily's house had taught him that. He had a bad panic attack when he realized she wasn't home and another bad one in the cab on the way back to his apartment. Alicia had tried her best to help him, but he'd gone to the dark place all the same. Of course, the circumstances were very unusual. In the first case, he'd realized the girl he loved had been lying to him. In the second, he was leaving that girl, probably for good.

When he got back home that day, he was too unnerved to do anything but sit in a chair with Alicia at his feet. He tried to think about Emily, but every time he did, he felt a stabbing pain in his chest. The worst part was how pretty she was in person, much prettier than in her picture, even prettier than in his imagination. Her smile was so genuine as she came up the front walk. She really was happy to see him, he felt sure, but what he didn't understand was why. Why would someone normal have chained herself to someone with his condition? Normal people want to go out to dinner and concerts and parties. Normal people don't want to get romantically involved with someone they can't have sex with or even kiss.

If she wasn't romantically involved with him, that would explain a lot, but he felt certain she was. She talked like she was, but then she talked like she was agoraphobic. Maybe he'd been wrong about all of it. Maybe she was just passing the time between writing her greeting cards, enjoying a weird friendship with a very weird guy. Something to tell her normal friends about. A story to tell her brother and his fiancée.

He tried to put her out of his mind, but it was so hard. She'd been such a big part of everything he did for so long—he couldn't imagine how he would get through the next few days without her, much less the rest of the week, the rest of his life. He couldn't bring himself to sign on to the internet, knowing he'd see her on his buddy list: "Emily2Paris." "I've always wanted to go to Paris," she'd told him as an explanation. It never occurred to him to ask her why she didn't go, because he thought he knew. He thought he knew her.

The present she'd given him remained unopened on his kitchen table. Judging from the size of the box, he thought it was probably a telescope. He'd told her he was thinking of ordering one. He didn't open it because the idea of using something she'd given him made him too sad. He celebrated his birthday by taking Alicia to a used CD store and stocking up on music. He bought jazz and some alternative but no classical. He knew classical would remind him of Emily, because that was what they used to listen to on the web.

He passed the next week listening to John Coltrane and Ben Webster, wailing a beautiful pain. His walks with Alicia got longer and longer, until he was making it all the way to Haverford, to let Alicia run in the college yard. It was spring now and getting warmer; maybe that was why he felt like he needed to start thinking about what he should do with the rest of his life.

He had about twenty thousand dollars left, but he couldn't go on forever without working. Yet he had no idea what he could do or how to go about discovering that. Finally he decided to make a call to Dr. Wilson. The combination of medication and Alicia had helped enormously, but he knew he couldn't rely on either of them forever. The first appointment wasn't until August, but he took it. He figured he'd still need therapy then.

On Thursday night, exactly a week after he went to Emily's house, he impulsively picked up the phone to call his old girlfriend Liz. He wasn't sure why, but he suddenly felt like he had to do this. He hadn't treated her very well before he left New York, and he thought it was time he apologized.

He assumed she'd be angry, but she wasn't. She said she understood several times; she said it was probably "fate." When he asked her what she meant, she said, "No offense, Jules, but you know you were never cut out for any of this."

"Any of this?"

"The high-stress job, the parties, the clubs." She coughed. "Big-city life."

"You're probably right," he said softly.

"I know I am. Your idea of fun was staying home, talking about some bizarre thing like the shadow of a tree."

He knew what she was referring to. There was a tree outside his apartment window, and he used to spend hours watching the leaves dancing on his dining room wall. He didn't remember talking to Liz about this, but obviously he had. And obviously, she'd hated it.

"Don't take this the wrong way, but you were always a

dreamer kind of guy, living in your own head. What you're doing now is like accepting it."

Alicia, who never barked, barked at that point. He took it as a sign that it was time to go. Liz said, "Take care of yourself," and put down the receiver so quickly, he realized she was waiting for this chance herself.

He sat down on the rug with Alicia and brushed her coat while he thought about what had just happened. His primary reaction was a strange kind of relief. The idea that he hadn't been a hundred-percent different when he was in New York had never occurred to him before. What if it was true? What if where he was now was only some kind of bridge to where he'd always been headed? What if it turned out to be just a temporary state, rather than a permanent illness?

This was the kind of question he'd always discussed with Emily, and he wished he could talk to her now, but he didn't pick up the phone. All of their talks about agoraphobia had been tainted by his new knowledge that she'd only been talking about him.

He spent the rest of the night absorbed in his thoughts. It was the only advantage to not having Emily in his life: he had to try to deal with his own problems. He would never regret being involved with her, though; he was sure of that. How could he regret happiness?

The night before Emily left for the wedding, she posted the whole truth to the online group. She'd been lurking all week, and she'd noticed how many people remarked on the fact that she wasn't around, asking one another if anyone had heard from her. Naturally they would worry about someone who had posted daily for nearly a year and a half. She owed it to them to let them know she was fine. Not happy because of what she'd done, but alive and well.

She spent the whole day preparing the post, even though it meant she was blowing a deadline at Perfectwords.com. Big deal. She wouldn't be working there much longer anyway. It was time to go out and get a real job, hopefully one she didn't hate. She needed friends, that was obvious from the last two weeks, when the only phone calls were David or Clara with another "urgent" wedding question. What about the proposed menu he'd emailed? The dress Clara had asked her to buy? The Friday rehearsal dinner—had she decided where she wanted to sit? Her answers were: Don't care what we eat, Dress already bought, and As far away from everyone else as possible. "You're such a misanthrope, Em," David would say and sigh. She'd become Em since she'd agreed to be part of the wedding. She'd become "misanthrope" because David loved words like that and because they'd talked so much recently, he really was starting to know her now.

She thought the post for the agoraphobia board was the most effort she'd ever put into a piece of writing. She wanted them to know that she'd never looked at them as anything but friends: that took two careful paragraphs, describing what they'd given her when she first came on the board, how much they'd meant to her since. She also ended up explaining how she felt about Jules—but hiding his identity as someone who'd never posted there, only lurked, and emailed her off the board because he lived nearby. "What he did for me," she wrote, "is at the heart of why I lied to all of you. I fell in love with him, which probably sounds strange, since I'd never met him. Even stranger since we never went anywhere: he was the first person who showed me how beautiful the world can be if you open your eyes."

She told them about the day she realized she wasn't agoraphobic, the same day she got this man's picture in the mail. She described her feelings then, and why she was afraid to alienate him with the knowledge that she was nothing like him. So she lied to him and to them, because she wasn't sure if he still lurked there, and she couldn't take a chance. And she got closer to him. So close his voice became like her mother's, soothing and gentle, and like her father's, wise and kind. So close she trusted him to know the stupidest things about her: that she liked to watch reality television and she still wore Hello Kitty pajamas. That she could eat a whole family-size bag of Cheetos in one sitting. That she could never learn a foreign language. No matter what she told him, he was still just as wonderful. Until the day he discovered that she wasn't agoraphobic.

The last paragraph was the hardest for Emily to write because she kept crying. "This man was the best friend I've ever had, and I honestly don't think I'll ever find another person like him. I would still do anything to make him happy. I worry about him constantly, hoping he's not too lonely. Hoping his open hands aren't trembling and his big heart isn't racing. Hoping he can someday go outside into a world he deserves, without the ugly parts of life that have never deserved him."

As soon as she hit Post, she turned off her computer and threw herself on the bed, which was covered with clothes she still had to pack for her early-morning flight. She fell asleep that way, without setting her alarm. It turned out to be a very lucky mistake, as she slept right through the plane taking off.

From the view of that plane that took off without Emily, if one of the passengers had had the telescope Jules thought she'd given him (or at least a damn good pair of binoculars), that passenger would have seen a man and a dog getting into a cab. Of course he was coming to her, but not for any of the obvious reasons. He still hadn't opened the present, although halfway to New Hope he remembered it and wished he had, in case she asked about it. He hadn't gone to the online agoraphobia board and seen her post, which was probably a good thing, as he might have felt so guilty for what he'd put her through that he wouldn't have been able to move that morning. He hadn't even realized he couldn't live without her, because that wouldn't change anything if, as he feared, the Emily he couldn't live without didn't even exist.

No, it was something much simpler that made him get into that cab. He couldn't stop daydreaming about her lips, turned up into that smile. It was probably the most beautiful thing he'd ever seen, better than the microscopic raindrop, better even than the field of wildflowers in Peru. A smile that said she was happy to see him: he kept returning to that one crucial fact.

Maybe she shouldn't have been happy—since she was normal, and he was a freak—but there it was, the unquestionable truth, written right on Emily's lips. She wanted him there, and so he got in the cab.

Maybe somewhere in his mind were the germs of all the other thoughts that would eventually have convinced him to do exactly what he was already doing. He knew, for instance, that he himself had lied many times in his former life, so why judge her so harshly? He also knew that she had brought out the best in him: not only by her reaction to the pictures he found and what he thought and believed but even by giving him a reason to search out Alicia, the dog that was enabling this very trip. And he knew he still cared about her, because every time he thought about never seeing her again, he felt the stabbing pain in his chest that was unlike anything he'd experienced before. Unless he was really dying this time. That thought had occurred to him too.

The morning rush-hour traffic gave him plenty of time to worry if he was doing the right thing. When the cab stopped in front of her house, his hands were shaking so hard that the cab driver had to get out and open the passenger door for him. Jules had to stop and pet Alicia for several minutes before he could convince himself to ring the doorbell. That was the way Emily found him: on his knees, petting his dog that looked so much like her old friend Fred.

Before she was awake enough to remember to be cautious, she smiled at him, but this time he smiled back. So she invited him in. Alicia found a spot on the throw rug in front of the fireplace while the two of them sat on the couch together, talking as long as they could stand to before they had to have that long-delayed kiss. They spent the next hour that way: kissing and talking and kissing again.

To Emily, it felt a lot like a dream. She said so a few times, the way you do when you're hoping that just by saying it, you're making it impossible—for who ever says something feels like a dream in a dream? She finally accepted that it was real when she remembered her brother's wedding and the plane she'd missed, but even then, she was so happy she didn't care much. It was Jules who insisted she get ready, and together they worked out a plan to make it by the Friday rehearsal dinner, if they hurried over to Ardmore to get Jules's clothes and medicines and Alicia's food and favorite toys, and then drove straight through to Santa Fe. That is, if Emily drove. Jules had let his New York license expire, and neither of them thought he was up to driving on the highway.

The trip was hardly perfect. Alicia threw up on the PA Turnpike barely past Harrisburg, and even with all four windows rolled down, the Toyota smelled like dog vomit the rest of the way. In the middle of Missouri, when it hit Emily that it was really true, she was really about to see David, she remembered how angry she was with him about her parents' funeral, and she had a meltdown about how she could possibly handle being with him without screaming. Jules managed to talk her down from that, but neither of them could talk the other out of their worry about what they were going to do in the future, since around about Oklahoma, it hit them both at once that they had no jobs or career plans or even marketable skills, at least none that they were willing to use.

Not surprisingly, Jules had several panicky episodes: one in Columbus, Ohio, and another in Terre Haute, Indiana, and yet another in Joplin, Missouri—pretty much every place they stopped. In each case, when it was over he told Emily that it wasn't so bad; it wasn't a full-fledged panic attack. Whether it was or not, by the time they reached Santa Fe, after traveling through eight states and 1,916 miles, he knew one thing for sure. The people on the agoraphobia board had been right when they'd insisted that the fear of panic is what really hurts you. If you can just manage to ride it out, you will find yourself on the other side. If you manage to ride it out, you might even end up like Jules and Emily did, standing on a hillside in Santa Fe dotted with shrubs and dancing hyssop, holding hands with the one person in the world who they knew understood loneliness, looking out on a view as wide as their hearts could reach. Wide as the limitless sky.

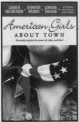